W9-BVZ-231

THICKER THAN WATER

Bruce Zimmerman

Thorndike Press • Thorndike, Maine

Library of Congress Cataloging in Publication Data:

Zimmerman, Bruce.
    Thicker than water / Bruce Zimmerman.
        p. cm.
    ISBN 1-56054-276-4 (alk. paper : lg. print)
    1. Large type books. I. Title.
[PS3576.I48T45   1991]   91-34932
813'.54—dc20   CIP

Although many of the places depicted in this novel
clearly exist, none of its characters represents or is based
on any person, living or dead, and all the incidents
described are imaginary.

Thorndike Press Large Print edition published in 1991
by arrangement with HarperCollins Publishers.

Cover design by Suzanne Noli.
Cover illustration by James Steinberg.

The tree indicium is a trademark of Thorndike Press.

This book is printed on acid-free, high opacity paper. ∞

This book is for Lynn

The darkest hour of any man's life is when he sits down to plan how to get money without earning it.

— HORACE GREELEY

1

I knew we were in trouble when the captain started going country on us. Quinn Parker theorem number seventy-three states that the severity of an airline problem is directly proportional to the pilot's tendency to drawl and chuckle and get folksy on the intercom, and the last message did not bode well. There were two "gosh durns," one "howdy," and several "we figgers," so I decided it might be wise to hazard a look outside. Put my nose to the little oval window and check the horizon.

Gosh durn, indeed. If a sky could go insane, it would look like this. Wild and dark and frayed at the edges. It wasn't possible that it was one in the afternoon. It couldn't be that almost directly below was rumor of golden sands, tropical palms, and turquoise water. A land where every paperback smelled of suntan oil, and where women wore bikinis that would fit neatly into a martini glass.

The stewardess tightened the bolts at the edge of her smile and made one last pass with the drink cart. Hank sat to my left.

Fixed. Immovable. Fingers dug deep into the fabric of the armrest.

"How're you doing?" I said.

Hank shook his head.

"We land in less than an hour," I said soothingly. "Fifty minutes. Terra firma. Cocktails at poolside and a plate full of shrimp."

Hank shook his head again.

I smiled and gave him a gentle elbow in the side. "What do you think of this captain? Ten bucks says he's up there with the co-pilot whittling sticks and playing checkers."

"Forget it," Hank said. It was the first time he'd spoken in a thousand miles. His voice was thin and dusty.

"Forget what?"

"The diversionary conversation. I appreciate the gesture, but the shamans of Peru teach that a man should die consciously."

"Consciously?"

"That he should exit the earth in full possession of his senses. No drugs, no hospitals, no painkillers . . ."

"No diversionary conversation."

"Precisely," Hank said. "So in these final moments I'm trying to briefly review the panorama that has been my life. The triumphs, the regrets, the things left undone . . ."

I shrugged and settled back in my seat.

10

When he's not shredding airline upholstery with his fingernails, Hank Wilkie is a stand-up comic, knocking around the local clubs in San Francisco. Three years of tagging along while Hank pursued his would-be career had convinced me that comedians come from the same gene pool that produces bullfighters, bomb defusers, and the guys who raided Entebbe. Nerves of stainless steel, unfazed by drunken hecklers, tattooed bikers, or a lynch mob masquerading as an audience. I would not have expected him to turn to jelly over a bumpy plane ride.

The jostling got worse, and Hank's grip tightened on the armrest. Fine. He was right. Forget the chitchat. I pulled down the little plastic window shutter, pushed the recline button on the side of the seat, leaned back, and closed my eyes. Though Hank would never suspect it, I had a sizable anxiety of my own, and it had nothing to do with turbulence at thirty thousand feet.

Psychiatrists say that if you can number your fear — if you can, for example, say that on a scale of one to ten this fear is a three and that other fear is a seven — you soon will master it. By labeling it, you control it. Nothing terrifies so much as the nameless, the formless, the endless. My job in San Francisco is to help people find these labels

11

for their fears. To seek out the number that will put a safety net under a free-fall phobia.

Okay then, Parker, do it yourself. Eyes closed. Visualize the source of your unease. Frame it like a photograph. Adjust the focus. Good. Now what do you see? A sandy beach? Definitely. Palms swaying in the gentle breeze? Absolutely. Little black boys selling coconut bread at the edge of the sea? Hopefully. Nice images, all of them. And Hank Wilkie — sallow, hardcore transplanted New York urbanite who was attempting to die consciously beside me — was about to inherit the whole delicious package.

Not much of a fear. On my one-to-ten scale it would be hovering somewhere around zero. So why was I squirming in my seat? Why weren't my thoughts full of pina coladas and panama hats and fans turning lazily overhead? Christmas just came early this year. Never mind that twelve bullets into the back of someone's head had set all of this good fortune in motion. Ignore the shadows extending into the picture of tropical paradise; the tinge of arterial red in the blue, blue water. Nasty things happen to people all the time. The lucky ones pick up the pieces.

2

The phone call had come three days earlier. It was a criminally beautiful Indian summer morning in San Francisco. Clear air, warm sun, the Golden Gate Bridge stark and majestic against the blue horizon. Hundreds of sailboats drifted on the bay. Bands were playing somewhere, and somewhere hearts were light. But at 1464A Union Street, top floor, home of the greatest dining-room view in Northern California, I was buried deep into the contours of the overstuffed armchair, laden with potato chips and onion dip, watching Arnold Palmer on the twenty-seven-inch Sony.

The situation was this. Arnie had hooked his tee shot into the left rough and was now standing over the errant ball, shoulders slouched, brow furrowed, mulling it over. Two options presented themselves. He could play it safe by turning sideways and flopping the ball out onto the manicured fairway . . . or he could chance it. Hitch the pants, steel the jaw, yank out a four-iron, and rip the ball through the narrow opening between the trunks of the trees, directly at the pin.

There were, of course, problems associated with the second option. The ball might not make it through the trees. The ball might hit one of the trunks at a solid 150 m.p.h. and come howling straight back in a screaming microsecond and make borscht out of Arnie's gonads. I hunkered deeper into the electronic darkness and felt around for the onion dip.

People handle depression in different ways. Some eat. Some stop eating. Others sleep excessively or shop compulsively or have an affair. Me, I watch meaningless television. Cartoons. Home Shopping Club. The bowling finals on ABC from Wonderbird Lanes in Dayton, with the difficult spares being replayed in slow motion. It wasn't something I was particularly proud of, but the doldrums are the doldrums and at least, I told myself, mine were being wallowed through in private.

It had been a tough year. An ex-lover had died, and a new one had moved away, leaving in her wake all sorts of personal fidgety questions of maturity and commitment and roads not taken. Not that the wounds were all emotional. A fresh four-inch scar on my stomach stared up at me from time to time as a tender reminder of my own fragile mortality, and my nostrils were

14

still filled with the sharp, antiseptic smells of the hospital. Recent events had made it difficult for me to reenter the world with a smile on my face and a song on my lips, so I kept to myself. Slept. Ate. Watched television and fretted the colossal decisions of Arnold Palmer.

That's when the phone rang. I pushed myself carefully out of the armchair, never taking my eyes off the tube. Arnie said something to his caddy and the caddy handed him a club. A four-iron! Son of a bitch, he was going for it! I groped, fumbled with the receiver, picked it up.

"Could you hold on just a second, please?"

Arnie stood over the ball and then backed off. Approached it again, lips pursed. One last practice swing. Tense-tendoned. Poised. He almost pulled the trigger, then backed off once more shaking his head. The four-iron went back in the bag. Out came the pitching wedge. I exhaled, rubbed my eyes, and re-adjusted the phone.

"Thanks for waiting."

The female voice pounced. "Put me on hold like that again and I don't care. I'll come down there personally and kick your butt!"

It was Carol. She's the only grown-up lady I let talk to me that way.

"Sorry, Carol. What's happening?"

15

"Hank's upset," she said. "He's on his way over to see you. Just thought I'd give you some warning."

"You guys have a fight?"

"No, nothing like that." Carol paused. "I don't even know where to begin, Quinn."

"Start with, 'Hank is so ridiculous that . . .'"

"Okay," she said. "I will. Hank is so ridiculous that he doesn't want to make one short plane trip to pick up a half-million dollars."

Carol is not prone to flamboyant statements and she suddenly had my attention. "A half-million what?"

"You heard me. Dollars. Green rectangles that enable small children and their parents to continue a diet of nice, hot, nourishing meals."

"You said a half-million?"

"Give or take a couple hundred thousand. Look, Quinn. This is important. I'm not letting out any family secrets if I tell you we're not doing all that great financially. Both kids are in day care now, Cort all day and Matty after school. That's six hundred bucks a month. I'm working free-lance and Hank . . . you know what Hank just did?"

"I'm afraid to ask."

"He just took a job as a fry cook at this

16

stupid restaurant out in the Haight! Eight hours a day flipping hamburgers and scrambling eggs! And so now we're both working and the kids are salted away with strangers all morning and afternoon and we're still slipping backward a cog at a time."

"How about allowing Uncle Quinn to extend a small loan? Hank doesn't need to know."

There was a five-second pause on the other end. "You're a sweetie," Carol finally said. "And six months from now I'll probably take you up on it. But for right now you can do me a bigger favor."

"Name it."

"When Hank gets to your apartment and starts in, just tell him to *do it!* All right? That's all you need to remember. *Do it!*"

Carol hung up before I could say another word. I moved my head and let the receiver fall into my hand. Strolled back to the armchair. CBS had gone to commercial. A wanton woman in some improbable desert. She was wearing a Paris-after-midnight gown and was sprawled over the glistening hood of an imported automobile.

I vaguely watched the television and tried to absorb what Carol had just told me. If information is too crazy, it simply doesn't register. Like cartoon characters who go run-

17

ning off a cliff and keep going on, sprinting across air, until they stop, blink, and notice that there's nothing below them but a thousand feet of empty space. Then they fall. I hadn't stopped to blink yet. A half-million dollars, Carol'd said. Tell Hank to hop on a plane and pick up a half-million dollars.

The commercial ended with the woman in her slit-to-the-thigh evening dress contemplating stick shift possibilities with moist lips. If you weren't going to buy the car after thirty seconds of that, you weren't going to buy it. Arnie had hit his third shot onto the green and approached the waiting gallery to a smattering of polite applause. The announcers talked about his maturity in taking the sure thing rather than risking disaster. That was the word they used. Maturity.

Read "chicken-shit."

I was on the verge of changing the channel when the hallway buzzer buzzed three quick bursts. Then I heard the front door open, and Hank started trudging up the stairs. He has his own key. My apartment takes up the entire top floor of a funky, pre-elevator-era Victorian. It's fifty-four steps from the top of the stairs to the bottom of the stairs, and Hank visits enough that I get tired of making the round trip to unlock the door for him.

"You're missing a gorgeous day," he said.

18

"I've been watching it from the dining-room window."

Hank had a manila folder under his right arm. He went to the window and stood there a moment, gazing out toward the Golden Gate. Hank has an angular, sharply defined face. Strong jaw, soft blue eyes, and longish brown hair combed straight back. He's not a big guy — barely five foot eight after an evening on the rack, but lack of height has never bothered him. Look to the insects, he'd once told me. An increase in size generally signaled the end of a species.

"You know what's really starting to annoy me?" Hank said at last.

"Toxic waste?"

"No. Interpretive National Anthem singers."

I snapped my fingers. "That was going to be my second guess."

"I was listening to the Giants-Braves game on the way over," Hank said, ignoring me. "Just started, but I thought I'd at least catch the top of the first. Unh-unh. They hauled out this faded star of yesteryear and he hot-dogged the National Anthem for three and a half minutes, like it was some great blues single. It went on and on and on and on . . ."

"Would some coffee help eradicate the memory?"

"Worth a shot."

19

I went into the kitchen and got a new pot going, and Hank filed in behind me. He leaned against the drainboard and folded his arms across his chest.

"All right," he said. "I guess we can both stop pretending Carol didn't call you. What did she say?"

"That you should get on the plane and pick up the half-million. Right off the top of my head, it sounds like a reasonable request."

"It does, huh?"

"Yep."

Hank held up a single finger for me to wait. He went into the living room and came back with the manila folder. "Read this," he said, "and then tell me what comes right off the top of your head."

I pulled out the contents of the folder. Very official-looking. Enough gold seals and silver stamps and flowery emblems to remind one of junk mail sweepstakes contests that everyone in the neighborhood is on the verge of winning. Except this ornamentation was real. A communication to Henry Ellsworth Wilkie of San Francisco, California, from the Honorable Nigel Brambley, Attorney at Law, Priest River, Jamaica, West Indies.

I glanced up at Hank. "Henry Ellsworth Wilkie?"

"Just read."

I read. The packet was thick with the tangled verbiage of legalese, but buried among the herewiths and aforesaids and here-inunders two cold and clear facts emerged. Somebody named Martin Greene had died, and Hank had consequently inherited Seven Altars — a house and fifteen acres of land near the town of Priest River. A small regional map was enclosed, the property circled in red ink. It was situated on the eastern coast about midway between Kingston and Port Antonio, and the fifteen acres looked to be mostly beachfront.

I put the folder down. "Somebody died and you got his house."

Hank stared at me. "I *know* that! What about the rest of it?"

"The rest of it? Hank, there are ten pages of single-spaced legal gobbledygook — "

Hank shifted into Impatient Mode. He picked up the document and flipped hurriedly through the pages, finally pointing at a solid block of paragraph the size of my fist. "There!" he said. "Right there!"

I gently pushed the document away. "Why don't you just tell me what it says."

"Okay," Hank said, starting to pace. "I will. It says that I have to go to Jamaica and sign the papers. Personally! Otherwise it doesn't happen."

21

"They won't just mail the papers up?"

"No."

"Why not?"

"Who the hell knows why not! They just won't, that's all! Terms of the frigging will!"

Hank turned, exasperated, and walked out of the kitchen to the dining-room window. I took a guess at the problem confronting the Wilkie household. Hank is not Tropics material. He does not like to travel, does not go ga-ga over blue-water splendor, hates rum, and has never achieved anything remotely resembling a tan in his life. Civilization is directly proportional to how high the buildings are, and quaint Third World-isms carry no weight at all. Cobblestones wreck shock absorbers. Burros leave burro shit. Police are draconian, authorities corrupt, and peasants exist primarily to foment revolution. He was a native New Yorker, and after eight years on the West Coast was having problems enough adjusting to California. Carol and I are able to drag him off to Baja now and then, but that was the only kind of nature he felt comfortable with. Stark, dwarfing, inhospitable. Jamaica, where fruit was rumored to grow right on the trees, might be enough to put him over the edge.

I joined Hank in the dining room. He was just standing there at the window, looking out at the Golden Gate Bridge.

"It doesn't seem to me that Carol is being particularly unreasonable about this," I said. "A half-million dollars, Hank. Think about it. You could quit working for good and concentrate entirely on your comedy."

"Carol doesn't know the whole story." Hank's voice was quieter. Subdued. He tipped slowly forward till his forehead touched the glass. "I called the lawyer in Jamaica last night. Marty didn't just die. He was murdered."

"Murdered?"

Hank nodded. "Some kind of drug deal gone bad. They found him shot execution style on his boat. Doesn't change the terms of the will, but the lawyer thought I should have some idea of what was going on."

I picked up the packet and leafed through it. "Martin Greene . . . Why does that name ring a bell?"

"I might have mentioned him once or twice. Marty was an old college buddy from New York. Matty's godfather, actually." Hank sighed. "Make that Matty's *ex*-godfather . . ."

"Did I ever meet him?"

"No. After graduation he went his way and I went mine. Godfather or not, we hardly swapped Christmas cards."

"That's it?"

"Practically. Never saw him after New York except once, about six, seven months ago. He came through town and gave me a call."

"And?"

"He came over to the house, met Carol, and played with his godson. Then he and I went out to the Cliff House for drinks. Boys being boys. You know how it is."

"Not really."

"Use your imagination. Anyway, Marty was fed up with Caribbean heat and humidity so he told me to pick the coldest spot in the city to have a drink. The absolute bone-numbing coldest. We sat out on the terrace there at the Cliff House in the middle of the night with the fog blowing straight in our faces and drank. Everybody else was inside, bunched around the fireplace. Wait-resses thought we were out of our minds." Pause. "That's when Marty told me he was going to leave me his house."

"Just like that?"

"We were horsing around," Hank said. "At least, I *thought* we were horsing around. I was giving him hell about being such a negligent godfather and he sort of stopped for a second. This look came over him. He put his glass down and slapped his hands and said by God, I was right. He *had* been

24

a lousy godfather. No excuse for it. So to make amends he was going to leave his property in Jamaica to Matty."

"What were you drinking?"

"Tequila."

I nodded. "That explains it."

"The tequila had nothing to do with it, Quinn. I hadn't seen Marty in ten years, and after we paid the tab and went through the good-bye hugs I figured it'd be *another* ten years between drinks."

"Was he the drug-dealing type?"

Hank shook his head. "Not when I knew him. But like I said, it'd been ten years. People change . . ."

I ran my finger along the embossed letterhead. "This looks like a pretty big deal," I said. "A house and fifteen acres of Caribbean beachfront. Why is it called Seven Altars?"

Hank shrugged. "No idea."

I put the paperwork aside. "Was Marty well off?"

"If you mean was he rich enough to hand out houses to his long-lost college friends, no. There was a little money floating around, but not what you'd call a fortune. From what I gather the place in Jamaica had been in the family for eons. Stephanie, his wife, she was rich as hell, but Marty was just an average guy, making a living. Taught high

25

school in Montana or someplace before moving to the islands."

"He was married?"

"Still is," Hank said, then corrected himself. "Make that 'was.' I'm not used to the past tense with Marty yet."

"You knew his wife, then?"

Hank nodded. "Sure. Stephanie and Marty met at Columbia. I was the one who introduced them, and we used to go on the town together, the three of us. Stephanie's from here, actually." Hank pointed at the floor. "San Francisco. In New York she was the one who first put it in my head to move to the West Coast. Anyway, it was one of those freakish marriages that really seemed to work. As of six months ago it was still going strong." Hank paused, shook his head. "That's another thing. Why didn't the property go to her?"

"You say she's rich?"

"Gobs and gobs of the obscene stuff. Her father was a multimillionaire, but not multi as in two or three. Multi as in forty or fifty. I used to give Marty a hard time about it. He had this image of himself as a real enlightened character, liberal politics, defender of the downtrodden, all that. Very sixties." Hank paused and smiled to himself, lost in a private memory. "At the grocery store he'd spend fifteen minutes in front of the coffee rack, trying to buy his beans from the least fascist country. Coffee-producing nations tend to be repressive. He wanted coffee from Sweden."

I dropped the packet on the dining-room table and looked Hank straight in the face. "So what are you going to do?"

"Do?" He seemed surprised by the question. "I'm going to go to Jamaica, that's what I'm going to do. I'm going to get on a plane and claim Matty's half-mil."

"You are?"

"Of course. I'd be stupid not to."

I contemplated his decision for a moment or two. "So what's the big problem?"

"There isn't one," Hank said. "Because you're coming with me."

"Wait a second — "

"Not open for discussion, Quinn." Hank held up his right hand and started counting off fingers. "You were in the Peace Corps. You knock around Mexico. You speak Spanish — "

"They speak English in Jamaica."

"Don't play dumb. My point is, you know the ropes in the Third World and I don't."

I laughed softly, but Hank wasn't laughing with me. "I can't do it, Hank."

"What's stopping you?"

"For starters, hotel row on the Jamaican coast is probably about as much like the Third World as Nob Hill. Besides that, I have obligations here. Responsibilities."

"Like what?"

"Like clients."

Hank laughed. "You haven't had a client in months!"

I smiled and shook my head. "Trust me, Hank. I can't just drop everything and fly down to Jamaica. My impetuous youth is behind me. I'm all grown up and well-adjusted now."

"That's it?"

"That's it."

"Final answer?"

"Subject is closed. What else do you want to talk about?"

Hank just sat for a moment and stared at me. Then he exhaled, pushed himself out of the dining-room chair, and began gathering up his legal papers. "Okay," he said. "Suit yourself. But if you don't go, I don't go."

"Hold it . . ."

"Never mind the half-mil. Carol's wrath. Forget the children's education." Hank's eyes fell to the floor. "I understand." He began walking away, back down the hall, toward the stairs, exaggerating a posture of gloomy defeat.

"Won't work," I called after him. "I don't respond to blackmail."

Hank just kept plodding down the stairs, each sigh more emphatic than the one that went before. He was carrying on an imaginary future conversation with Matty, his six-year-old. "Gosh, son. It's great that you were accepted to Harvard, but, well . . . your old dad's a little short of cash right now. How about a trade school? Air-conditioner repair? Or motel management? Don't cry. Please don't cry. It didn't have to be this way. I wasn't always a dishwasher at Der Wienerschnitzel. Ten years ago I had the chance to be rich. To turn my life around. *All* of our lives around. Ten years ago, when our future was bright and hopeful . . ."

His voice trailed off and I heard the door open and close fifty-four steps below.

I smiled and gazed up at the ceiling. Evaluated the performance. By Hank Wilkie standards, it was a subpar effort. He hadn't laid on nearly enough guilt, and the exit was far too hasty. But I liked the bit with the kid who couldn't go to Harvard. The pitiful urchin angle. That was good. That showed promise.

I got up and wandered into the back bedroom and pulled my suitcase down from the top shelf. Rummaged through the drawers

29

trying to find some warm weather clothing.

I was, of course, going to Jamaica. There was never any doubt. From the moment Carol had called it had been chiseled in granite that I would be escorting Hank to wherever he had to go. I just didn't want him thinking I was a pushover.

Three shirts, three shorts, a gathered handful from the underwear drawer, and the packing was done. I shut the suitcase and smiled. Arnie's pitching wedge notwithstanding, there were still a few of us risk takers out there. Drop everything and fly to Jamaica? No problem, mon. Let the word go out that the four-iron has been passed to a new generation.

The king is dead, long live the king.

"The only thing that sustained me through that nightmare called 'the friendly skies' — the *only* thing — was the thought of a nice, icy Scotch and soda at poolside."

"Come on." I smiled. "A quick look. Turnbull House isn't going to run out of Scotch and soda in the meantime. Then at least we'll know what we're talking about tomorrow at the meeting."

Hank gazed wistfully at Rodney washing glasses at the bar. "Not fair."

"Here." I shoved my Black Widow at him. "Finish this. I'd hate for that Scotch and soda to end up costing a couple hundred thousand dollars."

Turnbull House "maintained" a small cadre of luxury European touring sedans for the use of the guests at no additional cost. At five hundred dollars a night, they apparently didn't have the gall to dun us another fifty, plus mileage. Hank selected a powderpuff-blue BMW, and we were off.

The road heading south followed the coast for a few miles, then dove inland. The country was lush and green, and there was a lot of activity along the side of the highway like you see in almost every country except the United States. Children, dogs, island buses, and workers on bicycles, machetes dangling at their sides. Fishermen set up shop right next to the road, their catch facing the oncoming traffic, guts splayed and salted and hung in the sun to dry. Makeshift soccer fields dotted the landscape, filled with shouting boys and the thud of homemade soccer balls. Higher up, one could see the uneven patchwork of agricultural fields, planted at impossibly steep angles against the sides of mountains. An island bus was directly in front of me, brightly painted, jammed full. The axles were so out-of-whack that it gave the impression of sliding down the road in a permanent skid. Ragtag belongings were strapped to the roof, strips of cloth and rope fluttering in the breeze.

Solid ground and a reluctant polishing off of my Black Widow had made Hank expansive and philosophical as we sped down the highway. By God, Walt Whitman was right! The open road! The body electric! We'd grown too cautious these days. Too brittle in the face of adventure.

"Think about what we just experienced!" Hank said, pointing an incredulous finger to the sky. "Think of it! A roller coaster ride through storm-shredded clouds eight miles above the earth! Did Shakespeare know that?"

I shook my head. "Unh-unh."

"Beethoven?"

"Nope."

"Leonardo never experienced what we just experienced!" Hank said. "*Leonardo!* Think of it!"

I refrained from pointing out that Leonardo probably wouldn't have spent the entire roller coaster ride staring at the folded-up food tray in front of him. When Hank gets on a roll, you have to let him play the thing out.

I missed the turnoff to Seven Altars the first time around. According to the map the property lay at the end of a private dirt road that slanted off to the left of the main highway about a mile and a half short of the town of Priest River. When we hit the outskirts of Priest River I knew we'd gone too far, so I U-turned, backtracked at a slower speed, and located it. It was an easy road to miss. No signs marked the way, and it was not so much a road as an exaggerated footpath, widened to barely accommodate a smallish automobile. Branches from the overhanging trees softly scraped the top of the car as we drove through.

"I didn't think it would be this remote," Hank said.

"Secluded, Hank. The real estate people are going to lick their chops and call this 'secluded.' "

For a hundred yards or so the seclusion got darker and deeper and more overgrown.

37

Hank mumbled about Jonestown and Kool-Aid. Then the road hooked sharply to the left and we were suddenly out of it, in bright sunlight, at the edge of a small clearing. A driveway of white sand and crushed seashell led directly to the house thirty yards away. I was surprised at the size of the house. I was also surprised at the half-dozen cars parked out front.

I drummed my fingers on the steering wheel. "And who's been sleeping in my bed, said Papa Bear."

Hank sat up straight and looked concerned. "It's supposed to be empty. The lawyer told me it was empty."

"Apparently not."

"What should we do?"

To our right the Caribbean was glinting sunlight. The house sat up on a six-foot base of rock, and a jungly hill slanted up and away from it on the left. No neighbors. Sun and surf and complete privacy. The half-million suddenly seemed like a very conservative figure.

"We've seen it," Hank said. "That's enough. It's not a shack in the middle of some swamp, so let's go back."

"Can't," I said.

"What do you mean, can't? All you do is put the lever on the 'R' and go backward."

"Look." I pointed at the house. A black man had walked out onto the front terrace. He stood there for a second, watching us, then he smiled and leaned forward against the guardrail and wiggled his finger for us to keep on coming.

I had an elderly aunt in Fresno who — when properly loosened with a few sips of bourbon — used to peer over the edge of her glasses, look cautiously left and right, and tell you in a hushed voice about "falls" — the inexplicable dropping from the sky of objects that have no business dropping from the sky. Ancient coins, frogs, pieces of boats. "Biggest coverup in history," Aunt Betty used to say. "Einstein knew the whole thing but the government shut him up."

The time-honored family reaction to Aunt Betty was to pour more bourbon and usher the children out of the room, but now I realized she had been right all along. If ever there was a human "fall," I was looking at him. The man on the porch had tumbled down out of the sky from another continent and another century. He was medium height and slender, with a Medusa-like mane of thick dreadlocks coiling halfway down his back. He wore faded green bathing trunks and had the smooth, elongated muscles of an Olympic swimmer. The facial features

39

were fine and delicate, buffed to an unnatural shine. Stun-gun handsome. A dozen wind chimes filled the deck, and he stood there in the middle of the shimmering music, gazing down at us like an Old Testament prophet about to impart some bad news.

"Ignore him," Hank said. "Just back up and leave."

"Nonsense," I said with a smile. "We wouldn't want to be brittle in the face of adventure, would we?"

Hank glared, I put the car in gear, and we slowly coasted up to where the man stood waiting.

I parked next to the other cars, got out, and nodded to him. He returned the nod. The aroma of a barbecue drifted on the air.

"Hate to bother you," I said. "But we're looking for Martin Greene's house."

The man nodded. "This is Martin Greene's house. I am Bongo. Come with me."

It was not a point open to debate, so Hank and I did as we were told, up the five steps leading to the front porch and on through the front door.

Bongo indicated for us to wait in the living room while he went out onto the back terrace. Beyond the sliding glass door ten or twelve people stood around a dying barbecue, cradling drinks, stealing glances at us. The house

40

itself was every beach hideaway you've ever seen beckoning from high-budget travel posters — light and breezy, full of bamboo and wicker and the bracing scent of salt water. Hank and I looked at each other. A smile creased his face.

"Chez Wilkie," he said quietly.

The sliding door reopened and a woman came in, and Hank's smile evaporated. She was wearing a white silky summer dress, a colorful Mayan belt loosely knotted around the waist. Her eyes were locked on Hank and she walked directly up to him, ignoring me completely. For a moment they simply looked at each other in silence.

"Hello, Hank," she finally said.

"Stephanie . . ."

Hank stepped forward and they embraced each other awkwardly while I stood to the side, shifting my weight from one foot to the other. Then she turned from Hank and faced me.

The suddenness of her head-on beauty was momentarily disorienting. She had soft, shoulder-length brown hair streaked with occasional brushstrokes of ash blond. High cheekbones, one a little higher than the other. Full lips. Wide-set hazel eyes. The skin was smooth and full of sun. It was a face that hinted of good breeding, good schools, and

41

money enough to give such good fortune a big backyard to run around in. At first glance you would have said that she was merely run-of-the-mill gorgeous. Drag a net across Fifth Avenue at lunch hour and you'd have a thousand just like her. But closer inspection revealed more. There was pain in her eyes, tension at the corners of her mouth. A face contoured as much by suffering and grief as it was by anything as mundane as a bone or tendon or ligament.

She leaned forward to shake my hand, and her dark, olive-smooth breasts strained the confines of the low-cut summer dress. I felt myself start to fade like Con Edison on a hot August day. A mild brownout, then power was back to normal.

"I'm Stephanie Greene," she said.

"Quinn Parker."

"Pleased to meet you," she said, but she was neither pleased nor displeased. They were only words that needed saying.

She indicated for us to wait a moment and then went back out onto the porch, sliding the glass door shut behind her. I looked over at Hank.

"That's Stephanie," he said. "What do you think?"

"I think my blood type just changed."

Beyond the glass door I could see Stephanie

talking to the group, and several of the people around the barbecue nodded their heads. They set down half-finished drinks and began tucking in shirts. Then Stephanie turned and came back in.

"Let me give you a quick tour," she said. "Sorry for the confusion. I was under the impression you were coming tomorrow."

"The party doesn't have to break up because of us," Hank said. "We jumped the gun a little."

"It was breaking up anyway," Stephanie said. "To tell the truth, I'm glad you came. Everybody thinks that if I don't have a steady, nonstop diet of mirth and cheer I'll go into a tailspin. This was the last one, though. I'm headed back home to San Francisco myself tomorrow."

Stephanie forced a smile and folded her arms across her chest. She had a curious habit of now and then opening her eyes a little wider than usual, wider than you'd think necessary, as though she'd forgotten her contacts and needed to refocus. Sometimes it felt like scrutiny, other times it was a curiously involving gesture . . . a dilated intimacy that seemed to draw one physically closer.

We went down the hall, Stephanie in the lead. She pushed open various doors and briefly explained what the rooms were. At the end of the hallway was a wrought-iron spiral staircase. We climbed it and emerged into a large, sun-splashed room that occupied the entire top floor of the house. Floor-to-ceiling windows gave a spectacular view of the Caribbean. The bed was large and sumptuous, veiled by a gauzy mosquito net, and a fan the size of a B-17 propeller rotated lazily overhead.

"This was Marty's favorite room," Stephanie said. "We used to joke that if he had a hot plate and a bedpan he'd never set foot beyond these four walls."

"It's huge," Hank said.

Stephanie nodded. "There used to be mirrors up on all the walls and then the room looked like it went on forever, but the maid took them down."

"Why'd she do that?" Hank said.

"Superstition," Stephanie said. "In Jamaica they believe a living person reflected in a dead man's mirror will soon pine away."

That was a conversation stopper. We nodded awkwardly and wandered to the window and looked down on the terrace below. Most of the lunch guests had left. To the right a wooden boat dock stretched about fifty feet out to sea. No boat at the end of it.

"Do my eyes deceive me," Hank said,

nodding down at the terrace. "Or is that the 112th Street telescope?"

"The very one." Stephanie smiled. Then she turned to me. "Hank got Marty going on astronomy back in New York. It became an instant obsession."

"Hank's tried the same thing with me," I said. "It hasn't caught on yet."

Stephanie nodded. "Well, it caught on with Marty. Whenever he had to think or work something out, that's where he'd go." She sighed and shook her head. "Marty and his planets. I used to envy him. It was like he could look through that tube and drift right on up to Saturn and stay there awhile till his head cleared."

Stephanie looked down at the telescope, and at that instant was so hauntingly detached, so alone with her unshareable grief, that the slow, warm peace of utter resignation spread through me. It etherized the barking dogs that shouted at the kennel gate for a chance to kiss those lips, caress that face, stroke those breasts.

"So what did they tell you about Marty?" Stephanie said, abruptly breaking the mood. "That he was a drug dealer? That they shot him on his own boat because he was dealing drugs?"

"They didn't go into details, Stephanie,"

45

Hank said quietly. "It's not important."

"It's important to me." Her eyes widened and she folded her arms across her body. "You knew Marty, Hank. What do you think? Do you believe Marty was a drug dealer?"

"No," Hank said. "I don't believe that."

"Because Marty didn't have anything to do with drugs. He was against drugs. Somebody else killed him."

"Why?"

Stephanie shook her head. "I don't know. Marty kept things to himself. He had a lot of . . . secrets. But you were his friend, Hank. You should know the truth, and the truth is that Marty had nothing to do with drugs."

"Stephanie . . ."

She ignored Hank and pointed out at the bay. "That's where it happened, you know. Right out there beyond those rocks. Just right out there, a hundred yards offshore. You could see the boat from here. You could stand right here and look out and see it . . ."

Hank moved close behind her and put a hand on her back, and it was all the coaxing Stephanie needed. Her eyes grew bright with tears and she leaned her head into his shoulder.

"I'm sorry," she said. "I told myself I wasn't going to do this."

"It's okay."

"It's just that I still can't believe it really happened," she said, beginning to cry. "I can't believe I'm never, ever going to see him again. Never hear his voice. Nothing."

Hank reached out and gathered her in and she buried her face in his shoulder. My code of ethics is as suspect as the next guy's, but I don't rubberneck at traffic accidents, and I don't eavesdrop on someone else's private grief. I took the spiral staircase as quietly as possible, leaving Stephanie and Hank in their tearful embrace, swaying ever so slightly in the silent and mirrorless room.

4

Bongo and three of the other original guests were still out on the terrace. The inner circle. Those expected to stick around when others are expected to leave.

Bongo was smoking a joint that was of a size and shape to give Linda Lovelace pause. He dipped the end of it in the dying embers of the barbecue and drew from it deeply. When I came out on the terrace he nodded to me and I nodded back, and that was the extent of our communication. He just stood there, silent and peaceful, smiling at his own private amusement, peering through the smoke and scanning the horizon as though his depth of vision was just that much deeper than everybody else's.

A girl stood next to him. Correction. A girl *attempted* to stand next to him. Her name was Meredith Something and she had wild, every-which-way red hair and a Texas accent strong enough to warp floorboards. Houston debutante gone to seed in the islands. She laughed and squirmed and played with the tassel on Bongo's green swimming trunks, but it wasn't the flirtatious play of romantically involved people. I suspected the swimming trunks Meredith played with depended entirely on who had the drugs. She giggled and leaned into Bongo, and he ignored her as a lion ignores the silly, frivolous play of one of its cubs.

Norman and Jana were the other couple. Jana was an exotic beauty with Asian features who may or may not have just graduated from high school, and she lay flat on her stomach on the chaise lounge, sunbathing, while Norman rubbed oil onto her back. She wore a sarong with a bikini top and stared straight out at the water, her little chin resting on her little folded hands. When I came out on the terrace she slowly turned her head, gave me about three seconds' worth of her Vuarnet sunglasses, then turned back. There was the kind of hopeless ennui in her posture that only a certain breed of teenager seems capable of mastering. I couldn't tell if she was sleepy, bored, or merely assuming a when-oh-when-will-someone-ignite-me pose.

The guy oiling her up, Norman, was a ruggedly handsome character of about forty, and he was the one who introduced everybody while crouching over Jana. He wore his dark hair in a small ponytail and had a strong

49

jaw, chiseled features, deep blue eyes, and a winning smile. Tall. Deeply tanned. Very much in shape. His bright Hawaiian-print shirt was unbuttoned to reveal a manly pelt of chest hair. I had the nagging feeling that I'd met Norman before, and then in the next instant I placed him. He was the guy always holding windswept women on the covers of romance novels. The package was perfect except for a persistent nervous blink. It wasn't severe, but on such an otherwise impeccable specimen the defect stood out. After the introductions he turned away and concentrated on the contours of Jana's back. Nobody on the terrace was an immediate candidate to head up the Priest River Welcome Wagon, so I strolled to the far end, near the telescope, and looked out at the water.

The house was situated midway on a small and shallow bay that stretched perhaps two miles from one end to the other. Jagged outcroppings of rock on either end signaled the boundaries of the bay. The cove was mostly very white sand and very blue water. Palm trees grew right to the edge of the sea, and there were no other homes or buildings in sight.

Bongo came up beside me while I surveyed the area.

"Pitiful hospitality," he said with a smile. "Nobody here knows how to make a man feel welcome." He offered me the joint.

"Thanks," I said. "But I'll pass."

Bongo nodded and drew deeply from the spliff. Then he held it up questioningly. "You don't like the weed?"

I looked over at Meredith in the corner, folded up on the floor of the terrace like a fighter who'd just gone down from a savage ten-punch combination. "One puff of that thing and I'm afraid I'd end up like her."

Bongo glanced at Meredith, smiled, and nodded his head. "Yeah, mon. Meredith doesn't have the brains to smoke the weed. Her brains are too weak."

Bongo drew from the joint and looked out at the water. Though his voice had that lilting, singsong quality of the islands, there was a kind of precision in his diction that hinted of a life or an education spent somewhere other than Priest River. England, perhaps. Or even the States. Bongo turned from the ocean and looked up at the second-floor window. "How is Stephanie?"

"So so."

He pursed his lips. "It was a terrible thing, what happened."

"Did you know Marty very well?" I said.

"Yes."

51

Bongo didn't elaborate. He just stood there and let his gaze linger on the second-floor window.

"So you must live here, too?" I said.

Bongo turned away from the window and redirected his attention to the spliff. "Yes. Priest River is my home. Born here. Grew up here and in Kingston, but mostly here."

We stood for a moment in silence. The turquoise water rolled ashore. The cumulus clouds, so menacing from the window of the buffeted airplane, now hung overhead, blue in the Caribbean twilight. The air was sweet with the smell of sea grape. Fish now and then broke the surface of the water. I took a deep breath and let it out. Despite the grim purpose to the trip, this was good. This was nice. Next time I was taking Arnold Palmer with me.

"Why do they call this Seven Altars?" I said.

Bongo turned slowly, a smile on his face. "What?"

"The legal papers referred to this place as Seven Altars. I was curious why."

"Stephanie didn't tell you?"

I shook my head. Bongo peered up at me as though I surely had to be putting him on. "What do you say I go show you?"

"Show me?"

"Yes, mon." Bongo laughed, putting a finger to his open eye. "Show you."

"When?"

"Right now."

I followed Bongo as he unhooked a swinging gate to the left and maneuvered the half-dozen weather-beaten stairs leading down to the beach. My sense of anticipation was heightened considerably by Jana's decision to come with us. Anything that could wrench her from the lounge chair had to be special. Norman recapped the bottle of suntan oil and trundled after. Meredith wisely stayed behind. In her current state I doubted whether she had the technical expertise to mount a teeter-totter, let alone start hiking the length of beach.

For about fifty yards we skirted the edge of the sea. The jungle to our left crowded close to the shore, leaving only a narrow corridor of sand between the leaning palms and the sea. Now and then we had to duck under low-hanging branches, holding on to the smooth limbs, using them for leverage to swing ourselves around to the next patch of dry sand. Coconuts, faded and bleached by sun and salt water, washed ashore and rolled gently at our feet.

At the fifty-yard mark Bongo came to a

stop in front of a knee-high wooden sign that had been hammered into the beach like a crucifix. A crudely painted-on white arrow pointed to the left, and that's where Bongo went. We disappeared into the trees and began following a small jungle trail that rose steeply up the side of the hill I'd seen earlier when first driving up to the property.

I heard Seven Altars before I saw it. From the silence of the jungle it began as a slow trickle . . . the sound of a bathtub over-flowing. Then I felt it. Cool spray drifted into our faces. The sound of cascading water grew louder. The temperature lightened, the humidity eased, and suddenly we were there.

A canyon of rock had been carved out of the lush, tangled jungle. A hairline fracture in the skull of the mountain, camouflaged by dense foliage and thick tree cover. Two enormous slabs of solid, mossy cliff face rose perhaps a hundred feet on either side of us, illuminated here and there by rays of late-afternoon sunlight slanting in through the trees. It was narrow where we stood at the base. Four people, arms outstretched finger-tip to fingertip, would probably cover the distance. It tapered out as it rose, opening gradually to the sky, and at the top was as wide as a couple of school buses.

At our feet a small waterfall emptied into

a Jacuzzi-sized emerald pool. The spillover from the pool went off to the right and down the other slope of the hill. Just beyond the first waterfall was another. Then another. Then another. The eye kept moving from one level to the next, higher, deeper, a shimmering, liquid hall of mirrors, misted with rainbows. Beyond, the mountains leapfrogged each other — high, distant, hazy, the last one a fragile bluish outline against the huge dark blue of the sky.

"Seven Altars!" Bongo said, smiling broadly. "What do you think?"

"I think I'm hallucinating."

I reached out and touched the side of the canyon wall. The hard rock face had been blanketed over the years by a soft and spongy layer of moss, and moisture oozed from the green velvet at the pressure of my fingertip.

"It is real." Bongo laughed. "You don't need to touch to make sure. Come on. The best of it is all the way to the top."

We climbed higher. There was no more trail, only a cross-country journey of boulder hopping. Bongo moved ahead of me with remarkable agility, his two-foot-long dreadlocks swinging from side to side. Monkeys screeched in the trees above, and if you turned and looked back you could see the turquoise Caribbean through the narrow canyon formed by the jungle trail. The half-million-dollar estimate for the property was no longer a conservative figure. It was a down payment.

Each emerald pool we came to was a little larger than the one that went before, and the last one at the top was the size and depth of a large swimming pool. It faced a sheer wall of rock, twenty feet high, smooth and dark, over which the water cascaded. Bongo and I sat on the smooth, rounded rocks at the edge of the pool, breathing heavily.

"Fifteen feet deep," Bongo said. "The best pool for swimming."

I nodded and took a deep breath of the thick, honeyed air. It was so dense you felt it was solid. Digestible. Could fill the stomach and alleviate hunger. Norman and Jana were still working their way up the jumbled stairway of boulders.

"Are these waterfalls actually part of Marty's property?" I said.

Bongo nodded. "Incredible, yes?"

"Yes."

"It's why they call it Seven Altars. The Arawak Indians who lived here five hundred years ago, before the Spanish and before the British, they worshipped this place." Bongo felt around in his bathing suit pocket for the spliff. "I used to come to this spot many times as a boy. This was my meditation spot. I still come here when I need to contemplate a thing. Stephanie, she calls this my thinking rock."

"I have a thinking rock, too. Up near Mount Tamalpais, in California."

Bongo smiled, found his spliff and the box of matches, lit up, and took a deep, deep drag.

"Seems too good to be true," I said.

Bongo's smile faded. "Funny you should say that." He tapped the rock with his knuckles. "This *is* too good to be true."

"What do you mean?"

Bongo drew from the spliff again, peered through the smoke. He waited a long time before speaking. "Somebody asks you what does a bomb look like, what you tell them?" he said.

"A bomb?"

"Yes, mon. A bomb."

"I don't understand."

Bongo smiled. "What does it look like? What is the structure of a bomb? You might say a grenade, yes? Or a big long thing you strap to the bottom of an airplane. But then sometimes a bomb is in disguise. Sometimes a bomb appear in the form of a waterfall."

I stared at Bongo and he held my gaze without flinching. "Like this waterfall, for

57

instance?" I said.

Bongo brought his hands together and then let them push out, as though he were holding a balloon that was instantly inflated. He imitated the sound of a bomb exploding. "Yes, mon. This waterfall. Seven Altars is a bomb as sure and true as anything the army makes."

"Are you talking about what happened to Marty?"

"Yes. Other things, too."

At that moment Norman and Jana reached the top level and Bongo fell silent. Norman stood for a moment, hands on hips, trying to catch his breath. Jana wandered over to the far end of the waterfall, ran her hands through her long, thick hair, then stepped out of her bikini like you'd step out of a bathtub. She stretched flat on her back, nude, on one of the large, level rocks that rimmed the pool. Bongo watched me trying not to watch her.

"Bombs . . ." he said with a smile. "And then sometime it have the structure of a pretty girl with no clothes, eh? We talk about it another time." Bongo stood, winked at me, and took one long, last drag of his spliff. He held the smoke in his lungs and dove into the water. I watched his dark body knife to the bottom of the pool. Norman wandered over to where I sat. He took his shirt off and undid his ponytail.

"That fucking climb kills me," he said. "Jesus. Straight up."

Bongo was still at the bottom of the pool. Then suddenly air bubbles began to rise to the surface, in five-second intervals. They popped, and when they did thick puffs of ganja smoke drifted up into the fragrant air. The impression was of a submerged fire, of flames smoldering somewhere down in the water, and it lent a degree of menace to the otherwise paradisal setting. Then Bongo finally surfaced and Norman slowly applauded.

"Don't know how he does that," Norman said, shaking his head. "I tried it once and all I got was a mouthful of water. These fucking locals, man . . . these Rastas . . . they're from another planet."

While Bongo swam back and forth Norman and I talked. I try to resist snap judgments, but with Norman it was hard. He was a fairly predictable guy. You see a lot of Normans in resort areas. They tend bar. They give ski instructions. They spread oil on the backs of beautiful girls and drink imported beer. Their personalities tend to be formed by whatever it takes to get laid, and on a net worth of about five hundred bucks they live the life most men would kill for. In the fifties they were football heroes. In the sixties they grew long hair and marched on the Pentagon. In the seventies they were vulnerable, lugging their newfound ability to cry from one sexual hotspot to the next. In the eighties they were getting old enough to start looking for cover. The Aspen-Rio-Jamaica portfolio.

"How's Steffie doing?" Norman asked at last.

"Okay."

"She say anything about Marty?"

"Not really. Only that he didn't have anything to do with drugs. That his death was something else."

Norman laughed a small, bitter laugh, and then imitated Tammy Wynette, twang and all. "Stand by your man . . ."

"What does that mean?" I said.

Norman shifted his haunches on the hard rock and sighed. "Just between you and me and the green fucking jungle, I admire Steffie's loyalty. I really do. Just like how Lee Harvey Oswald's mama went to her grave saying her little boy never did anything wrong. But fact is, Quinn . . . it was Quinn, right?"

"Right."

"Fact is, Quinn, Steffie doesn't know shit about what's been going on around here. Last couple of years she's spent most of her time over the hill, in Kingston, going to college. Head off in the morning, come back late at night. Three or four days a week. Books and term papers. She got a little out of touch about what was happening on the home front."

I watched Bongo swim back and forth under water. "Bongo just said Seven Altars was like a bomb ready to go off."

"Bongo says lots of weird shit, but on that he's right." Norman exhaled as though frustrated at even trying to decide where to begin. "It's such a mess . . ."

"Jamaica?"

"Jamaica, sure. Jamaica's always been screwed up. Poverty. Politics. But I'm especially talking about this." Norman pointed at the ground. "Right here. Priest River. This little slice of the island. What happened to Marty was just business as usual around here. Drugs. Guns. Crime. We even got a goddamn ghost running around town!"

"A ghost?"

"Once a month like clockwork, out on the road to Los Rodriguez. Shit, you name it, Priest River's got it. I've been here five years and thought I'd finally found a home, but I'm about to pack it in myself."

"Where would you go?"

Norman nodded his head and covered

his top lip with his lower lip. "Got my eye on Spain. Spent a little time there back in the sixties and it sucked, but now that Franco's croaked things've loosened up. That's what my friends tell me, anyway. And it's cheap, too."

"So you think Marty was killed because of drugs?"

"Look," Norman said, "let's not get off on the wrong foot. The last thing I'd ever want to do is bad-mouth Marty. He was my friend, for Christ's sake. And who knows? Maybe Steffie's right. Maybe what happened to Marty didn't have shit to do with drugs. All I'm saying is Marty wouldn't have been the first to go for some easy money and end up getting wasted. The ganja trade here can be lucrative as hell if you nail it right. I dicked around with it a little myself when I first came down."

"Dealing drugs?"

"Shit, yes! In fact, that's kind of what inspired me to come in the first place. I was up bartending in Aspen and there was this guy who came in all the time, good tipper, and one night he told me about Jamaica. About the easy money. He didn't come right out and broadcast it, you know. He didn't scoot up a barstool and say, 'Hey, I'm a drug dealer!' But it also didn't take a genius to figure out how come he was able to spend all winter skiing in Aspen with no visible means of support."

"So you toyed with it?" I said.

Norman nodded. "Toy's the right word. Strictly nickel-and-dime stuff. Small-time. But the money was un-fucking-believable. My first deal — not here, but over in Negril on the other side of the island — it netted me more than what I made busting my ass fixing Mai-Tais in Aspen all winter. One little piss-ant deal! Second deal bought me my little piece of property down the beach here. Third got me my boat. I'm telling you, it's hard money to walk away from."

"But you walked away."

Norman nodded, blinked his nervous blink. "Look what happened to Marty. You start thinking, okay, one small score and I can kick back all winter. Lay on the beach and play with the girls and laugh at all the poor suckers at home who're bustin' their asses off nine-to-five so they can hook up fucking HBO and watch some dumb-ass movie. But then you start to think, wait a second. A bigger score, I can kick back all winter *and* go to Europe for a while, too. Then you think about even a bigger score than that and hey, we're starting to talk about *retirement*. Blow off ever having to work the rest

63

of your life. *Two* big scores gets you the Lamborghini. Three gets you the yacht, crew and all." Norman shook his head. "It's bad, man. Bartending I used to see a lot of alcoholics. You can imagine. I remember I used to look at those guys and the way their eyes would glass over when I'd set down the first drink and I never really got it."

"Got what?"

"Got how a person could get so fucking addicted to something. Then I dealt a little ganja, got the taste of quick and easy money. All of a sudden, click. I understood what addiction was all about. Overnight, I got it like that. How something gets in your blood and just won't go away."

"You think that's what happened to Marty?"

Norman suddenly seemed bored with the subject. Talked out. "I only know what happened to me. I don't know what the hell happened to poor Marty. Probably nobody ever will know what happened to Marty."

Bongo climbed out of the pool on the other side and worked his way up a fifteen-foot shelf of rock. He stood at the very top, eyes closed with concentration, and executed a perfect swan dive, surfacing right next to us. Norman smiled and flipped over an imaginary scorecard.

64

"Eight point five," Norman said.

Bongo smiled and pushed off and swam away to the opposite end of the pool. Norman watched him swim.

"There's still something I don't understand," I said.

"What's that?"

"I realize the temptation of big bucks and all that, but I was under the impression that Marty was more than comfortable. That he had all the money he could ever want."

Norman shrugged. "Could be. Steffie has some. Marty, I don't know. He poor-mouthed a lot about how much it cost to keep this place up. But like I said, just because you have money doesn't mean you don't want more."

"Strange that they killed him right out in front of his house," I said. "That they didn't try to just get rid of him in a quiet way."

Norman turned his gaze to Jana. A wedge of sunlight had angled down into the canyon and come to rest directly on her nude body, like a spotlight. It brought every slope and contour into sharp relief. I only had a portion of Norman's attention now, and I couldn't blame him.

"They didn't want to be quiet about it," he said at last.

I'd forgotten the question. "Quiet about what?"

"How Marty was murdered," Norman said. "He took twelve bullets to the head, you know. Twelve. Can you imagine what he must have looked like? Means whoever it was emptied their clip, reloaded, and did it all over again. Bam, bam, bam. Twelve times. Just firing into red pulp after a while. You don't do that to make sure somebody's dead. Marty was dead before the first bullet came to a stop. You do that to send a message."

"The message being . . . ?"

Norman shrugged. "The same message that always gets sent in the drug business. Don't fuck with people. Marty probably double-crossed somebody or got double-crossed. Toward the end he was real paranoid. Looking over his shoulder all the time. Things going bump in the night. Something was up." Norman finally broke off staring at Jana and focused on me. "Can't blame Marty. This thing with my eyes? The blinking? That only started when I moved to Jamaica."

"Nerves?"

"I don't know what it is. I had an uncle who got shot down over Germany in World War Two and it scared him so bad the next day his hair went completely white. Boom, just like that. Twenty-year-old guy with a head of white hair." Norman took a deep breath and licked his lips. "Now, if you'll excuse me, that lady over there looks like she needs a little more oil."

Norman stood and pushed off into the emerald pool. He swam under water to the other side, where Jana was sunbathing. She sat up as he drew near, stretched her arms to the sky, arched her back, and rolled languidly over onto her stomach. The when-will-someone-ignite-me theory won out. Norman got out the bottle of oil and began casually massaging her back.

I sat there by myself and thought of Marty and his paranoia. Norman and his nervous blink. Having once lived in Guatemala, I knew the syndrome. Your phone was tapped. Your letters were steamed open. Men with reflector sunglasses beamed radar into your room as you slept. A friend in Guatemala City had once had his apartment ransacked by heavily armed soldiers who turned the place inside out before ultimately confiscating his coffee table book on Cubism. Cubism, Cuba, Castro, insurgency . . . the connection was obvious. Enough of that and you get a little jittery. If there was a common thread running through all of us who spent time in the Third World, it was a slightly above-average share of anxiety. It came with the territory, like booster shots and Pepto-Bismol.

The twilight thickened. Hank eventually found his way up to the top of the waterfalls. Stephanie wasn't with him. He was badly out of breath and spent fifteen minutes simply sitting on one of the rocks mopping the sweat from his face. I left him alone.

At sunset we all headed back. On the terrace the embers of the barbecue were dead. Meredith was gone. Norman said good-bye, wished us luck, and drove away with Jana and Bongo in tow.

"Where's Stephanie?" I said.

Hank pointed out at the end of the boat dock. Stephanie was out at the very end, legs tucked up so that her chin rested on her knees, looking out at the spot she'd pointed to earlier. The spot where Marty had died.

I thought for a moment of going out to say good-bye, offer condolences, whatever. But something held me back. She was wrapped in the resonance of Marty, and to go out and put a comforting hand on her shoulder would only break the spell.

Hank went back to the car, but I stayed on the terrace a moment longer, watching her. She stared out at the spot with such unwavering intensity that one had the feeling a great event was about to occur. An incomprehensible door out there on the surface of the water, and if she only stared hard enough, and with enough devotion, she might be given one last glance of Marty leaving this earth.

The world might not be as cruel as it seems. Maybe the exiting was slow.

5

"Coffee, sir?"

The uniformed black woman stood over my breakfast table with a pot in her hands.

"Good and strong?"

"Yes, sir."

"Sold."

She poured me a cup, left a menu, and moved to the next table without another word. The dining room at Turnbull House was not a place for howdys and hellos between servants and guests. I dumped in some cream and watched while the coffee changed color. Yawned. Yawned again. Then Hank appeared around the corner and pulled up a chair.

"You look bright and bubbly," he said.

"Didn't get much sleep."

"At five hundred bucks a night I'd think you'd feel a moral obligation to get a good night's sleep."

Hank signaled the waitress over, and she poured him some coffee and left.

"So what was the problem?" he said. "Stephanie have you tossing and turning?"

"Remember that young couple out by the

70

pool yesterday?"

"Vaguely."

"They share the bed on the other side of my wall and they don't spend the wee hours watching Johnny Carson."

"Loud?"

"Yes."

"How loud?"

I gave Hank a look.

"I'm an entertainer," he said. "I need to be on top of this stuff."

"Okay. You know in the movies when the woman gets mugged by three punks on a crowded street in New York and it goes on and on and nobody comes to help?"

"Yeah?"

I nodded. "That loud."

Hank let out a long, low whistle and scanned the dining area. "She down here?"

"I don't know where she is. Probably upstairs trying to dispose of the body."

Hank leaned back in his chair and linked his hands behind his head. "Come on, Quinn. You haven't forgotten already what it's like to have noisy hormones?"

"Hank . . . hormones can be as loud as they want for a reasonable period of time. It's one of those truths I hold to be self-evident. But this dragged on for three solid hours. There comes a time when it's both

71

acceptable and prudent for the screamer to have a sock shoved in her mouth. Lovingly, of course."

"No jury would convict you." Hank unlinked his hands and opened his menu. "What are you eating?"

"Bacon and eggs."

"What a bore." He paused, inspecting the breakfast choices. "I'm going to have the . . . *folie de matin.*"

"What's that?"

Hank folded the menu, pushed it away, and smiled. "In a few minutes we'll both find out."

"You feeling okay?"

"Why?"

"The Hank Wilkie I know had to be dragged, kicking and screaming, into the concept of wheat toast."

A wistful smile drifted across Hank's face. "Coming down the trail from the waterfalls yesterday I asked Bongo what his head felt like, smoking that much dope."

"And . . . ?"

"He said his head felt like barley." Pause. "What an image. Barley! My head *never* feels like barley. My head always feels like my head."

"Your point being?"

"I'm living life too tame, Quinn. I'm forgetting William Blake's edict."

"Refresh my memory."

" 'The road of excess leads to the palace of wisdom.' "

I shook my head and rubbed my eyes. "It was excess that kept me awake all night. Not a good subject this morning."

The waitress came to our table, took our order, and we set aside Hank's midlife crisis for a few moments to discuss the business at hand. The meeting with Nigel Brambley was only two hours away, and we had to be prepared in the event he threw us some unexpected curveballs. There were tax liabilities to consider. Hidden costs. The rumor of exceptional violence in the Priest River area. Did Marty have any family, and might they not contest this revised, tequila-induced will? And what about Stephanie? All was fond and chummy now, but what if things got ugly down the road and she decided that she couldn't live without a waterfall in her life? What recourse did she have?

I made Hank write down the points, one by one, on a napkin so we wouldn't forget during the meeting. Finally, we decided that there would be no buying or selling between anybody until Hank could have an independent appraiser come and take a look at the property and give an estimate.

"There," Hank said. "Does that cover it?"

"That's it."

Hank capped his pen and slid it back in his shirt pocket. "Maybe I ought to grow a beard."

I groaned and shook my head. "Carol's going to love this development. What about all us little people who have to put up with you while you travel the road of excess?"

"Blake covered that, too."

"Enlighten me."

Hank held up his right forefinger. " 'The cut worm forgives the plow.' "

"Easy for the plow to say."

The waitress suddenly appeared at our table and put the plates before us. Silence fell. Hank and I stared at his *folie de matin*. God knows what it was, but if you said shredded raccoon intestine on a bed of month-old cottage cheese, you'd be very, very close. Hank looked at my bacon and eggs and hash browns, then back to his *folie de matin*.

"What . . . in the hell . . . is this?" he said.

I shrugged and put my fork into the crisp, steaming potatoes. "Some of those cut worms that forgave the plow. *Bon appétit.*"

Priest River proper was a ramshackle town of perhaps five thousand people. The wooden houses were mostly up on stilts, and old men sat out on the broken-down porches, watching the world go by. A half-assed attempt had once been made to pave two of the roads and put in sidewalks, but the notion didn't stick. Heat and neglect had cracked the concrete, clumps of grass grew out of the buckled pavement, and the few cars we did see in Priest River didn't use the paved road at all, but drove along the shoulder in the dirt. The town was only a slightly more civilized extension of the jungle itself, and I had my doubts that it would survive the next good rain.

We found the lawyer's office without much difficulty, and one thing became immediately apparent. The lion's share of Nigel Brambley's budget had gone into his stationery. His office, 57 Livingston Road, Suite III, was nothing more than a worn-out, single-story structure at the end of one of the two paved streets in town. It was set up on about four feet of cinderblock and was warped out of shape like an image in a fun-house mirror. If it had ever had a paint job it hadn't been in my lifetime. Thick underbrush tapered off on both sides of the building, separating it from a rum shop on one side and a mud-and-wattle home on the other where naked children played in the yard.

Hank and I sat for a moment in the car.

"Suite III?" Hank said.

"Makes for good letterhead."

We climbed the three steps and Hank knocked on the screen door, and a little, silver-haired, roly-poly black man of about fifty-five immediately answered.

"Yes?"

"Is this Nigel Brambley's office?" Hank asked.

"Yes."

"We have a ten o'clock appointment," Hank said. "Hank Wilkie. Regarding Martin Greene's property . . . ?"

The man smiled and opened the screen door and waved us into the office. There was no secretary, no waiting room. The office was dark and shadowy, smelling vaguely of jungle rot, and the wooden floorboards creaked as you walked across them. Two uncomfortable-looking chairs faced a solid, no-nonsense metal desk. Glass-encased diplomas hung on the back wall. On the desk was a globe the size of a basketball, and I noticed that the island of Jamaica was clumsily circled in Magic Marker, an arrow drawn to it like the "You Are Here" maps in shopping malls.

The silver-haired man had little round eyes, little round ears, and wire-rimmed glasses with little round lenses. I had this immediate, unshakable image of him rolling back and forth in his empty office all day long, a lone marble in an empty toy box. He simply stood and smiled at us and made no effort to get the proceedings under way.

I cleared my throat, and at that moment a door leading off to the right opened and another man walked into the room. The jolt of recognition temporarily disoriented me. It was Bongo. His dreadlocks were tucked up under an oversized beret. He wore new American-style jeans and very white tennis shoes. He smiled at my unabashed surprise, held his forefinger and thumb up an inch apart, and quietly conferred with the little round man. The round man nodded and shook Bongo's hand and exited through the front door. Bongo motioned at the two empty chairs before the desk.

"Mr. Wilkie," he said, grinning. "Please sit down."

"What are you doing here?" I managed at last.

"Me?" Bongo put his hands to his chest. "This is my office. I am Nigel Brambley."

"I thought you were Bongo."

"At the waterfalls I am Bongo." He laughed. "In this office I am Nigel Brambley. I try very, very hard not to confuse the two. But for you let's pretend I'm Bongo all the time."

He laughed again and got up and disappeared into a side room and came back with three paper cups of Pepsi on ice.

"You're the lawyer?" Hank repeated.

"Yes."

"You're the one who mailed me the packet?" Hank went on. "The one I talked to on the phone?"

"That was me," Bongo said. "University of the West Indies, here in Kingston. Then UCLA, in California. So!" Bongo put his hands on the desk and smiled. "How are your accommodations at Turnbull House? Satisfactory?"

"They're fine," Hank said in a numb monotone.

"Good!" Bongo leaned back in his chair. "You know, I must tell you that I dislike Turnbull House enormously. It embodies the very worst of whatever residual colonialism we have here in Jamaica. But Marty left a provision in the will that insisted Hank be enthroned in the finest hotel in the area, and Turnbull House is certainly that. The decision was out of my hands."

"Why didn't you tell us you were Marty's lawyer yesterday?" I said.

Bongo shrugged. "Yesterday I was not necessarily Marty's lawyer. Yesterday I was Stephanie's friend who had been invited to a going-away party. Besides, I thought it might be good to talk to you first when you didn't know who I was. Marty's will, the way he died . . . I try not to be a suspicious person, but I have natural concerns."

Bongo removed a folder from the right-hand drawer of his desk and began going through the stack of onionskin paper. "Now," he said to Hank, "let's get on with it."

The conversation was suddenly all business and I shut up. Sat quietly and kept the radar tuned for odd frequencies. Things seemed to be straightforward enough. Brambley-slash-Bongo had been handling Marty's affairs in Jamaica ever since he and Stephanie had come there six years earlier. Marty had no family with claims to the property, Stephanie had made it clear that she would not contest the will, and all that remained were a couple of dotted lines for Hank to sign.

"If I were to sell this," Hank said, "what do you think I could realistically get?"

Bongo cleared his throat. "Actually . . . there is a stipulation I haven't yet told you about."

It grew very quiet in the warm, dark office.

Hank turned and looked at me, then faced Bongo.

"What stipulation?"

"Simply this. You cannot sell, lease, or rent the property on a long-term basis until your oldest son graduates from high school."

Until that moment I'd never really understood the expression "silence fell." But it fell hard in the tiny office. Started at the ceiling and whooshed down over the top of us and thunked solidly on the wooden floor. Hank sat with his mouth open, pen poised, eyes wide and vacant.

"I can't what?" Hank said.

Bongo sat up straighter in his chair. "When Marty drew this new will up, he indicated that the property was to be a gift to your children. That it was based upon a discussion the two of you had had in San Francisco a few weeks earlier. It was my understanding that he was the godfather of your oldest son, correct?"

Hank was still a little dazed. "That's right," I said, answering for him. Bongo swiveled his chair and faced me, relieved at the chance to explain the situation to somebody other than Hank.

"Of course," Bongo went on, "Marty was laughing the whole time he was revising this will. He was still treating it as something of a joke. Marty had every intention of living a full and useful life. Who could have foreseen this tragedy?"

Hank started to come out of his fog. "So what are you telling me? That the property is just going to sit there till Matty graduates from high school?"

Bongo shrugged. "It doesn't have to just sit. You may live there. You simply cannot sell, lease, or long-term rent."

"But Matty doesn't graduate for twelve years." Hank was almost talking to himself. "Twelve years!"

Bongo exhaled deeply, shook his head, and looked over at me. "I was against the provision. It was Marty who insisted."

"Did Marty say why?" I said.

Bongo steepled his long, slender fingers beneath his chin. "You must understand that Seven Altars has been in Marty Greene's family for many, many years. My father knew his father quite well. The Greenes were a clannish, territorial sort of family. Marty not so much, but his father and grandfather certainly. Outsiders. They had very strong beliefs, and one of those beliefs was in the sacredness of land. They could be difficult people at times, but they were people of principle, and everyone who knew them respected them. Marty was not nearly so head-

81

strong as his father and grandfather, but the genes were there, nevertheless. One cannot argue with genetics." Bongo smiled and glanced over at Hank, who was still gazing into space. Bongo turned back to me. "At any rate," he said, "Marty felt the weight of tradition and was firm that Seven Altars was not merely going to be auctioned off to the highest bidder like a prize steer. He always spoke of this imaginary dentist from Toledo, Ohio, and how Seven Altars would never fall into this dentist's hands. I'm sure that's why he left it with you. Though the circumstances were unusual and we had a laugh or two, I must emphasize that Marty did not treat this as a joke. Quite the contrary. The passing along of Seven Altars to you was a very serious thing."

Hank had roused himself from his stupor and was trying to think logically. "No long-term rental. What about short-term? The season?"

"A short-term rental is perfectly fine," Bongo said. "But I must tell you that things are very bad in Priest River now. Very bad. The likelihood of securing a seasonal rental in the current atmosphere is not good."

"Are you talking specifically about what happened to Marty?" I said.

"That, yes. And other things."

"What other things?"

Bongo eased back into his chair. Then he took a blank sheet of paper and a pencil and began drawing a series of concentric circles. "When I lived in Los Angeles there was a big earthquake. I remember the diagram on the television of where the middle was. The strongest part. They called it . . ." Bongo bit his lower lip and thought.

"The epicenter?" I said.

"Yes." Bongo nodded. "The epicenter. They showed on the diagram how the shock waves emanated out from that. That is what Priest River has become to the rest of Jamaica. The epicenter. I don't know why. In West Kingston you expect crime and violence, but not here. Things weren't like this before. Something has happened to Priest River. I went away to law school in UCLA for two years and when I returned things had changed. Something very bad had happened but nobody seems to know what."

Bongo finished doodling. There was a dot representing Priest River, with rippling waves of violence and trouble radiating out from it. Bongo tapped the dot with the tip of his pencil.

"So I've inherited something that's just going to sit for a dozen years," Hank said.

"People here are frightened," Bongo said

with a shrug. "Crime is very bad and prices are plummeting."

"And nobody has a clue?" I said.

Bongo smiled. "Many of the local people here blame it on the duppy."

"The what?" Hank said.

"Duppy," Bongo repeated. "A ghost. Zombie. Phantom. It is called different things in different countries. The spirit of a dead person who comes back to the world of the living."

I laughed a little, but Bongo was not laughing with me. "It comes every month at the new moon," Bongo said. "Out on the road to Los Rodriguez. Less than a mile from here. The whole town has seen it. *I* have seen it!"

I turned to Hank. "Norman mentioned a ghost yesterday at the waterfalls."

Hank looked from Bongo to me and then back to Bongo. "But what is it really?" Hank said, growing more exasperated by the second. "Somebody dressed up in a sheet?"

Bongo smiled condescendingly. "It is a foolish man who only believes what he can understand, Mr. Wilkie. Even Marty came to believe in the duppies. You know, there is a saying here in Jamaica that no black man ever dies a natural death, so when he does die he must come back to haunt whoever caused this unnatural thing to happen to him. He 'rides' the living, as one would ride a horse."

"What about the white man?" I said.

Bongo hesitated a moment. "White man is on his own."

"So Marty died a natural death?"

Bongo leaned back in his chair, and a slow, sad smile creased his lips. "Quinn, I'm afraid in Priest River these days that being executed on a boat is a very normal death. You might say Martin Greene died of natural causes."

A half-hour of paperwork lay ahead for Bongo and Hank, so I left them to their business and wandered a few blocks down to the main square — an incongruously tidy little park in the center of town. A gazebo dominated the plaza, all white and ornate and filled with la-dee-da carvings and metalwork.

I found a bench and sat by myself and mopped the sweat from my face. After the doomsaying of Norman and Bongo I was not the most impartial observer, but there was definitely something sullen and mean in Priest River. An expressionless old man at the next bench ate peanuts. Two young black men standing at the other end of the plaza glared at me. One had his dreadlocks tucked up under a red beret, the other wore a thin, white headband. I did my best to ignore them. A skeletal dog came up to me, sniffed, and wandered away, delirious with heat and hunger, glazed eyes fixed to the ground. The air smelled of milk left out in the sun. I rubbed my eyes and shook my head. Marty needn't have worried about that imaginary dentist from Toledo. No Midwesterner in his right mind was going to sink vacation money into this town.

I got a shoeshine that I didn't need from a retarded boy of about sixteen named Winston. The other kids made fun of him while he buffed away, calling him "genius," "Einstein," "brains," and the like, but he just kept buffing and smiling. At the end of the shoeshine he winked in an exaggerated fashion and asked for five dollars.

"Five dollars?" I said.

He nodded hard. "Five dollar."

"How about fifty cents?" I said.

He smiled and winked some more. "Five dollar."

"Fifty cents."

"Five dollar."

I gave him a buck. Winston folded the bill three times and stuffed it through a slot in his shoeshine kit and wandered away, smiling.

Time dragged on. I looked at my watch. Twenty minutes yet to kill, and after the polishing of my shoes I suspected I had just about exhausted Priest River's cultural extravaganza. It was getting hotter. I was just about to get up and stroll back to Bongo's office when I heard a low rumble on the horizon, and a Land Rover with four men in uniform appeared to my left. The Land Rover coasted slowly around the plaza, engine whirring at an unnatural r.p.m., as if to suggest power beyond what you see. The men looked this way and that through reflector sunglasses. They came to a stop at the far end of the square, next to Beret and Headband. The driver cut the engine, and the two cops who were sitting up front began slowly climbing out of the vehicle.

Beret didn't hesitate. He flashed into a full-out, breakneck run, past the gazebo, toward me, high-hurdling a bench just to my left and disappearing between two shabby buildings on the other side of the street. Nobody chased him. Nobody seemed unduly alarmed. I looked back and saw that Headband hadn't budged. He planted his short, muscular body and faced the approaching cops head-on, hands on his hips, defiant.

The lead cop was big and solid and had a smile on his face, as though bemused at the speed with which Beret had bolted. I could see his lips moving as he spoke to Headband. He finished saying what he had to say, waited, then his lips moved again. Headband had his back to me, but suddenly I saw his shoulders pinch tight together, his head lurch forward, and even from my distance it was impossible to mistake the enormous gob of spit that hit the policeman square in his reflector sunglasses.

For two seconds nothing happened. Then a white blur streaked from the cop's side and there was a sickening crack like a split watermelon and Headband went down in a heap. The cop put his truncheon back on his belt, took off his sunglasses, wiped them off, and then, almost as an afterthought, gave Headband a swift, solid kick in the gut. My body involuntarily clenched. Then the second cop moved in and dragged Headband into the Land Rover, and the engine started up and they drove around the plaza to a nondescript building almost directly behind me. I turned around on my bench to watch. They parked and lugged Headband into the building, his shoes dragging along the floor as they walked. His white headband was splotched with red.

I glanced around the plaza to see if anybody else had noticed the incident. If they had, it was no special cause for alarm. The old man ate his peanuts, the shoeshine boys milled about the gazebo. Dogs kept sniffing for scraps.

The smart thing was to get up and walk quietly back to Bongo's office as planned. What cop? What spit? Priest River has a central plaza? No kidding! I sat on the bench and contemplated the smart thing for about ninety seconds, then I stood and brushed off my pants and strolled over to the building where the Land Rover had come to a stop.

A sign just inside the door informed me that I was in the Priest River police station. The empty room was just a marginal upgrade from Bongo's office. Hot and echoey and filled with flies. The floor was a kind of smudged white linoleum that crunched grittily underfoot, and the drab green walls were completely bare. A ratty couch was pushed up against the left wall, and a large, metallic desk sat in the exact middle of the room, and that was the extent of the interior decorating. A door, half-opened, led to another room to the right. There were sounds coming from the room on the right.

They weren't good sounds. They were the sounds of somebody having the shit beaten out of him. Muffled thumps and laughter and the squeak of shoes bracing for leverage on the slippery floor. I was about to turn and leave when the cop who'd been spit on in the plaza appeared in the doorway and looked at me.

"What you be wanting?" he said.

"I need some information."

The cop scowled and came into the room. Two other cops followed him. They were breathing heavily from exertion. The lead cop slowly took his place behind the solitary desk. A nametag on his shirt said "Chief L. Gordon." He still had his sunglasses on, and the armpits of his khaki shirt were discolored with semi-circles of sweat. The other two cops ambled over to the ratty couch and settled in. Gordon leaned way back in the chair and put his feet up on the typewriter, boot heels crunched right down into the keys so that they clustered in a tangled jumble.

"What information?" he said.

"I'm interested in buying a boat," I said.

"This look like a boat store?"

They all laughed. The three pairs of meaty shoulders jostled in mirthful unison. Big, bulky, well-fed men. They reminded me of something you herded together and slaughtered and then hung from refrigerator hooks. I laughed along with them to show what a regular guy I was.

"No," I said. "I'm interested in a particular

90

boat. Martin Greene's boat. I was told the police had impounded it."

"Who tell you that, man?"

"Guy in the street."

Chief Gordon slowly shook his head and sucked at his lower lip. It made a bad sound. "You got wrong information. Anyhow, you no want that boat."

"Why not?"

"Body been roastin' inna sun all day. Hundred pound of ganja don't tek away the stink of death. Body so bad even de fockin' blood-clot flies die on it. Mus' scrape dem off wit a knife."

Chief Gordon took off his sunglasses to look at me. He had a scaly, reptilian blink. Prolonged, deliberate. The slow closing and opening of a window shade. His pupils never wavered. The tip of his bright pink tongue ran along the edge of rounded baby teeth. The silence in the room thickened.

"So you don't think I'd want the boat?" I said.

His reptilian eyes hardened. "You don't be hearing what I say. We don't got de boat."

At that moment the door to the right opened completely and the fourth cop came into the room. He was smiling, holding a pair of garden shears aloft.

"Archie look so much better wit him hair

91

cut," the fourth cop said. "Mebbe him get a new career as a model." The room rumbled with laughter again.

I could see Archie through the parted door. He was down on the floor, apparently unconscious. His face was puffy and bleeding and all of his hair had been hacked off in uneven rows. I turned back to Chief Gordon, and he was watching me very carefully. There was something in his eyes that dared me to comment. Dared me to disapprove.

"Okay." I stood there, nodding to myself and trying to look disappointed. "You don't have any boats to sell. Wild goose chase. Thanks anyway."

They didn't tell me I was welcome. They watched me leave the room, and as I headed back down toward Bongo's office I noticed that Chief Gordon had come out on the street to monitor my exit.

When I got back to Bongo's office they were just finishing up. Hank still seemed slightly dazed at the sudden evaporation of his millionaire status. I thought about telling them what I'd just seen in the plaza, but there was no point. When the last form had been signed, Bongo stood and Hank stood and we shook hands one last time.

"I hope I haven't scared you," Bongo said. "But it is important to know what is happening here."

"Maybe things will get better," I said.

It was a feeble line, and Bongo just shook his head. "This island is a troubled place. You know, when Columbus went back to Spain, the king asked him what the new land called Jamaica looked like. Columbus took a piece of paper . . ." Bongo picked up the paper he'd been doodling on and slowly crumpled it in his fist. Then he set the crushed paper on the desk. " 'Jamaica looks just like this,' Columbus told the king. 'Just like this.' "

We drove back to Turnbull House, packed our bags, and took the same single-engine Cessna back across the island to the airport in Montego Bay. Our flight was late taking off and I found myself getting nervous for no reason at all. To pass the time I scanned the other passengers. Stephanie had said she was leaving for San Francisco today as well, and I thought she might be on the same flight. She wasn't.

When they called us for boarding at last and the doors sealed shut, I breathed a sigh of relief. We taxied to the end of the runway and took off with a gentle lift of the nose. The mood was morose. The flight down had been the festive, vacation-beginning crowd.

This was the vacation-ending group. Sun-burned, hungover, facing another fifty-one weeks of Business As Usual before the next brief drive-by of paradise.

I took one final look at Montego Bay as we flew over. The shiny hotels rose from the golden sand like futuristic gravestones, and beyond them the rugged mountains stretched into the hazy distance, toward Priest River. Columbus was right. Jamaica *did* look like something that had been crushed in an angry fist.

Then the airplane banked west and we were in the clouds once again.

6

A light, cool rain was falling on San Francisco when we landed. It was almost dark. I got my van out of long-term parking and took Hank directly home. Freeways full. Billboards harsh. Carol asked me to stay for dinner but I ignored the aroma of seasoned meatloaf and gracefully declined. They had plenty to talk about and the talking would be easier with me elsewhere.

Driving home on Union Street I suddenly remembered it was Friday night, and I winced. Most people don't wince at the thought of Friday night. For the bulk of the civilized world, Friday night looms out there on the far side of the work week as a beacon of hope, rich with the promise of romance, relaxation, movies, and pizza. But in my neighborhood Friday night conjures up only one harrowing image: the utter, complete, and absolute impossibility of ever finding a parking place.

Round and round and round I went, peering through the dark and rain, cursing under my breath and hitting the steering wheel with the palm of my hand. I finally found a spot way the hell out on Scott near Pacific, a good dozen blocks from my apartment. I got out, locked the door, and turned my collar to the rain. The damn suitcase could wait till I was able to park somewhere in the vicinity of my own zip code. Seven Altars, warm and fragrant, was a million miles away.

By the time I reached 1464A Union Street I was drenched. I said halfhearted hellos to Oscar the parrot and Lola the cat, and after that a five-minute shower was all I could muster. Jet lag, the strain of the events in Jamaica, and lack of sleep from my Triple-X night at Turnbull House all ganged up on me at once. I collapsed in bed and slept a deep, dreamless sleep.

A few listless days passed. Nobody called, nobody came by. A dreary, steady rain fell on the city night and day. I'd spent less than thirty-six hours in Jamaica, but was having trouble readjusting. My apartment reminded me of those tree stumps you see in natural history museums, the kind that have pins attached to the various rings marking important events. Birth of Christ. Battle of Hastings. Signing of the Declaration of Independence. Scorch marks from century-old lightning bolts. That was my apartment. Five rooms of dings and dents and almost-great events. A furnished and carpeted chronicle of the haphazard life of Quinn Parker.

A "normalcy" attack was coming on. No doubt about it. The affliction was a strange one, characterized by a burning desire to once again commute on crowded buses, put up with trivial office politics, and be grossly underpaid at a job where I was pitifully underutilized. These attacks swept over me two or three times a year, and there was nothing to do but ride them out.

It was, in a way, merely a curious homesickness for my old life. My life "BPD," as Hank puts it. "BPD" stands for "Before Power Drill," the power drill in question being the one that blew up in my hand a few years back. The damage had not been significant and I was ready to forgive and forget until some nefarious legal research brought to light the fact that the power drill company knew full well about the defect before it left the factory, and had decided to save a few pennies.

The revelation cut severely into my sweet nature, and while I'm not the litigious type, I decided perhaps this was one of those times to unleash the frothing lawyers and let them seek red meat. We settled out of court, and thus began my life After Power Drill.

I drank a beer and told myself to forget about it. This wasn't a normalcy spasm. It was just a mild attack of the post-travel blahs. After the Caribbean's dazzle of heat, color, and intrigue, the old homestead was a bit dull. My world was getting too familiar.

On the morning of the third day Carol finally called and asked me to come over. Something had come up and she needed to talk. There was nothing terribly urgent in her voice, but I was so lonely and eager for companionship that I found myself practically sprinting to the van.

Hank and Carol live on Woodland Avenue, a nice, quiet, dead-end street behind the University of California Medical Center. I rang the doorbell and Carol answered immediately. She stood on tiptoes and planted a solid kiss on the lips. "Come on in."

Carol Scardino, a. k. a. Carol Wilkie, is a living, walking New Year's Resolution. The kind of person you vow to be more like in the coming year. Athletic, healthy, full of drag-you-along energy. I'm not comfortable with relentless optimism, but Carol's brand got me every time. It was pure and strong and had nothing to do with innocence. She was five feet six inches of authentic, certifiable fifth-generation San Francisco Italian. Her black hair was short and shaggy and gave her a crazy, youthful look, like the kind of girl who would have fainted at Beatles' concerts.

The two kids, Matty and Cort, were sprawled out on the rug, watching television. A fire crackled in the fireplace.

"Hello boys," I said.

Silence.

"Hello boys," I said again.

"Hi, Uncle Quinn," Matty said. Matty was the six-year-old. Cort was four. Cort didn't say anything. He just lay on his stomach, chin propped in his hands, lost in the blue glow of the television.

"Great conversationalists, eh?" Carol said, rolling her eyes. "Matty's got a sore throat, so I've got double duty this morning. Hold on a second. I'll be right back." She headed down the hallway and I sat on the couch and looked at the television. Cartoons. Robots fighting other robots.

"How do you know which are the good robots?" I said.

Silence.

"How do you know which are the good robots?" I said again.

"They have the shields with the snakes," Matty said without moving his eyes from the screen.

"Oh."

I leaned back in the couch and watched the cartoon. The carnage was horrific, and at the end of it, amid the smoking rubble and charred metal and tangible throbbing of leftover bloodlust, the good robots stood together in the desolate aftermath and uttered a half-dozen perfunctory sentences about how sharing was the most important thing and just because you can beat people up doesn't mean that you're *really* strong, because true strength comes from the heart. I have a pretty good handle on my gag reflex, but this was pushing it.

Carol came back in the room.

"Where's Hank?" I said.

Carol patted her stomach. "Where he's been all night and most of the morning. On the pot."

I smiled and Carol sat down next to me. She sighed a very deep sigh and stared me straight in the eyes. "What do you think we should do?" she said.

"Kaopectate."

Carol shut her eyes. Opened them again. "Unfunny, Quinn. I *mean* what do you think we should do about the property."

"What can you do? Wait twelve years and then sell it for a million dollars."

While she continued to peer at me, Hank came staggering down the hallway in his bathrobe, hair rumpled, pale as a ghost.

"Speaking of a million dollars . . ." I said.

Hank grumbled, plopped down on the couch, and ran his fingers through his hair. "Don't say a word."

"Your *folie de matin* catch up with you?"

"My *folie de matin* was just fine," he snapped. "It was that damn Black Widow you forced on me."

Carol looked back and forth at us. "Are you speaking in some secret code?"

Hank stood on wobbly legs. He looked like one of those baby deer in Disney films trying to take its first step. Carol bit her lower lip and decided something.

"Hank," she said. "You're feeding the kids this morning."

Hank looked puzzled. "What?"

"Pancake batter's already made. Temperature's set on the electric pan. All you have to do is plug it in." Carol went to the hall closet and pulled out her jacket.

"Where are you going?" Hank said.

"Quinn's taking me out for breakfast."

"He is?"

Hank looked at me and I shrugged.

"Come on, Hank," Carol said. "Try being an enlightened husband for just a couple of hours, okay? While you were in Jamaica watching nubile nymphets swim naked at waterfalls, I was washing the pee-pee out of your youngest son's Teenage Mutant Ninja Turtles bedsheets. Give me a break."

There wasn't much he could say to that. Carol and I headed out the door and left Hank standing forlornly in the living room. I wanted to toss off some zinger by Whitman or Blake, an over-the-shoulder exit line to really finish him off, but I refrained. Poor guy was having a tough enough time as it was.

Sometimes I'm just staggered by the depth and breadth of my own maturity.

Mel's Drive-In on Geary Street is that rarest of rare commodities — an institution that, despite being an institution, has not become precious, self-conscious, or phony. Okay, they don't let you forget that it was used as the locale for a couple of big Hollywood movies. And yes, they sell T-shirts and visors at the cash register and the menu occasionally deviates into mentioning San Francisco personalities. But it's still the best place in town to eat a good solid utensil-clattering breakfast at a reasonable price.

Carol and I got a booth at the front window looking out at Geary, and Brenda was right with us, pouring coffee.

"Where you been, Quinn?" she said.

"Oh, you know. Millbrae. Daly City. Montego Bay. The usual."

"Tough life."

Brenda had been waitressing at Mel's for years. She was a hard-looking woman of nearly forty, brown hair pulled back, permanent fatigue pouches under her eyes. She was small and bony and used to be a cocktail waitress at a casino in Vegas till she decked some high roller who pinched her butt. Left hook to the jaw and down he went. To hear Brenda tell it they had to cart the guy out on a stretcher and then she found out he was a close, personal friend of a close, personal friend of the owner of the casino, and that was the end of Brenda's Las Vegas career. I didn't doubt the story for an instant.

"Putting on a little weight," I said.

"Weight, bullshit," Brenda said. "Got another in the hopper."

The coffee cup stopped at my lips. "You're kidding?"

"Due in February."

"How many will this make?"

"Number four." Brenda flipped through her order pad and nodded her chin at me. "Regular?"

I nodded. She looked at Carol.

"I'll have what he's having," Carol said.

"You ever thought about birth control, Brenda?" I said.

103

"Piss off, Quinn," she said. "You wouldn't believe what I had shoved up me. Foam, gel, ointment, IUD. You think Love Canal had chemical waste? You shoulda seen me in the bathroom every time I wanted twenty minutes of the old in-and-out. Didn't matter. Squiggly little bastard swam through all of it." She shook her head. "Naw. That's it. I done enough. Frank wants to keep banging me, he goes under the knife."

Brenda demonstrated the proposed severing of Frank's vas deferens by looping an imaginary pair of shoelaces and yanking them tight with the final, bone-cracking snap of a hangman's noose. My knees instinctively came together under the table.

"Back in a second," she said. Brenda turned and headed off back toward the kitchen. Carol lifted her eyebrows.

"Demure little thing, isn't she?"

"That's Brenda." I shrugged. "And she only talks that way with me."

I flipped through the jukebox selector attached to the table, put in my fifty cents, and chose "The Banana Boat Song."

"Mood music," I said.

Carol clasped her hands together and set them on the table. "The lawyer from Jamaica called this morning."

"Bongo?"

Carol wrinkled her forehead. "No. The lawyer. Nigel Brambley."

"Same guy."

"What?"

"Bongo and Nigel Brambley are the same guy. It's a little confusing. Did he talk to Hank?"

Carol shook her head. "Hank was in the bathroom doing his thing, so I talked to him myself."

"And?"

"He said the last couple of days an anonymous buyer has been pestering him about the land at Seven Altars. Offered two hundred fifty thousand cash."

"And?"

"And Mr. Brambley told them it wasn't for sale."

"He called just to tell you that?"

Carol cleared her throat. "He was concerned. He said the people who contacted him are having trouble taking no for an answer."

"In what way?"

"He didn't go into it."

I played with the information a second. "Did you tell Hank?"

"Sure. He just laughed. When he heard the two hundred fifty thousand figure he said they were still a decimal point off."

"How come you're not laughing?"

Carol unclasped her hands and began playing with the fork. "I'm an old-fashioned girl, Quinn. I don't talk about my vaginal foam at breakfast tables. I don't swim naked at waterfalls." Pause. "I don't believe that million-dollar houses fall out of the sky without serious strings attached."

"I think you should reconsider swimming naked at waterfalls, but on the other things . . . you're right."

"This isn't a joke, Quinn. The lawyer said these people might contact us directly. I'm worried."

"Last time we talked you wanted Hank to just hop on a plane and pick up the money."

"Last time we talked I didn't know that Marty had been murdered." Carol looked me in the eyes. "Quinn, I dragged you out of the house this morning because I wanted to hear your version of what's going on. Hank and I have been talking, but he's got moonbeams in his eyes and I can't really trust what I'm hearing. Know what I mean?"

"Okay," I said. "I have two versions. The first version assumes a kinder, gentler world where everybody tells the truth and you won't get spun, folded, or mutilated by taking things at face value."

106

"In other words, the version you don't buy for a second?"

"You said that. Not me."

Carol forced a tight, reluctant smile. "Let me hear it anyway."

"Marty Greene left Hank his property. Why not? He was Matty's godfather. His wife was rich and there wasn't going to be any squabbling over community property. Bongo said — I mean, Brambley said . . . For simplicity's sake can I just call him Bongo?"

Carol shrugged, bewildered. "Go ahead."

"Okay. Bongo said Marty had no family. Where else would the property go? Besides, Marty was young and healthy and it hardly seemed an immediate concern."

"And the drugs?" Carol said.

"In Version One yes, we assume Marty was involved with drugs, exactly as reported by the upstanding and incorruptible Priest River police. Shot on a boat full of ganja. He hadn't made much of his academic career. People do strange things when they sit and idle. Maybe the intrigue of drug smuggling appealed to him. Or he was having financial troubles none of us are yet aware of. He crossed somebody or was crossed by somebody and that was that."

"And the will?"

I shrugged. "It was in keeping with everything else. Almost a practical joke that shockingly came true. All the funny little provisions. Making Hank get on a plane and come to paradise. Forcing him to get a tan. And if the property truly was to help the kids through school, it is perfectly plausible that the twelve-year wait would be a part of the will. Keep Hank from cashing out and starting his Rolls Royce collection."

Carol listened carefully. "Okay," she said at last, "and what's Version Two?"

"Version Two is my gut feeling. I trust Stephanie when she tells me Marty wasn't the drug-dealing type."

"Why do you trust her?"

"Because she has high cheekbones and full lips. Why else?"

Carol put on her long-suffering look. "Sorry I asked."

"Just kidding, Carol."

"I know. Keep talking."

"Okay. I had a chat with the local police — swell bunch of guys, by the way — and they let slip that a hundred pounds of ganja was left on the boat. I haven't checked the *Wall Street Journal* lately, but I figure the street value of that much dope is at least thirty or forty grand. If I'm in the drug business I don't kill Marty and then walk away from inventory like that. Not unless I'm sure I'm going to recover it later. So what other reason is there to leave it on the boat except to frame him?"

"And Mr. Brambley? I mean . . . Bongo?"

"I think he's on the level, but I also think it would be naive to totally rule out the possibility that he isn't. Bongo might very well have some silent partners in this. Partners who have money. Bongo told us that Marty's estate picked up the tab for our trip down, but we don't have any proof. Suppose somebody else bankrolled our two-day junket."

"Maybe Bongo paid for it himself," Carol said. "Maybe he's the anonymous buyer who wants it for two hundred fifty thousand dollars."

I shook my head. "Believe me, Carol. Bongo's capacity to shower riches began and ended with Pepsi in a Dixie cup and a few cubes of ice. The hotel alone cost a thousand dollars a night for the two of us. Airfare. Private planes. Gourmet food." I paused and took a gulp of coffee. "Another thing. I don't think it was an accident that Bongo put the fear of God into Hank about Priest River. The way he talked up the violence. The danger. How you'd never want to raise your kids there. Put the needle in enough and a quarter of a million cash might be something the Wilkie family would jump at in a second. Then the anonymous third party resells it for a couple of million, maybe tossing a five-thousand-dollar bone to Bongo as a little thank-you."

"But isn't this all a moot point?" Carol said. "Hank can't sell it to *anyone*, no matter what the price. Bongo himself told the anonymous buyers that."

I smiled. "Come on, Carol. Where there are lawyers there are loopholes. You know that."

Brenda was back with our breakfasts. She set the plates in front of us, gave me a wink, and left. Carol concentrated on the steam rising off her eggs.

"Let me ask you a real basic question," Carol said at last. "What would you do if you were Hank?"

"Bide my time. Let the dust settle and not do anything impulsive in the meantime. But I wouldn't let Seven Altars go for less than a million dollars no matter what. Your financial concerns would be gone for the rest of your lives, the kids can go to Princeton, and the third party'll still make a killing when they resell it."

"Bad choice of words," Carol said.

"Sorry."

I smiled but Carol didn't smile. We simply

ate our respective breakfasts in silence, and when there was no more food on the plates we drove home.

My apartment hadn't changed much since breakfast. No waterfalls had sprung up in the living room. There was no need to hang mosquito netting over the bed. I went into the world headquarters of Amalgamated Tropical Enterprises — also known as my spare bedroom — and checked the telephone message machine. No calls. There hadn't been a call in a month. The Bay Area populace had their phobias temporarily under control.

I killed an hour catching up on some correspondence, then the doorbell rang three short bursts and Hank started up the stairs. It was an especially slow ascent. He came down the hallway and dropped into the chair across from me.

"How was breakfast?" he said.

"Great."

"Brenda?"

"She's fine. Pregnant."

"Again?"

"Frank doesn't know it, but he's about to have some delicate surgery."

Hank nodded. "Give her my congrats next time."

"I will."

111

Hank kept nodding. Ten long seconds of silence passed.

"Okay," I said. "Let's have it."

"Have what?"

"What's the problem?"

"No problem," Hank said. "I'm just curious if the word 'loophole' by any chance dropped from anybody's lips during the eating of aforementioned breakfast?"

"Maybe once."

"That's what I thought," Hank said. "Carol decided we should tell Bongo to start digging for loopholes in the will and take the two-fifty. I left the house before things got ugly."

"Don't blame me. I advised holding out for a million."

"She's scared, Quinn. She wants out."

I shrugged. "It's not a completely unreasonable emotion, Hank. Let's face it. Marty didn't live to be eighty and die peacefully in his sleep. Somebody blew him away. Emphatically."

"But two hundred fifty thousand," Hank moaned. "The goddamn *driveway's* worth two hundred fifty thousand! You know what this means, don't you? This means I can't even afford to quit my job flipping hamburgers yet!"

"Relax."

"How can I relax? Food and beverage is

a bad profession. Language skills start to deteriorate. I'm using rice and gravy as verbs. 'Ain't those potatoes been gravied yet?' 'Hell no, not till somebody rices the plate.' " Hank winced and clutched his stomach. "Jesus Christ . . ."

"Cramps?"

" 'Cramps' is far too soothing and joyful a word to describe what I'm going through. My lower intestine is staging an exact reenactment of the firebombing of Dresden."

I smiled. "William Blake say, he who travels on road of excess must also be prepared for periodic bouts of honorable amoebic dysentery."

I went into the bathroom, dug through the medicine chest, and came back with a bottle of pills I'd picked up in Mexico City the year before. "Take three of these six hours apart and you'll be a new man."

Hank scrutinized the bottle, read the label. "Third World antibiotics," he mumbled. "What the hell's in here? Hydrolyzed auto parts?"

"Just take them."

Hank tapped three pills out of the bottle and put them in his pocket. Then he sighed and shook his head. "In my weakened state some of this has had a chance to sink in. How unreal it is. Like a nightmare. Marty dead, Stephanie a widow . . ." Hank continued to shake his head. "*Twelve* bullets! Jesus!"

"Norman said when drug dealers get irritated they tend to underscore their irritation."

"But why did they have to shoot him so many times in the face?" Hank went on. "I sit in bed now and try to remember what Marty looked like and it's almost impossible. Know what I mean? I can't reconstruct his features, even in my memory, because all I see is what he must have looked like after the murder."

"Maybe that was the point," I said.

Hank focused on me. "What?"

"Did we ever find out who it was that identified the body?"

Hank stared at me a good, long five seconds. "What are you talking about?"

"Body identification. Positive ID. You know, the person who goes into the morgue and somebody pulls down the sheet and they say, 'Yes, officer. That's Marty.' Who identified him in Priest River? Stephanie?"

Hank shook his head and abruptly stood up. "I don't know, and I'm not going to ask her. In fact, I'm sorry I brought the subject up in the first place." He dug around in his right pants pocket and pulled out a scrap of paper. "Almost forgot. Here."

Hank tossed the wad of paper to me. I unwrapped it and smoothed out the wrinkles. An address was scribbled in red ink.

"What's this?" I said.

"Stephanie called this morning. She's back in the city. Her brother's throwing a welcome-home party for her Saturday night and we're invited. I've got an actual cash money paying gig at the Zoo, so I can't make it. But I thought you'd want to go. Catch up on your drooling."

"Her brother?"

"Russell. Never met him, but from what Marty told me at the Cliff House he's the family ne'er-do-well. Sails, skis, twiddles his thumbs." Hank sighed. "Why is it that the people who don't know what the hell to do with their lives are the ones who have all the goddamn time in the world not to do it in?"

"Can you repeat that?"

"No."

Hank began his trudge toward the stairs. "Anyway, you're invited. I'll give you a few minutes to pretend that it doesn't matter, then you can dive for the phone and accept. But when you see Stephanie just try to remember one thing."

"What's that?"

"She's still in mourning."

7

The party was held at a sprawling, multilevel home in Seacliff, one of San Francisco's tonier neighborhoods, perched above the cliffs on the rocky bluffs just west of the Golden Gate Bridge, tucked neatly between the Presidio on one side and Lincoln Park on the other. I tooled my van past the long line of imported automobiles and parked way down at the end of the street.

The evening was fresh and cool. The rain had finally lifted and a low blanket of thick fog hugged the bay, foghorns blowing. Above, the sky was a fragile dome of deep, dark blue. I started to stride right by, but then I slowed, slowed even more, and came to a complete stop to stand a moment and take it in.

In recent years I found myself waxing philosophic in the tired and predictable way of how much the city has changed for the worse. Good-bye to the offbeat characters who gave neighborhoods their charm. Hello to an army of bankers and insurance executives who cared intensely about their home wine cellars and whether it was correct to have the Chardonnays on the bottom and the Cabernets on top. I had grown cynical and irritated, grumbling like an old man who loved the world when he was young and full of juice, and now hated the watchdogs of his decline and blamed them for the withering of his soul.

It reached a point where I fled temporarily to Mexico, heavy with outrages at modern vulgarity. I had come to look at San Francisco as nothing more than an expensive call girl, gorgeous only because she had no choice in the matter. But, alas. The call girl called me back. Stroked my forehead and smiled. Forgave me the occasional infatuation with cobblestoned streets and tropical waterfalls. The easy dream. The effortless narcotic. San Francisco had a subtler magic, and I was beginning to simply walk right past it the way a museum guard at the Louvre must come to see the *Mona Lisa* as just another painting that stands between him and the employee bathroom facilities.

Russell Axton's house was from the Star Trek school of interior design. Cubes and sharp angles and spaceship austerity. It was built on the slope of a cliff, so once you went through the front door you began a gradual descent. Nothing that you would notice, especially; three steps here, four steps there, little by little, room by room. But by the time you reached the far end of the house you were a good twenty feet below the entrance level.

At least two hundred people were already on hand. I recognized some of them. Local mini-celebrities. Hometown media luminaries. There were the rakish young lions, and there were the wealthy, face-lifted females who looked like they wouldn't mind being raked. Only about a dozen people seemed the type you'd like to roast marshmallows with, and they mostly drifted to the corners. Stephanie was nowhere in sight.

I counted five bars going full tilt, but the one out on the back terrace looked the least crowded and most inviting, so that's where I went. An elderly, white-suited bartender stood at his station, arranging glasses and bottles. I ordered a Scotch on the rocks and wandered to the edge of the terrace and peered over the guardrail. A rocky cliff went straight down three hundred feet into the pounding surf of the Pacific Ocean. A couple miles to the right, eerily lit in the foggy night, was the Golden Gate Bridge. There were several other cliffside homes nearby, but the terrace was laid out in such a way as to ensure total privacy.

I was on my way back into the main house when I saw Stephanie among a crowd of well-wishers. She noticed me at the same time, smiled, and managed to break away from the group.

She was even lovelier than I remembered, wearing a black sequin dress that was tight at her throat and low-cut in back, black nylons, and three-inch heels. Her sun-streaked blond hair was pulled back away from her face. The Caribbean tan was as deep and layered as varnished mahogany. A vivid contrast to the rest of us pale fog-dwellers.

She walked straight up to me with her right arm extended. "Quinn," she said. "I'm glad you could come."

We shook hands and she looked up at me. "My goodness, you're tall."

"Only six-two."

"Really?"

"Really. On a basketball court the other guys kick sand in my face."

Stephanie looked down at her shoes. "Must be these heels. I'm eyeball to eyeball with most of the men here. Come on. Let me introduce you to some people."

I followed as she took me from room to room, from conversation cluster to conversation cluster. I cradled my drink and smiled

119

and gave the thirty-second version of my life and times to those few who bothered to ask.

"A shame Hank couldn't come," Stephanie said at one point. "He always loved a party."

"Hank Wilkie?"

"You sound surprised."

"I am. The Hank I know is the last to arrive and the first to leave."

Stephanie shook her head. "Not in New York. People who didn't even know him would invite him to their parties because of his reputation. I think that's what made him decide to go into entertainment. If everybody was going to laugh so hard, he might as well get paid for it."

I took a sip from my drink. "Hank said this is your brother's house?"

"Uh-huh. Russell. Actually, this was the family house. I grew up here. It wasn't quite so severe when Mother and Father were doing the decorating." Stephanie smiled and craned her neck and scanned the crowd. "There he is. That's Russell."

Stephanie pointed to a man standing near the entrance to the kitchen. He was in a heated discussion with a woman. From a distance Russell looked younger than Stephanie. He had an oddly shaped head, thin and narrow at the chin, wide and flat at

120

the temples. A rounded-off triangle, like a Yield sign on the highway. Yet he was still handsome in a rich-man's-son way, with a bumper crop of carefully tousled blond hair and smooth, unblemished features. The mouth was thin as an incision and a little too large for his face. It started off fine but then ran out of room and had to hook up slightly on the end, as though a child had drawn it on and miscalculated. An unruffled, manicured fellow whose demeanor effortlessly implied the backup inventory of Porsches and ski condos and summers spent at tennis camps.

I was so focused on the brother that it took me a couple of seconds to register the woman he was talking to. When I did, I executed the kind of double take that would've gotten me thrown out of acting school. I'd seen her before. Recently. Very recently. Then it clicked. Meredith. The stoned redhead from the patio in Priest River who was last seen giggling up against Bongo's swimming trunks. I looked at Stephanie and she stopped me before I could say a word.

"Russell's girlfriend," she said wearily. "Not a subject the family brings up at the Thanksgiving table."

Russell was trying to keep the argument hush-hush, but Meredith made no attempt to disguise her anger. She was quite a sight, all cleavage and panty lines, her body shoehorned into a Ferrari-red evening gown. She pouted and stomped her foot and shook her head. The other guests stayed clear.

"Maybe this isn't the best time to introduce you," Stephanie said. "They seem . . . involved."

"I'll take a rain check."

We small-talked for another minute or two and then Stephanie recognized someone in the crowd.

"Oh, no," she said. "Aunt Rose just came in."

"Sounds ominous."

Stephanie nodded. "The matriarch."

A dour, thickset woman of about seventy was slowly clumping down the stairs from the direction of the front door. Her face was heavily powdered and she was sagging beneath the weight of her jewelry. Gold and diamonds and emeralds and sapphires assaulted the eye from every angle. If Aunt Rose went down in a storm it would be worth the effort to send along a salvage team.

Stephanie turned and gave me a brave smile. "I've got to spend some time with her. But don't go before we have a chance to talk."

"I won't."

"Because I really need to talk to you before you leave. It's important."

"I'll be around."

"Promise?"

"Promise."

Stephanie gave me an innocent squeeze on the arm and winked. "Thanks." Then she excused herself and disappeared into the fawning multitude that had begun to swarm Aunt Rose.

I nursed my drink and turned my attention back to the argument by the kitchen door. Russell said something. Meredith just laughed. Russell said it again. Meredith shook her head, looked bored, and swatted her hand in Russell's direction as if fending off a particularly bothersome gnat. Then she turned while he was in the middle of a sentence and disappeared through the kitchen door. Russell fumed. Then he drained the last of his drink in one swallow, clenched his jaw, and looked out across the sea of merrymakers. Someone called to him from across the room and he reattached his host-of-the-party smile, waved, and went to the dining-room bar for another drink.

Meredith had exited like a woman who needed to be followed, but Russell wasn't going to be the one to do it. I set my drink down on the nearest table, glanced this way and that, and began edging through the crowd.

The door led to the kitchen itself, now empty but for three Latin maids fiddling with trays of food. They looked at me with blank, employee eyes. I asked in Spanish if they'd seen the young woman with the red dress, and they pointed at another door. I went through it and another hallway stretched out before me. A crimson velvet cord blocked the entrance to the hallway. A sign was attached to it, politely informing all wayward guests that this was a private section of the house and not for general perusal. Beyond it, at the far end of the corridor, I caught a glimpse of Meredith ducking into a room on the left. I nimbly slipped under the cord and took a quick look back to see if anybody had seen me. Nobody had. I walked to the last door on the left. It was partially open. I stood outside for a slow count to ten, then entered.

It was a bedroom with gold satin wallpaper and black silk sheets on the king-sized bed. Gaudy as the honeymoon suite in a so-so Vegas hotel. The carpet — blindingly white — was thick enough to lose a golf ball in. Meredith stood before a full-length mirror at the foot of the bed, reapplying makeup. When I walked in she simply gave me a side-glance and went back to the makeup. There was no recognition in her eyes.

"This is a private room," she said. It was a statement, not a threat. There was no malice in her voice.

I put my hand on my stomach. "Felt a little sick. Thought I'd better get as far away as possible from the rest of the guests."

"Any port in a storm, hunh?"

"Something like that. Mind if I sit a second."

Meredith shrugged. "Go ahead. It's that smoked oyster shit they're passing around. Bash like this, you'd think they wouldn't buy the hors d'oeuvres at K Mart. That's what they did, you know? At one of those discount stores I forget the name of. Labels come off, or the cans get dented . . ."

I sat down on the edge of the bed. "Generic caviar?"

"You got it."

Meredith fiddled in front of the mirror for another couple of seconds. Thumped her stomach, slapped her thighs, fluffed out her hair. Then she turned and faced me, hands on hips, legs set wide apart.

"How do I look?" she asked.

"Fine."

"Really?"

"You look fine. Honest."

She smoothed out an imaginary belly. "Everybody says I shouldn't wear red because I'm a redhead, but I don't care. I like red. Red and purple. Do you like red?"

"On you it's my favorite color," I said.

She gave me a naughty-boy look and then went into the bathroom and left the door half-open. I could see her nyloned kneecaps jutting out as she plunked down on the toilet.

"If you gotta puke," she said above the steady gurgle of splashing urine. "Do it in the toilet. Russell'd shit the colors of the rainbow if you bailed all over his precious rug."

"Okay."

The kneecaps straightened and the spindle of toilet paper spun and the toilet flushed. She came out fluffing her hair. "Jesus . . . every time I come to the States I put on five pounds and you know where it goes? Straight to my gut." She sucked in her breath and her cleavage clamped shut with enough force to crack walnuts. "How old do you think I am?"

"I don't know."

"Take a guess."

"I really don't know."

"Take a guess anyway."

I thought for a second. "Twenty-five."

She whirled on me, eyes wide. "Twenty-five! I only just turned twenty last month!"

"You told me to guess."

"Oh, that's great! That's just great! I'm gonna look horrible when I'm thirty. My boobs are too big, that's part of the problem. They're getting saggy already. Look."

She cupped her hands beneath her breasts, hoisted them skyward, and then let them drop. She did it again — up, down, up, down — as if her nipples were doing chin-ups.

"See that?" she said.

I nodded that I saw it, but Meredith wasn't paying any attention to me. She turned, gave herself one last percussive primp in front of the mirror, and sighed. "You really think I look twenty-five?"

"You seem mature, I guess."

She grunted at my feeble diplomacy.

"You don't recognize me, do you?" I said.

That stopped her for a second. Meredith came over, sat on the edge of the bed, and looked at me. "No," she said. "Who're you?"

"The barbecue at Stephanie's house in Priest River."

Meredith continued to stare, and gradually the short-term memory started to kick in. "Oh, yeah. You and that other guy, the one who got Marty's house."

"Right."

She nodded and smiled. "I was kinda

wasted that day."

"You left before we could say good-bye."

She continued to nod and smile, a little wistfully, as though I had summoned from the deep, dark past a long-forgotten pleasant memory from childhood. Then little tiny shards and slivers of reality debris started to fall into her consciousness, Skylab breaking up over the wilds of Australia, and the smile faded. "So what're you doing here?" she said, glancing down at the bed. "And don't tell me you're about to puke because you're not sick one little bit."

"I'm curious about Priest River."

Meredith just looked at me. I hadn't answered her question.

"Stephanie invited me to the party," I said.

"Oh." Meredith nodded and ran a long red fingernail along the side of her throat, as though absentmindedly retracing the ridge of a scar. "How come you're interested in Priest River?"

"I'm concerned for my friend."

"What for? He got the house, right?"

"He's also got a family, and if there's a lot of drug dealing in the area . . ."

Meredith shrugged her shoulders and glanced around the room. "There's a lot of drug dealing in *this* area."

128

I smiled. "Suppose you're right." Pause. "Did you know Marty?"

"Sure. Everybody in Priest River knew Marty. He was a popular guy."

"Do you think he could have been mixed up with drugs?"

Meredith's expression darkened. "Are you some kind of cop?"

"No."

"Don't bullshit me."

"Believe me, Meredith, I — "

The door suddenly swung open and a man took two steps into the room and stopped. He had on a suit and tie but I didn't think he looked like a guest.

"Oh, shit," Meredith said under her breath, more annoyed than frightened. "Here we go . . ."

The man said, "Excuse me, Miss Nelson," then turned to me. "What are you doing back here? This is a restricted area of the house."

"I didn't realize that."

"There's a sign right in the hallway."

He stood with his legs planted as though I might at any moment spring for the door and attempt a desperate getaway. He was tall. Taller than me. Significantly taller than me. His neck was thick, the face scarred by acne. Brass-knuckles personality. He must have had eyes, but I swear to God from where I sat I couldn't see any.

"He's a friend, Gary," Meredith said wearily. "I'm not balling him."

Gary kept looking at me. He had his hands linked in front of him, left hand holding the right wrist, covering his crotch, Secret Service style. "This wing of the house is not for guests," Gary said. "Please leave."

"Take it easy, Gary," Meredith said.

"Please leave," Gary repeated.

One didn't argue with Gary. After two or three of his "pleases" your intestines needed defrosting.

Meredith looked at me and shrugged. "Better go. Russell's the jealous type." Then she smirked and wandered back into the bathroom, shutting the door behind her.

I got up and headed toward the door, but as I passed Gary he unclasped his hands and put a firm grip on my shoulder and held me where I was. It was like walking into an unexpected chest-high clothesline. The thumb dug more than necessary into my neck muscle. Much more. A bright and quick flash of pain lit me up from my shoulder to my kneecap.

"Wise up," Gary said. "Leave Miss Nelson alone. One warning's all you get, pal."

I nodded and Gary let his grip linger and

tighten just long enough to let me know he meant it. Then he released me and I continued on my way.

Even from that close range I couldn't tell for certain if Gary had any eyes.

8

By the time I reached the outdoor bar I had thought of three nasty and cutting things I could've said to Gary when he dug his thumb into my shoulder. My personal favorite was: "A little more to the left and down about an inch." I rehearsed how it would've gone. Me unflappable, tough as nails. Meredith giggling because she'd never heard anyone mouth off to Gary before. Gary himself turning purple with impotent rage at having been so succinctly put in his place.

"Yes, sir," the pale bartender said. "Scotch on the rocks?"

"Good memory."

"Actually, sir, memory has very little to do with it." He fixed the drink and handed it to me. "I have a system. Every good bartender has a system."

"I break out in hives when people call me 'sir.' Name's Quinn."

"Very good, Quinn. My name is Edward, but I would prefer that you call me Eddie."

We stood together and talked for a while. Eddie was quite a character beneath his

132

Caspar Milquetoast facade. He'd worked one of the Financial District's more popular watering holes for decades, calling it quits a few years back, then taking it up again when his wife died. Eddie believed that there were two kinds of people who should never retire — saloon keepers and orchestra conductors. He had a passion for Richard Wagner and the St. Louis Cardinals. Traveled once a year to England to visit the grave of Milton. That sort of thing.

While we talked I kept one eye on the party. Stephanie was nowhere to be seen. Ditto Meredith. My old deep-muscle massage buddy Gary was also scarce. Once in a while I'd catch a glimpse of Russell moving with cultivated ease from one person to the next, but that was it. I glanced at my watch. I'd log another hour or two, have my talk with Stephanie, and then head across town and catch Hank's performance at the Holy City Zoo.

Eddie started to get some business so I took my drink back inside and passed five dull minutes at the hors d'oeuvres table, shoving celery sticks into a beige-colored dip and carefully avoiding the smoked oysters. Somewhere around my seventh celery stick I suddenly saw Meredith across the room, over a sea of heads, chatting in a flirtatious

133

way with three elderly gents in funeral-home suits who were doing a rotten job of not staring at her cleavage.

Meredith tossed her head back to laugh at something one of them had said, and her eyes found me. The smile changed slightly. A subtle crease of come-hither fire. She patted her stomach and put a finger down her throat to indicate vomiting. I laughed and gave her the A-OK sign. Russell's precious rug was safe. She turned back to the three men who stared uncomprehendingly, openmouthed.

"There you are!"

A hand fell on my shoulder and I instinctively pulled away. Stephanie blinked and stepped back.

"Didn't mean to scare you," she said.

"My mind was a million miles away."

"Sorry I took so long," she said, shaking her head. "That was a particularly rough session with Aunt Rose."

"No problem. I'm enjoying myself."

Stephanie looked around the room with a slightly troubled expression on her face. "We need to talk, but not here. Let's go where it's quiet."

"Lead the way."

We maneuvered through one last gauntlet of so-good-to-see-you and how-terrible-about-Marty and what-are-your-plans. A

134

couple of teen idols fleeing a throng of adoring fans. Then we ducked down a wide hallway lined with paintings and went all the way to the end and through the last door on the right. A spiral wrought-iron staircase almost identical to the one in Seven Altars took us up to a cozy one-room studio that perched on the roof and overlooked the dark Pacific and the terrace where Eddie tended bar.

"This is Russell's study," Stephanie said. "We won't be bothered up here."

I liked the room immediately. It was rich and warm and cluttered with knickknacks. A refreshing change from the sparse, minimalist atmosphere of the rest of the house. A high-backed C-shaped couch the color of vanilla ice cream faced the ocean and took up most of the floor space. Thirty pounds' worth of hardback Goya sat on a glass and chrome elongated oval coffee table. Muted landscape paintings hung on the wall. The hardwood floor was covered by a lush burgundy carpet with intricate designs and gold tassels at the edges. To the left was a wet bar and a music system and a small television built into the wall. There were two cherry-wood bookshelves on the right, filled with trinkets rather than books. No desk. No chairs.

"What does Russell study when he comes

to his study?" I said.

Stephanie shrugged. "Who knows? I think it's more like a meditation room, like Marty was with his telescope."

We sat at opposite ends of the C-shaped couch. Stephanie leaned her head all the way back and stared straight up at the ceiling.

"Quite a party," I said.

Stephanie gently shook her head from side to side and kept looking at the ceiling. "This isn't a party. A party is a place where you relax and let your hair down and enjoy yourself."

"And you're doing none of the above?"

"I'm too busy defending Marty."

"Who's attacking?" I said.

Stephanie chuckled. "Aunt Rose was the final straw. White flag time. Throw myself at the mercy of the Party Gods and hope they understand why I can't do this anymore."

"Your Aunt Rose reminded me of the Queen of Hearts in *Alice in Wonderland*," I said.

"Off with their heads, off with their heads?" Stephanie laughed.

"Exactly."

We both laughed for a few seconds. Then I leaned back on the couch and linked my hands behind my head. "How does it feel to be in the Old Country again?" I said.

Stephanie exhaled. "Strange."

"How so?"

"Just your basic culture shock, I suppose. Nothing serious. You have to remember that I haven't lived in the States for almost six years. Requires a bit of readjusting."

I nodded. "There *is* a vague dissimilarity between Priest River and Seacliff."

Stephanie motioned for me to hold on for a second. "Let me demonstrate just how vaguely dissimilar it is."

She got up and went over to a hidden control panel that had been built into the wall. She bent from the waist, both hands on her knees, and stared at the switches. The clinging black dress accommodated her wonderfully, and the study was beginning to smell of her fragrance. Light and fresh. Gardenias after a soft tropical rain.

"Here we go," she said, flipping a couple of switches. There was a second of silence, then the room was suddenly flooded with the sound of crashing waves.

"What's that?" I said.

"Russell has microphones down at the bottom of the cliff."

"You're kidding."

"Took eight hundred feet of cable." Stephanie laughed. "And practically killed the two guys who installed it. That's what I mean about culture shock."

She came back to the couch and settled in. "Russell can be incredibly indulgent. From a distance it was more palatable, but now that I'm up here, living around it . . ."

"Did Russell ever come visit in Jamaica?"

"Now and then."

"And none of it rubbed off?"

Stephanie shook her head. "He just wanted to sail and play golf. Russell didn't come to Jamaica to immerse himself in the local culture."

"How did he and Marty get along?"

"They didn't. I remember the first time Russell came down to visit. Marty went out on the boat to catch fish for dinner. Spent the whole day in the sun, blistered his hands, got sunburned, everything. He came back around dusk with a bucketful of fish only to find out that Russell was having a half-dozen lobsters flown down from Maine. Marty was furious. When the lobster arrived in this special refrigerated van, he took his portion outside and threw it to the dog. I thought Russell was going to die. That sort of set the tone for future visits. They tended to go their separate ways."

Stephanie smiled and lowered her eyes. "Anyway, I didn't bring you up here to rehash old memories. There were a couple of things I wanted to say to you. To you and Hank both." She cleared her throat and kept her eyes lowered. "First of all, let me apologize for being so rude in Priest River."

"Rude?"

"I barely said hello and didn't bother at all with good-bye. But when I went out on the patio Meredith said you'd all gone up to the waterfalls . . . I just couldn't do it. Marty and I spent so much time up there together . . ."

"Please, Stephanie. You don't need to apologize for anything."

She wasn't really listening. Her gaze was focused on a spot beyond me and to my right. "A few days after the . . . after Marty died, I went up to the waterfalls by myself. To forget. Or to remember. I don't know which." Stephanie hesitated, tried to smile, then averted her eyes again. "I haven't told anybody about this except Bongo."

I nodded and sat quietly.

"I was up there at the waterfalls, and at one point I dove all the way to the bottom of the pool at the top, the deep one. I touched the rocks on the bottom and came back up, and when I surfaced . . ." Stephanie shook her head and kept looking off to the right.

"What happened?"

"Marty was there."

"Marty?"

"He was there. Just his reflection, though. Right there in the water next to me. He was smiling, and his black hair was all puffed up like it got after he'd been swimming and it had dried in the sun. It scared me so badly I screamed and screamed. Hysterical. Fought my way out of the pool and ran all the way back down the trail, falling and cutting myself." Stephanie finally shifted her eyes to look at me. "Does that sound crazy?"

"No."

"It sounds crazy to me."

"We have different notions of what crazy is, Stephanie." I smiled. "To me, installing eight hundred feet of cable so you can listen to the waves is crazy."

We sat for a few moments in silence. Then Stephanie exhaled and put a false, brave smile on her face. "No more digressions," she said. "Promise. It's just that things ended kind of abruptly in Jamaica and I want to make sure that there's no misunderstanding about the land Hank inherited."

"What misunderstanding?"

Stephanie sat up a little straighter. "I'm not sure how to convey this without it sounding mushy or sentimental. I was hoping that Hank would be here tonight, but since he isn't I'd appreciate it if you could tell him what I'm about to tell you."

"Of course."

Stephanie licked her lips, frowned down at the book on Goya. "I want Hank to know that I'm glad Marty left Seven Altars to him. I don't want him to think that I'm resentful or feel that the house should have been mine or whatever. I'm not. Marty told me he was changing his will months ago, why he was doing it, everything. We were in complete agreement. I have enough money. Marty and I never had children of our own. We tried, but it wasn't meant to be." Stephanie smiled self-consciously. "Never mind about all that. I'm going off on a tangent again. Too much wine . . ."

"I'll tell Hank," I said. "It'll mean a lot to him."

"The point I'm trying to make is that Marty took his role as godfather very seriously. Not at first, but more and more as the years went on. Matty sort of became the child Marty was never going to have, and he felt guilty about not seeing him or sending him birthday cards or doing all those fun things a godfather does with his godson."

"Hank said he'd been a little delinquent, but there were no hurt feelings."

"Well . . . I'm not going to belabor the

141

point," Stephanie said. "I just wanted you to know that I'm glad the property has gone to Hank and his family and that he should please not think that I'm harboring any kind of resentment. He's probably not thinking anything. This is probably just me being neurotic."

"It'll mean a lot to him," I reiterated.

Stephanie relaxed. Her speech was over. She put her hands on her knees and straightened her shoulders. "There! Now I better get back to the party before Russell sends out a search party." She stood abruptly and I took the hint.

Stephanie went over to the control panel and flicked a switch and a particularly nice wave was interrupted in mid-slosh. I followed her back down the wrought-iron spiral staircase.

I walked over to the guardrail again and stared down at the churning foam of the dark Pacific. Stephanie had been immediately swallowed up into the crowd and I suspected that I wouldn't be talking to her again. At least not in an atmosphere where we didn't have to shout at each other over the din of rattling cocktail glasses. The realization filled me with a curious sense of ache and loss and chances blown.

I nursed my drink and leaned against the guardrail and looked up at the tinted window of the studio perched on the roof above the terrace. Poor, lonesome me. Silhouetted against sea and sky like some loner from a Rod McKuen poem. All I needed was a trusty sheepdog and a raspy voice.

I leaned further over the guardrail and gave some vague and juvenile thought to climbing down the cliff and murmuring obscenities into Russell's microphones. Then Meredith was suddenly beside me, her bright red shoulder rubbing mine.

"Gonna jump?"

"Something like that."

"I might join you," she said. "Anything to get away from these bores. I thought Frisco was supposed to be an interesting town. Don't think we've been properly introduced." She held out her hand. "Meredith Nelson."

I shook it. "Quinn Parker."

"How's the stomach?" She smiled.

"Much better."

"You here by yourself?"

"Yes."

"Me, too. Except my mother and daddy who're gassed over at the other end of the house."

"I thought you were with Russell."

Meredith made a fart sound with her mouth. "Just barely. When my folks are in town I stay with them over at the St. Francis. That way they can pretend I'm still a virgin."

Meredith leaned her elbows against the guardrail and cradled her chin in her palms. A little-girl smile came over her face, like she was about to play Princess and I was going to be the handsome Prince.

"Do you live in Priest River?" I said.

"Montego Bay, but only part of the time. Mostly I'm in Houston or here."

"You like Jamaica?"

Meredith brushed back her hair and reached into her purse for a cigarette. "What's not to like?"

I shrugged. "Everybody I talk to thinks the place is going to blow up."

Meredith smiled and looked at me. "Do you like me, or is all this just an information pump?"

"A little of both."

"Well . . . I could tell you some things about Priest River that'd stand you on your head."

"No kidding?"

"That's right."

I took the lighter from Meredith and did the honors for her while she sheltered the cigarette from the ocean breeze. "I'm all ears," I said.

"*All* ears?" She took a deep drag from her cigarette and leaned her back against the guardrail and looked me up and down and then up again. "What a shame."

Meredith was the kind of woman who exuded horizontal even when she was vertical. She sprawled across the guardrail as one would sprawl across the satin sheets of a king-sized bed. There was challenge in her posture, a sudden licentiousness in the line of her mouth . . . a thirty-car pileup of sexual mayhem in her hazel eyes. "You sure you're still not sick?" she said.

"Never was."

"That's too bad. See, I was thinking maybe what we oughta do is get this nice man here to fix us two more drinks and then we could go back to the bedroom and, you know . . . make sure there's enough Pepto-Bismol."

"Meredith!" I said with mock alarm. "You shock me."

She blew out some smoke and watched it drift away with the night breeze. "Honey," she said, "I don't think you know what shocked is."

"You'd regret it in the morning." I smiled.

"I doubt it," Meredith said. "I mostly regret things I didn't do, not things I did. That's the way it is with most people, don't you think?"

"I haven't really thought about it."

"A brainy guy like you?" Meredith smiled, crushed out the cigarette on the guardrail, and flicked the butt over the side. "You should give more thought to these things."

She walked away before I could answer. Across the terrace, into the house, among the crowd.

I turned back toward the ocean and finished off the rest of my drink in one swallow. I was preparing to brood a bit on Meredith's words when I became conscious of somebody standing right behind me. It was Gary, the security man.

"Could I speak with you a second?" Gary said.

"I was about to have another drink."

"Just for a second."

"Look," I said. "She was the one who came out here. I was minding my own business. Nothing I can do if she decides to follow me around."

Gary held his right thumb and forefinger an inch apart. "One second," he repeated.

We strolled over to the far end of the terrace, around a protected corner where we were out of sight. I leaned against the guardrail and Gary looked out at the Golden Gate Bridge and cleared his throat, trying to figure out how to convey to me what needed conveying. There was something wrong with his features. The proportions were off . . . a blundered statue abandoned by a beginning sculpting student. I finally located his eyes, but one's instinct was to avoid his gaze. He was like some biblical figure, a parable in flesh, and to stare at him would mean turning to salt or going blind or dropping endlessly through the deep chasms of an eternal hell.

"What'd I do wrong now?" I said. "If Russell doesn't want her talking to other people he'd better — "

With the sudden swiftness of a striking snake, Gary's left hand swung out and hit me high and hard on the chest and kept pushing. I went against the guardrail, up and over, felt the sickening swell of a backward somersault, and was off the terrace, legs flailing in the starry sky. The hand still clutched my chest. A nightmarish collage of sky, rocks, and three hundred feet of cold emptiness below me. My drink fell from my hand and the glass plummeted into the nothingness. Then the hand yanked and I was upright, on solid ground, staring wildly into Gary's face.

"Stay away from the girl," he said, "or next time I lose my grip." He lingered just for a second to let me know he meant it, then he slowly walked away, around the corner, back into the festive din of the party.

I took a few moments to compose myself. Let my pulse return to the low three figures. Nobody else was out on the porch. On shaky legs I went back around the corner where Eddie was intensely concentrated on realigning the bottles behind the bar. I adjusted my collar and strolled over to his station.

"Seem to have misplaced my drink," I said.

Eddie kept his head down and started fixing me another. "That happens."

"You didn't by any chance see what just happened over there, did you?"

Eddie finished up my drink and slid it toward me. "From our previous talk I gather you are a student of baseball, Quinn."

I nodded, puzzled. "That's right."

I was bathed in sweat, and Eddie handed me one of the white bar towels without comment. "Then you must remember Early Wynn," he said.

"The pitcher?"

Eddie kept his eyes to the table. "He had a reputation for throwing at batters."

"I remember that."

"Yes, well . . . a reporter asked him about it one time, whether or not it was bad sportsmanship."

"And . . . ?"

"Early Wynn said he would put a fastball under his own grandmother's chin if she tried to crowd the plate." Eddie finally looked up and stared me straight in the eyes. "And he meant it."

9

The Holy City Zoo is an informal comedy nightspot out in the Richmond District on Clement Street. Hayloft ambience with table service and ashtrays. Hank was just finishing up his routine as I walked in. There was applause and enthusiastic whistling. He climbed down from the stage and into the middle of a small group of fans who shook his hand and slapped him on the back and talked excitedly in his face. He saw me from a distance and winked. I sidled up to the bar, absurdly overdressed, and ordered a beer.

I hadn't bothered to say good-bye to Stephanie. My usual impeccable sense of style and grace had gone tumbling down three hundred feet of cliff along with my spare change and Swiss army knife. If the patron saint of car keys hadn't intervened, I'd've been walking home.

"You missed it, didn't you?" Hank said, climbing atop the barstool next to me. "You missed my whole routine!"

"I was detained."

Hank's face wrinkled with pain. "You *al-*

ways miss my triumphs! Always! You're front row center whenever I bomb, but if I have a hit . . ."

"Won't happen again."

Hank's anger with me was mostly fabrication, summoned up for effect. He had that sweet glow of success on his face. Cheeks flushed, eyes bright and alive. He rubbed his hands together and told Howard, the bartender, to break out the Tequila 1800.

"Brand new sketch tonight," he said. "About a guy who wins an all-expense paid trip to Jamaica and the thing is just one disaster after another. Sound familiar?"

"Frighteningly so."

"How was Stephanie's party?" Hank said.

"Remember that redhead from Houston? The one who passed out on the porch in Priest River?"

"How could I forget?"

"Her name's Meredith Nelson and she's the steady squeeze of Russell Axton, Stephanie's brother."

"No kidding." Hank didn't care.

"I made the mistake of talking to her twice, and the second time some goon with a face that looked like somebody'd walked on it with golf shoes gave me a new perspective on the Pacific Ocean."

"So it was a good party?" Hank said.

151

"Have you heard a single word I've said?"

Howard put down the bottle of Tequila 1800 and set up a shot glass for each of us. Hank filled our glasses, picked up his, and clinked it against mine where it sat on the bar. He tossed the drink down and rubbed his hands with delight. "I really was good tonight," he mused. "Hey, Howard. Was I good tonight or what?"

"Yep," Howard said.

"See that!" Hank said. "Unsolicited praise!"

"Meredith said she knew something about Priest River that would turn me upside down."

"Oh yeah? And what would that be?"

"She didn't have a chance to tell me. Gary the Goon came out and dangled me over a cliff."

Hank's smile faded and he focused on me as if for the first time. "Did *what?*"

I shook my head. "Forget it. Let's continue this discussion after you've come back down out of the ozone."

Hank winked. "Fabulous idea."

I downed my shot of tequila. Mistake. It rear-ended the Scotch and soda on the way down and the two started fighting. Hank stood and tucked in his shirt and announced his intention to use the bathroom facilities.

The bathroom was all the way at the other

end of the club, and Hank edged past the bunched-in tables, nice and slow. He didn't have to go to the bathroom any more than I did. This was an excuse to make another handshake-filled voyage through the adoring crowd. Give his fans a chance to glimpse the legend up close.

I put the beer to my lips and drank. Since conversation with Hank was going to be temporarily impossible, I turned to idle speculation. Like why, for instance, Gary didn't want me talking to Meredith.

There were several possibilities . . .

Russell was a possessive kind of guy, and while he normally allowed a free spirit like Meredith to siphon out her nymphomania in dribs and drabs, he'd never before seen her drift toward the back bedroom with any stud quite as drop-dead gorgeous as me. So he flew into a jealous rage and had Gary break it up.

Or . . .

Gary, passing through the house collecting UNICEF donations, overheard me talk about being sick and merely urged me in his idiosyncratic way to throw up into the ocean rather than on the white rug.

Or . . .

Meredith really did know something. Something about Priest River and what was going on there that ranked above mere gossip. Something that Gary or whoever he worked for didn't want spread around.

I glanced to my right. Hank was smiling and talking with two young guys and they disappeared together down the hallway leading to the bathroom. A new comedian was up on stage, a plump fellow, balding, thick glasses. The MC had introduced him as the World's Smartest Comedian.

"First of all," the comedian said, "how many of you here tonight are familiar with the dialectical imperative?" He held up his hand and cast an eager eye out at the beer-swilling crowd. Nothing. His face fell. "Great!" he muttered. "There go all my Schopenhauer jokes!"

I thought the World's Smartest Comedian was pretty funny, but the routine bombed. The MC sensed the crowd drifting away so he yanked the guy after ten minutes and brought on a scatological nimrod whose instant talk of farts and hard-ons got the crowd roaring again.

I turned back to my beer and noticed Hank's empty tequila glass and suddenly realized he'd been in the bathroom for an awfully long time. I craned my neck and looked down the hallway. Nothing.

I sighed and put both hands flat on the

top of the bar, palms down, and pushed myself up. This was my night to follow after people. I told Howard to top off Hank's tequila glass and began edging through the crowd. The bathroom was empty, and the hallway didn't go anywhere else except to an emergency exit door at the back that led to an alley. I came back out and stood near the stage and scanned the audience. No Hank.

I went back down the hall past the bathroom and pushed the emergency exit door. It opened onto an elevated concrete delivery platform. Five stairs to the right led into the alley itself. I looked this way and that into the chilly night. A few illegally parked cars, but that was it.

I was just about to head back into the club when I heard movement at the far end of the alley to my right. The rattle of a garbage can . . . a cat bolting from one hiding place to another. I stood at the edge of the delivery platform, watching, and in the next instant I saw a body hurtle through the air as if shot out of a circus cannon.

Hank's body.

For a moment I was frozen where I stood. Hank slammed up against the side of the brick building, and two men rushed into view, legs kicking, arms flailing. Then instinct took over. I leaped over the rail of the platform, hit the concrete hard, and raced down the alley, shouting.

The two men stopped and looked up. I expected them to bolt, but they didn't. They didn't seem particularly alarmed at my appearance. For a few perilous seconds they simply stood and watched me with indifferent curiosity as I closed the gap. Weaponless three-piece Quinn, running down the alley. With each stride the likelihood of stilettos and small-caliber weapons intensified, and a different kind of instinct kicked in. The instinct for self-preservation. I felt myself slowing up. I was only twenty yards away when the attackers suddenly turned and fled into the night, not running real, real fast. They knew I wasn't going to come chasing after.

Hank was on his back. There was blood smeared all over his face, and his eyes were wide open, trying to focus.

"Jesus . . ." he said.

"Take it easy."

He pushed himself up onto his elbows and then sank back. "Jesus . . ."

I took out a handkerchief from my jacket pocket and swabbed off the blood. It was immediately replaced by more blood. His face was a mess.

"Stay calm," I said. "You're going to be all right."

"All this blood . . ."

"Head wounds bleed. Just take it easy."

Hank was determined to push himself up to a sitting position, so I let him. He leaned back against the cold brick of the adjoining building. "I got beat up," he said.

"I know."

"Just now," he said, pointing down at the pavement. Blood seeped out of the corner of his mouth.

"I know. Come on, let's get you to a doctor."

"Beat up . . ." he said. The reality of what had happened was too much for him to assimilate. He just sat there in dazed wonderment before the majestic fact.

I left him where he was and ran to get my van and pulled into the alleyway. I hauled him in, getting blood all over the damn place, then drove as fast as I could to Mount Zion Hospital.

They worked on him for about an hour in the emergency room, and when he emerged he looked worse than he had in the alley. All the blood had hidden the damage. Hank's right eye was swollen shut. Stitches here and stitches there. His ribs were taped, and his right hand was in a temporary cast.

"At least the nose isn't broken," he mumbled through puffy lips.

157

"Let's get out of here."

I drove back to the apartment on Union Street and fixed up the bed in the spare room. Hank looked far too dreadful to go home. Good robots may slaughter bad robots, but the kids would need some debriefing before they gazed upon the results of real violence. Dear old dad was a frightful sight.

While Hank stretched out on the couch I called Carol and told her what had happened and that she was to just sit tight, and if she came rushing over I'd break Hank's nose and finish off the job. She could come and get him in the morning, after she'd had a chance to digest things. Then I hung up and went out and sat next to Hank on the couch.

"Break your hand?" I said.

Hank shook his head. "No. Bad sprain. I hit one of the guys on the forehead."

"Only movie stars punch people in the face without breaking bones. Jesus, don't they teach you anything in Comedians School?" I tried to smile a cheer-up smile. "Do you know who they were, Hank?"

"No idea. Fans, I thought."

"Fans?"

"Yeah. They said they were opening a comedy showcase in Marin and wanted to talk to me about performing there."

158

"Nothing else?"

Hank shook his head. "We went out back to talk in private. Next thing I know . . ."

"Did they say anything? Ask for money?"

"Nope. It was hi, how are you, let's talk, pow."

I sat down next to Hank on the couch. "You and I've had quite a night. Understand now why Carol has slight misgivings about this whole thing?"

Hank wasn't really listening to me. "Finally have a hit routine," he said, "and now I'm going to be laid up for two weeks, minimum. Can't win." Hank gently touched his swollen right eye. "So what do we do now? Sit around and see what tomorrow brings?"

"Meredith offered to tell me something important about Priest River. I was going to let it slide, but now I think I'd better find out what she knows."

"She 'offered' to tell you something?"

"Everything has its price," I said. "She wants my body. Can't blame the poor girl."

Hank smiled through his puffy lips. "Hate to pop your bubble, but Meredith strikes me as the type of girl who wants *everybody's* body."

"Not Russell's."

"But I thought you just told me she was Russell's steady flame."

"I didn't say it was a strong flame. Just steady."

"Uh-huh . . ." Hank said.

"Define your 'uh-huh.' "

"Normally this sort of thing is repugnant to you," Hank said. "But in the interest of us not getting trashed anymore you may be forced into bouncing the bedsprings with Meredith. Sacrifice yourself. Impale your virtue on the stake of what-must-be-done."

"You're confused about who has the stake."

Hank closed his eyes, and his head drifted back toward the couch pillow. "Not my fault. I got kicked in the skull."

"Come on," I said. "Beddy-bye time."

I helped Hank to his feet and began angling him toward the spare bedroom. He was stiffening up and in considerable pain. I shoved a pill the doctor had given me down Hank's throat and tucked him into bed. The doctor said it'd knock him out faster than a Sonny Liston uppercut.

"Gonna be a long night . . ." Hank mumbled.

"If it'll help you sleep any better, I have no intention of boffing some twenty-year-old drunken girl just so I can get a few facts and figures. I'm going to go have a talk with Meredith and that's all it's going to be. Talk."

"No tearing of sheets?"

"No."

Hank closed his eyes and smiled. "Not even for the greater good?"

I turned off the light and stood at the door. "Don't tempt me. You know what a slave I am to the greater good."

Hank was asleep before I even finished the sentence.

10

Meredith saw me before I saw her. She was leaning against the grand piano in the lobby of the St. Francis Hotel, all purple velvet and reined-in flesh. I was sitting about forty feet away in one of the armchairs near the revolving front doors that faced the hustle and bustle and cable-car clatter of Powell Street.

I'd just spent ten minutes in the lobby crossing and recrossing my legs, watching a parade of elegantly dressed people walk by. The women were poised and immaculate. The men looked like they were on their way from one cognac commercial to the next. Piano music filtered down from the Compass Rose Room, and I could hear the soft and distant clink of breakfast utensils. In the lobby of the St. Francis it was easy to pretend that the world was still a sane and civilized place, and my resolve began to weaken. Suddenly I wasn't in the mood for an illicit rendezvous with a shoehorned-in Lolita, no matter how chock full her satchel might be with Priest River scandal.

I looked at my watch. Carol would have come to fetch Hank by now, and he would probably be easing down into his own bed. I pictured the look on Carol's face. The kids creeping up to the door and peering in at beaten and battered daddy. My resolve steadied.

That's when Meredith saw me. I gave her a long-distance salute and she began slowly walking over, a skeptical smile on her face.

"Well, well, well," she said, easing into the chair next to me. "What a surprise."

"I don't think you're surprised at all."

"Did I tell you I was staying here?"

"Yes."

"No I didn't."

"Yes you did."

Meredith folded her arms and her smile grew bigger. "Shit, I must really like you then. I usually don't do that." Pause. "Why'd I tell you I was staying here?"

These were not rhetorical questions. Meredith was the kind of girl who needed a constant recapping of her life — a daily summary, just to keep current.

"You were having a fight with Russell and wanted to tell me something about Priest River."

"Okay," Meredith said, tapping the side of her head with her forefinger. "Now it's all coming back." She crossed her legs and leaned back in the chair. "How come you left the party so early without even saying good-bye or nothing?"

"Gary and I just couldn't seem to get along."

"He mess with you again?"

"Yes."

"Because of me?"

"Yes."

Meredith smiled. She liked it when men messed with other men because of her. "And you came here anyway?"

I held my hands up and let them drop. "What can I say? Always was a sucker for the St. Francis."

Meredith looked around the lobby, sniffed the air. She seemed unimpressed. "What for?"

"Atmosphere."

"Atmosphere," she repeated heavily. "I'm sick of atmosphere. Tell me something I don't know."

"That's supposed to be your job."

Meredith put on her little-girl smile. "You first."

I sighed. "What do you want to know about?"

"Anything. The world."

"I don't know anything new about the

world. You'll have to narrow it some."

"San Francisco, then. This hotel."

"This hotel . . ." I thought for a second. "Okay. There's a full-time guy at the St. Francis who does nothing but sit in a back room and wash the coins so the guests get nice sparkling change."

"Get outta here."

I nodded. "Scout's honor. He irons the paper money, too."

Meredith gave me a long, leery look. "Do you have a five-dollar bill?"

I dug into my wallet and handed one over. Meredith stood up and pointed a finger at me. "Wait right here."

She strolled over to the jewelry counter and spoke for a moment with the saleswoman. The woman nodded and Meredith gave her my five-dollar bill, and the woman counted out five ones in return. Meredith strolled slowly back, thumbing through the bills as she walked. The money was as starched and crisp as a handful of Wafer Thins.

"I'm impressed," she said.

"You didn't believe me."

"I don't believe anybody. Not at first."

"Why not?"

"Don't take it personal," Meredith said. "I just got a policy of calling all bluffs. Always."

165

"Why do you do that?"

"So I don't never get bluffed."

"Bad poker strategy," I said.

"That's all right." She smiled and gave her shoulders a small, suggestive shrug. "I don't play card games."

She reached into her handbag and withdrew a cigarette. I took the matches from the drink table between us and lit it for her.

"Are you always so dashing?" she said.

"Only in the St. Francis. It brings out the David Niven in me." I put the matches in my shirt pocket and leaned back in the chair. "Okay. Fair's fair. I told you about the ironed money. Now *you* tell me something *I* don't know."

Meredith drew from her cigarette and her eyes assessed me. "I'd rather do it like in school."

"School?"

"Yeah. The school I went to, you didn't just tell. You showed. Show-and-tell. Didn't you ever do that in school?"

"We're not in school now, Meredith."

She paused, then put out her newly lit cigarette in the ashtray after only three quick drags. "Suite 200. Wait five minutes and then come up. Don't hammer on the door. Knock softly, three times, then two." She demonstrated by knocking on air. Knock,

166

knock, knock . . . knock knock. Then she stood and smoothed the wrinkles from her purple velvet dress. "Five minutes."

She moved back toward the grand piano and disappeared into the crowd. Meredith the Unbluffable. I looked down at the table. Okay, Parker. Let's see you get out of this one.

Five minutes was not long enough to devise an escape from Meredith's show-and-tell, so at the appropriate hour I pushed myself out of the armchair, wandered up to Suite 200, and knocked the secret knock. Meredith answered and ushered me in without a word.

Unlike the Honorable Nigel Brambley, when the St. Francis Hotel calls something a "suite," they mean it. The room was more along the lines of a small, elegant apartment. Expensive furniture, wood-burning fireplace, well-stocked library with leather-bound books, pipe rack, hunting lithographs on the wall. A glossy magazine lay on the coffee table. The cover story was about the opening of grouse season in Scotland. Wet bar in the corner. Straight ahead a single large window overlooked Powell Street and Union Square. There were two doors on the right and one on the left. Meredith took me by the hand and led me through the door on the left.

Once in, she closed it and smiled. It was

a small bedroom with its own bath and closet space. The sheets on the double bed were still rumpled. Meredith leaned against the closed door.

"I'm glad you came," she said.

"Meredith . . ."

"What?"

"I don't think we should do this."

She blinked and looked surprised. "You don't?"

"No."

"You married?"

"No."

"Girlfriend."

I shook my head. "No."

Her face darkened. "Gay?"

I laughed and she sort of laughed along with me. I'd left her an opening, and she moved quickly to expand her beachhead. Her voice turned playful.

"Then what have you got to lose?" she said. "Come on, Quinn. I thought we had a deal. Ain't polite to make a girl come right out and ask for it."

Before I could say another word she reached behind her purple velvet dress and unhooked something and seemed to come sliding out of her clothing all at once. She wore no underwear and was instantly stark naked. Her skin was surprisingly pale for someone who lived in the islands, the breasts large and well-shaped. Despite the abuse it obviously took day in and day out, Meredith's body had the good fortune bestowed upon all twenty-year-old bodies. Resiliency. I instructed my eyes to ignore what stood before them, but they took off anyway like a couple of mutinous soldiers heading south, down the slope of her neck, over the breasts, sliding across the flat expanse of stomach before ducking into the deep, pubic undergrowth.

"Still not interested?" she said.

She walked up to me and linked her hands behind my neck and eased her body up into mine. Then she stretched up as high as she could stretch to kiss me and I let myself be kissed.

Until the kiss I didn't know what I was going to do. It is my reluctant but decided opinion that the average male's sexuality is about as complicated as a paperweight. No matter how stalwart the moral resolve, put a nude, willing, twenty-year-old woman in most men's arms and you're asking for trouble. At the party Meredith had scoffed that I didn't know what "shocked" was, and now here she was; soft, pliable, eager. A hardcore Webster's Dictionary, anxious to redefine a few of my favorite adjectives. Like the lady said, what did I have to lose? There was no salt-of-the-earth faithful wife back on the ranch whose face would crumble with pain and hurt. No children to be a lousy role model to. Geologic shifts would not hinge on my decision. This would be pure and simple pleasure. Tab A into Slot B.

But the kiss stopped me cold. It was dry and passionless, planted on my lips only because it was one of those things you did first before tearing the bedsheets. And when she drew back from the kiss her eyes were curiously vacant. I need involved eyes, filled-up eyes. Nobody lived in Meredith's eyes, and suddenly the sensation spread to the rest of her body. Empty throat, empty arms, empty breasts and legs.

Meredith sensed my hesitation and took my right hand and placed it on her left breast, and there it stayed as though affixed with Super Glue. Then she put her lips on mine and kissed me again. This kiss had a little more voltage, but my hand refused to do what she wanted it to do. Meredith drew back again, and I removed my hand from her breast.

"What's the matter?" Meredith said.

I shook my head. Her eyes narrowed and a look of slight disbelief came over her. "You really *don't* want to do this, do you?"

"No."

"Why not?"

I exhaled and looked away. "I don't know why not."

Meredith unlinked her arms from around my neck and let them fall to her sides. "Great . . ."

"Meredith, I like you. I think — "

"Save it."

She went over next to the bed, picked up a terrycloth bathrobe, and slipped it on but didn't tie it. She lit another cigarette and sat on the edge of the bed, blowing out the smoke and staring gloomily at the dresser drawers. She suddenly looked twice her age. "Fine," she said. "I never had to beg to be fucked before and I ain't gonna start now. So let's have it. What do you wanna know about Priest River?"

Meredith sucked on her cigarette. She wasn't really mad. She wasn't upset or hurt. She wasn't anything. She just sat heavily on the end of the bed like a burnt-out furnace waiting for the next arrival of coal. Sedate, depleted, monogamous, no life of her own. The most monstrous suburban extension of a "good little housewife."

"You're an attractive woman," I said. "It's not that I don't find you attractive."

"Super," she said. "I'll have to make a note of that."

"But you're Russell's girlfriend," I went

171

on. "He asked me to his party last night."

"So?"

"So I think it would be a tad indiscreet to sleep with his woman the very next morning."

Meredith smiled. "If that's all that's stopping you then don't worry because next week I'm blowing Russell off."

"You're breaking up?"

"Yep. This time for good." Meredith shifted on the bed and her terrycloth robe fell open a little. She cinched it back tight. "Relax. I'm not gonna start pawing you again. Believe it or not, I still got a thimbleful of pride left."

"Does he know this yet?"

"Russell?" Meredith made a face. "Let me tell you about Russell. He could be standing right there in the corner, watching all this, and he'd still think that I'm his one and only. Anyway, I'm sick of talking about him. I'm sick of everything."

She worked nervously on her cigarette and turned her head away so I couldn't see the bright sheen of tears that crowded her eyes. I came up behind her and put my hands on her shoulders and she leaned into me. It was the first honest thing we'd done with each other all morning.

"I'm sorry," I said.

"It's all right," she said. Her voice was

thick. "You probably wouldn't've liked it much anyway. I'm finally figuring it out that I'm the kind of woman men like once and that's it. When people don't ask for seconds you think that maybe they didn't like it all that much the first time."

"Russell doesn't feel that way."

Meredith coughed out a short, bitter laugh. "Right. Almost forgot about Russell. Always got Russell. Lucky me."

Meredith moved away, giving me a small pinch on the arm as she did. She scooted down a little further on the bed and cinched her bathrobe up tight. Tight enough that there was no danger it would fall open again. Then she fumbled for another cigarette. I lit it for her again and she tried to smile. "David Niven, right?"

"Right."

"That's my problem. I want David Niven and I end up with Bozo the Clown."

I pulled up a chair and sat on the very edge of it. "Come on. Russell can't really be *that* bad."

"Yes he can."

"Stephanie thinks the world of him."

Meredith blew out a small cloud of smoke. "Gimme a break. Stephanie feels guilty, that's all. She was the older sister, smart and pretty, and her folks always favored her over Russell. When Russell was a kid he had a problem with his eyes. Or his brain, I guess. Where everything gets mixed up . . ."

"Dyslexia?"

"Right. Dyslexia. So when he kept getting older and older and still could hardly read the family more or less wrote him off and concentrated on Stephanie. That's why she can't see him the way everybody else does."

"Why did you hook up with him in the first place?"

"Shit, I was only a high school senior!" Meredith crossed her legs and looked at the unmade bed. "My folks have a vacation home in Montego Bay where I always used to go for spring break and stuff, and I met him there when he was down visiting Stephanie. I thought he was kind of fun. More fun than I was used to with the college boys in Houston."

"How so?"

"Okay. If I said I wished I could ride a motorcycle through Spain, Russell'd go off and be back in two hours with plane tickets to Madrid. He did that once. That exact thing. A seventeen-year-old girl, that's pretty impressive. But it wasn't just him throwing around his money. I mean, my family's got money, too. There was other stuff."

"Like what?"

Meredith pulled on her cigarette and thought about it, and something resembling a smile actually drifted across her face. "Okay. One time I remember I was listening to some of Russell's tapes, some new group I hadn't heard of, and I told him how much I liked it. A week later he gave me three blank tapes filled up with the music. But you know what?"

"What?"

"When I listened to the tapes they all ended exactly when the tape ran out. I mean, there wasn't any dead time at the end like there always is when you dub your own tapes. I asked Russell about it and he'd spent two whole days writing down all the different songs and exactly how long they were, and then figuring out which songs could go together on one side so it'd work out. So it'd be perfect for me. Wasn't that sweet?"

I nodded.

"Course, that's what drove me nuts about Russell, too. Fiddle two whole days with a tape recorder like that . . . he wasn't like a regular grown-up."

Meredith drew from the cigarette and continued to concentrate on the folds in the unmade bed as though they were as

inscrutable and important as Mayan hiero-
glyphics. I shifted my butt on the edge of
the chair. Meredith was slipping away. The
seven-minute attention span of the video generation was taking effect.

"How do you think Russell will take the
break-up?" I said. My curiosity was not high,
but I wanted Meredith to keep focused. The
way you nudge a wind-up toy that has come
to a stop and needs a little push.

"He practically raped me last night," she
suddenly said. "Bastard. We had a huge fight
and I called him some names, so he decided
that he was going to prove what a dark,
smoky, virile beast he was after all, and
how unstoppable he was when he decided
he was going to 'have his way.' "

Meredith started to cry. Soft and quiet
and contained.

"I'm sorry, Meredith."

She nodded and swiped at her nose with
a Kleenex tissue from the bedside table.

"I read once about how long sperm live.
It was in some magazine that I shoulda kept.
Last night I was trying to remember how
long it was. How many hours. I think it
was six. Or eight, maybe. I pretended eight,
just to be safe. Jesus, last night it was so
important I almost phoned my gynecologist
back in Houston to ask him. I didn't want

one bit of Russell's disgusting life swimming through me. I spent most of last night just laying in this stupid bed by myself counting the sperm dying off. I imagined them dying, one by one. Shriveling up. It made me feel good. I tried to concentrate so that the inside of my body would get hotter, kill them faster." Meredith laughed again. "Most people count sheep to get to sleep, right? Me, I'm counting dead sperm. I mean, am I fucked up or what?"

Meredith's assessment of herself was so painfully accurate I didn't quite know what to say.

"Let's forget it, Meredith."

"I think they're all dead now. It's been a good ten hours. They couldn't have lived longer than that."

"Meredith . . ."

For the first time in several minutes she looked away from the rumpled sheets and focused on me. The tone of her voice became businesslike. Practical.

"You wanted to know about Priest River, right?"

"Right."

"What for?"

"Hank's my best friend in the world. His wife's my next best friend, and they have two terrific kids. I'd like to know more about the land he inherited."

"Okay," she said, putting out the cigarette. "Gimme a chance to get dressed."

"Are we going somewhere?"

"Russell's office."

"Why?"

"You'll see when we get there."

Curbing my urge to ask more questions, I went back into the sitting room, dropped into the leather couch, and thumbed through the grouse-season magazine instead. A clock ticked on the fireplace mantel. Through the bedroom door I could hear Meredith pulling on her clothes. There was another sound that I couldn't quite identify. I don't get many headaches, but I could feel a dull one coming on.

Meredith emerged five minutes later, wearing jeans, tennis shoes, and a T-shirt from Montego Bay. "Let's go before my mother wakes up."

"Your mother?"

Meredith nodded at the other door opposite her bedroom. "In there."

I looked at the door, then back to Meredith. "Are you telling me your mother's been in there this whole time?" I whispered.

"Don't worry. She's out cold."

Meredith went over to the door, nudged it open, then signaled me to come look. The

178

room was dark and shadowy and smelled of alcohol and stale sweat. A woman was passed out on the bed. She was still in her evening dress, shoes off, lying flat on her back. The sound I couldn't identify in the living room was the sound of Meredith's mother snoring. Loudly. Very, very loudly. If Suite 200 was a jail cell and I was the guard, I'd think she was faking it to cover the sounds of other prisoners hacking out a tunnel to freedom.

"Drunk as a skunk," Meredith said disgustedly. "Daddy and one of the bellboys had to haul her up here last night. You shoulda seen it. People in the lobby all looking. Her panty hose showing. Man, was Daddy pissed."

The mother continued to snore. Still Life with Deflated Socialite. Then I turned back to Meredith and watched her profile watching her mother's profile. Meredith looked quickly at me and she knew what I was doing. What I was comparing. What I was thinking. Then she soundlessly closed the door and went back into the living room.

"Let's get outta here," she whispered.

11

The trip over to Russell's office wasn't as awkward as I thought it would be. Meredith threw on a sweater and we walked across Union Square and toward the Financial District, arm in arm, like a couple of eager tourists who'd just polished off breakfast and were ready to see the sights. It was as if nothing at all out of the ordinary had passed between us in Suite 200. Meredith was accustomed to making rapid emotional adjustments.

Russell Axton's office was in the Embarcadero One Building. It was Sunday morning and quiet. Red lights and green lights clicked at empty intersections. There were a few businessmen in sports clothes and tennis shoes, kids in tow, stopping by the office to take care of loose ends. But nothing serious. Nothing rushed. Cities are always more human on weekends.

The guard in the lobby nodded at Meredith as though he recognized her and we took the express elevator up to the thirty-third floor. The door dinged and opened up and we were facing a double door with "Axton Enterprises" painted across it. Below was the company's logo, a rather unimaginative reproduction of the earth as photographed from the moon, with a network of criss-crossing lines going from one end of the earth to the other in a manner meant to convey rapid-fire communications. There were no other doors in sight.

"They have the whole floor?" I said.

Meredith nodded and dug through her purse looking for keys. "Whole thing."

"What if Russell's here?" I said.

"He isn't."

"But what if he is?"

"Trust me. Russell's never here."

"Why not?"

"They don't need him. I came in here once to meet him for lunch and all he was doing was sitting around, chewing his fingernails. He might drop in maybe once a week, just for show, but that's it. He hardly ever leaves his boat over in Sausalito. Russell isn't exactly a workaholic."

Meredith found the key and unlocked the door. We stepped inside and she punched in a series of numbers on an alarm unit mounted on the wall to the left. Then she flicked on some lights and signaled for me to follow.

We walked past an empty reception area and turned down a long, long hallway. The hallway walls were glass, and on either side of us were rows of empty desks with computer terminals. The fishbowl workplace. You see it more and more now. Interior designers use words like "clean" and "crisp" and "streamlined" to make the employees feel good, but it was strictly a toy for management fresh back from their Maximizing Efficiency Seminar. There were no cubbyholes in an office like this, no tiny private places where humans can engage in the crucially human activity of goofing off once in a while. Peeking at a magazine. Filing a nail. Placing a quick personal phone call or chewing on a pencil eraser because you like the taste. Unh-unh. At Axton Enterprises it was business, business, and more business. This was one of those offices that an employee was going to go berserk in one day. I could feel it. Could already see the future bulletholes zigzagging the walls and shattering the glass.

"Big outfit," I said.

Meredith nodded and kept walking. "Two hundred people on the payroll. Used to be a lot bigger, but business is bad."

"What do they do here?"

"Who the hell knows? Satellites, computers. Something. Russell doesn't talk about it much."

"And this is all his?"

Meredith nodded. "Now that his daddy's dead, yeah. Russell just took over a few years ago."

"Is that when business started going bad?"

"You got it. Good thing he inherited money, because Russell, he wouldn't know how to sell a hot dog at the World Series."

We kept walking and at the end of the hallway turned left, and we were in a new section of office. Upper management. You could smell the newness of the carpet, see the upgrade in the wall art. No peek-a-boo-I-see-you glass here. The individual offices were very private. Heavy doors. Tinted windows. There was another empty reception area in the shape of a half-circle, and beyond it was a double door with "R. H. Axton" on the front. We went past that door to another one that said "Conference." Meredith flipped through her keys again.

"Feels like 'Mission Impossible.' " I smiled.

"Practically," Meredith said. "Nobody goes in this room. I mean *nobody*."

"Why not?"

"You're about to see." Meredith brushed a strand of hair from her eyes and concentrated on the keys. "Damn! I know it's in here."

183

I paused a moment and watched Meredith. "Why are you doing this?" I said.

"Doing what?"

"This. Taking me up to the inner sanctum and showing me secrets. You don't know me. You don't have to do this."

"I told you Russell practically raped me, didn't I?" she said. "This'll serve him right."

"Come on. It's more than that."

Meredith found the key at last and looked up at me. Her slight irritation at my endless questioning melted away, and for the first time her eyes weren't empty. Something had filled them up. "You're right," she said. "It *is* more than that."

Her gaze lingered on me for a moment. It was humid, moist, exposed. If she'd had that look in Suite 200 we might still be there. Then she broke it off and put the key in the door and swung it open. Meredith flicked on the overhead light and gestured at a ten-by-ten architectural mock-up that stood by itself on a raised platform in the middle of the room.

"You wanted to know something interesting about Priest River," she said. "Well, there it is."

She stayed at the door and I moved toward the center of the room. It was a scaled-down model of a proposed development. There were green, papier-mâché mountains slanting down to a turquoise-painted sea. Little sailboats were glued onto the azure plywood, and tiny sunbathers stretched out on the golden sands.

The scope of the resort was huge. It sprawled up one hill and down the next — luxury hotel, rows of condos, boat docks, tennis courts, golf course. But no matter where you looked, the eye was drawn to one thing in particular. The centerpiece, the shimmering showcase of the entire development. Cascading down from one of the canyons was a waterfall. A seven-tiered waterfall. Affixed to the side of one of the papier-mâché mountains was a small plaque. "The Resort at Seven Altars: An Axton Enterprises Development."

"Did Russell show you this?" I said.

Meredith nodded sullenly. "Once. When he was drunk."

"When?"

"I don't know. Couple months ago." Meredith cleared her throat. For the first time she looked a little antsy. "We better go."

"Did he ever talk about it again?"

Meredith shook her head. "Never. I kinda got the feeling he was pissed at himself for showing it to me in the first place. But that night I was ragging on him about being

185

such a flunky and he said he was going to show me something that would shut everybody up once and for all. This was like his secret weapon. You know, his super-duper bomb that nobody knew about and was going to win the war. It was going to be the best resort in the world, Russell said, and everybody was gonna come crawling back to him, saying they were sorry."

"How did he plan to pull this off?"

Meredith held up both hands, palms facing me. "Hey, I just told you everything I know. Russell brought me in here and puffed out his chest and that was it. Except that same night on the boat he woke me up, shaking me like hell, and said that I'd better not ever tell anybody about what I just saw. His eyes were weird. It scared me."

"And have you?"

"Have I what?" Meredith said.

"Told anybody else?"

"Nope. Only you." Meredith glanced back out at the empty reception area and shivered against an imagined cold. "C'mon. We better get outta here."

I nodded and took one last look at the model. Located the spot where Marty's house should have been. It was gone. In its place, six miniature vacationers smiled at a miniature volleyball court. The boat ramp was also gone. The terrace, the telescope, the favorite room with no mirrors . . . all of it had vanished. There wasn't a trace of Marty left at all.

I walked Meredith back to her hotel, and neither of us said another word about what she'd shown me in Russell's office. When we reached Union Square we stood in the middle of the park, and she put out her hand so I could shake it good-bye. I ignored her hand and leaned down and gave her a kiss on the cheek. She tried to smile and gave me a tight, earnest hug and then disappeared across Powell Street and through the revolving doors of the St. Francis.

I got my van out of the Sutter garage, made a right on Stockton, and inched my way through Chinatown toward home. I caught the red light on Clay Street. It was going to be a long, long light. The three cars in front of me all wanted to turn right, but the steady flow of pedestrians was only going to allow one car per green light to sneak through. So I leaned forward on the steering wheel, took a deep breath, and thought about the Resort at Seven Altars.

If an innocent alternative would have presented itself, I would have explored it. But none did. Instead it seemed to me that it

187

had to have gone something like this . . .

At some point in the past Russell Axton had come to Jamaica to visit sister Stephanie and husband Marty. He looked upon it, saw that it was good, and began fostering the notion of a resort built around the seven-tiered waterfall. He quietly bought up the surrounding land and then approached Marty about purchasing the final jewel in the crown. For one reason or another, Marty wouldn't sell. Not enough money. Or — as per the lobster story — they simply didn't like each other. Bongo had said Marty's family was somewhat prehistoric about the sanctity of land, so maybe that was a stumbling block. Or Marty might have seen Russell Axton as just a very wealthy extension of the Toledo dentist. Whatever the reason, the sale of Seven Altars wasn't happening.

The three cars in front of me decided to take matters into their own hands and formed a kind of battering ram through a small gap in the pedestrians, and I was suddenly free and sailing down Stockton Street. I stretched the kinks out of my back, shifted gears, and leaned back in the seat.

Okay. The Seven Altars story could end right there if I wanted it to. Russell Axton writes it off to bad luck, the mock-up in the conference room gathers dust, and everybody moves on to the next thing. But Marty's murder was problematic. Hank getting the shit kicked out of him was problematic. I had been threatened, and an anonymous interested buyer was leaning on Bongo, not taking no for an answer. There were too many dark threads to ignore, so I continued to speculate.

Initially, panic in the Axton camp was probably at a minimum, since Marty was married to Stephanie and the land was more or less in the family anyway. Except Marty continued to refuse to sell. Maybe he would refuse to sell forever. The waterfalls, the resort, all of the preliminary blueprints began to recede in the misty distance. Unless . . .

Jamaica is a violent place. Lots of people die for lots of reasons. Like drugs, for example. Next thing you know, Marty's dead. Russell hurries down to Jamaica to comfort his distraught sister. While there he takes a long enough break from dabbing her tears to find out that Marty willed everything to his wife. Everything.

Except the property at Seven Altars.

Russell is stunned. The elusive final piece to his expensive puzzle went to some character named Hank Wilkie. Once the numbness wore off perhaps Russell did a little research into the Wilkie family's finances and he figured they might be overjoyed at the prospect of a quick quarter of a million. No creative financing or balloon payments or problematic fee schedules. Just a two and a five and a bunch of zeroes on a smooth, long check drawn on a Swiss bank account.

Back at the apartment a grumbling stomach reminded me that I'd skipped breakfast and it was closing fast on lunch. I rummaged through the refrigerator. Slim pickings. A few beer bottles and some ancient takeout containers tucked in the back. I opened the foil of a couple of them and peeked inside. It wasn't quite like identifying bodies in a morgue, but awfully damn close.

I dumped out the containers with my head turned away, and while I was down in my crouch the telephone rang. I let the machine take it.

"Quinn, this is Russell Axton calling. Stephanie Greene's brother . . ."

I stopped short. The voice on the machine continued, businesslike, with the studied formality of a dictated letter.

"It has come to my attention that one of my security people went overboard last night at the party. I regret the incident very much and would like to apologize. Let's see . . . it's almost twelve noon. Granted this is short notice, but if you would like to join me for

190

lunch and a sail this afternoon I'd be de-lighted. Salmon and wine. Please come. If your friend Hank would like to make it a threesome, that would be fine. I will be on my boat until, say, two-thirty."

I stayed in my crouch and listened while Russell gave directions to his yacht. Then the machine clicked off. Only the night may have a thousand eyes, but I was rapidly com-ing to suspect that Russell Axton sure as hell had more than two.

I grabbed my windbreaker and headed for the stairs.

12

Years ago I used to spend a lot of time in Sausalito. Back then it was a cozy cluster of funky houses clinging to the side of the fog-swept Marin hills, peopled with artists and oddballs, with a gravel-voiced ex-madame sitting in the mayor's chair. On chilly, drizzly afternoons with the foghorns bellowing, Hank and I liked to go to the No Name Bar on Bridgeway and sit in the back and warm our souls with hot Irish coffee and homemade pastries.

But Sausalito was too lovely for its own good. The tag team combo of Wealth and Speculation rolled into town one day and that was that. Now it was a swift and swishy burg of upscale wine merchants, fancy restaurants, and pricey art galleries, clogged to the gills with tourists every weekend of the year and most weekdays. Even the No Name Bar decided to cash in and hung out a sign announcing itself as the No Name Bar. Hank determined that that constituted a name, and he refused to drink there anymore.

I drove across the Golden Gate Bridge

and took the Alexander Avenue turnoff and amazingly found a parking place in the lot next to Flynn's Landing. I left my windbreaker in the van and walked down the two-hundred-foot gangplank where Russell's yacht was docked. The sun was bright and cool. On the left the slips were small and the boats modest. People were working topside, the men with their shirts off, the women in swimsuits. They all seemed to know each other, and they shouted jokes and insults back and forth in the lazy air. Two women struggled with a very heavy ice chest, and everybody was laughing.

To my right were the large slips. The floating dinosaurs. Mammoth things that sat there in the water as inert testimony to both their owner's wealth and their owner's inability to enjoy the fruits of that wealth. The right side of the gangplank had all the vitality and sense of fun of an ostentatious graveyard.

I spotted Russell's boat from way off. It was the last craft on the right; easily the largest and sleekest of all the yachts. It was as streamlined and graceful as a flashing marlin, and from a distance I could see Russell up on deck by himself. He had on white shorts and a navy blue shirt and no hat. He wore deck shoes with no socks and had that all-over, just-back-from-Bermuda tan. As I approached the boat he stood and smiled and offered his hand.

"Quinn Parker?"

"That's right."

"Great! You got my message. Russell Axton." He shook my hand with surprising vigor. "Pleased to meet you at last."

I climbed aboard and he opened a small cooler and held up a half-empty bottle of white wine. "Care to help me finish this?"

"Sounds good."

Russell fished out another glass, set it next to his, and began pouring. "There's so much poverty in the world," he said, "the least we can do is empathize. Cheers."

"*Salud.*"

Russell leaned back in his deckside chair and crossed his legs. "You found me quickly enough."

"You give good directions."

"Your friend Hank couldn't make it?"

"Hank's a little under the weather," I said. "But he doesn't like boats anyway."

"Good God!" Russell gave me an exaggerated look of disbelief. "What kind of man doesn't like boats?"

"Hank claims there isn't enough traction."

Russell paused for a second, then leaned his head back and laughed. "Not enough traction," he repeated. "That's a good one. I'll have to remember that one."

When Russell laughed his eyes sparkled with an artificial mirth, as though they'd mistakenly been treated with lip gloss. He spent a few more seconds savoring Hank's line, then allowed some seriousness to gradually settle on his face. "First of all," he said, "let me apologize for the incident at the party."

"Forget it."

"No, I won't forget it. What happened was inexcusable."

"Did you witness it?"

"I was told about it."

"Who told you?"

"One of the bartenders."

I nodded. "Must have been Eddie."

Russell stared at me for a second. "I don't know the names of my bartenders."

I studied Russell's face. The deep tan and general demeanor didn't go together. He was not instinctive jet-set material. His was an indoor face, an indoor attitude, and I could imagine him much more at home in a bowling alley with fluorescent lights and the scores showing overhead and the anxious avoidance of gutter balls. You felt that only the pressure of his heritage had forced Russell Axton out into the open skies of Aspen and Monaco and Sausalito.

"Apology accepted," I said. "Forget it ever happened."

Russell relaxed at that. He twirled the wine in his glass and looked at me sideways. "I suppose Stephanie gave you the rundown on Meredith," he said.

"Not really. Only that the two of you were together."

"She's been living with me, off and on, for almost two years now. I met her down in Jamaica when she was just out of high school." Pause. "Look, Quinn. I didn't invite you aboard to tell you my personal problems, but . . ." Russell held his thumb to his mouth, pinkie extended, and tipped. "Meredith has a drinking problem."

I nodded understandingly. You'd need a Rolodex to keep track of all Meredith's problems, but the way Russell'd said it I was supposed to think that alcohol was the one stumbling block in an otherwise pure, dynamic, and motivated woman.

"We all have our vices," I said diplomatically.

"Yes, well . . . Meredith tends to be sloppy and stupid with her vices."

"Is that why Gary roughed me up?"

Russell didn't answer for a second. He continued to twirl the wine in his glass.

196

"What did you think of Gary?"

"What did I think of him?"

"Yes. What was your opinion?"

"I think he's the kind of person who doesn't take four-way stops very well."

Russell glanced up from his wine. "Who doesn't what?"

"My opinion is that Gary's a little high strung."

Russell put his glass down, stood, and adjusted one of the ropes on the boat. "I asked because I'm thinking about canning him. It's a hell of a tough decision. He and I go back a long ways. Used to room together at college."

I couldn't keep the astonishment from my face. "Gary went to college?"

"Football scholarship," Russell quickly explained. "Linebacker. A sensational prospect out of high school, broke every prep record there ever was in Pennsylvania, but he ended up not making the pros. Gary had good instincts, but he wasn't quick enough. Didn't really have the strength or size, either. Not for the NFL."

Russell finished tightening the rope and stepped back down to his seat. "Anyway," he said, "when Gary didn't get drafted the poor guy was desperate. He's not real big in the brains department, so I gave him a job."

I took a sip of my wine and thought about

Gary not having the strength or size to play linebacker in the pros. This was the guy who'd easily dangled me with one hand over the ledge at Russell's house. The guy who'd collarboned me in a flashing instant and had effortlessly dug his thumb into my shoulder like I was the Pillsbury Dough Boy. The man with no eyes. This was a guy deemed neither powerful nor agile enough to chase after quarterbacks and tear their heads off by the roots? All of a sudden I realized why Joe Montana got paid so much money.

Russell leaned forward and looked at me, man to man. "There's a lot of hush-hush in my business, Quinn, and we have to be careful about people snooping around. That's all. I don't know what the problem is with Gary. In the last few months he's gone a little off-kilter. I just wanted you to know that I'm sorry. Okay?"

"Okay."

"Enough said." Russell slapped his hands together and looked out at the bay. "What do you say we take her out?"

"How's the traction on this thing?"

Russell laughed again and began putting the food stuff away. "Traction's great. Traction is absolutely terrific!"

We cast off and eased out of the quiet harbor, heading on a southeast diagonal toward Alcatraz. It was a restless ocean, with aimless gray swells and froth blowing across the surface of the water like sand in a wind-swept desert. Currents seemed to be tugging in different directions at once, as though confused about the shore. We tucked up close to Angel Island and dropped anchor.

Russell went below and came back with a tray of cold smoked salmon. He opened another bottle of wine and we stretched out on the deck.

"So tell me, Russell," I said. "Exactly what is your business?"

Russell smiled. This was a question he liked. A question he felt comfortable with. "Telecommunications. Fiber optics. The marketing of same. Now and then we trouble-shoot at a high level."

"Troubleshoot?"

Russell nodded. "For example . . . say somebody out in Philadelphia needs a hundred thousand clothes hangers by Wednesday. We arrange it. Remember the oil crisis in the seventies?"

I nodded.

"Okay," Russell went on. "The Winnebago people found themselves sitting on a huge inventory of aluminum siding with no re-creational vehicles to put it on. We found a guy in Ecuador who bought the entire thing for thirty cents on the dollar. Shit, Winnebago didn't care. They were ready to eat the whole thing. Thirty cents was thirty cents."

"What did the guy in Ecuador do with it?"

"Built houses!" Russell said. "I mean, *hundreds* of houses! Whole suburbs! Go down there now and you'll see that half the Indian population of northwest Ecuador are living in homes with 'Winnebago' written on the walls." Russell laughed again and passed the plate of salmon. "Our profit on that little deal bought this boat. One point two million."

I held out my glass of wine and let Russell top it off from the new bottle. One point two million. In Mexico a farm worker slaves away in the broiling sun six days a week for about twenty-five bucks. Times fifty-two . . . thirteen hundred bucks a year. Roughly a thousand years of work to buy this boat. The labor of fifteen generations. Sometimes I have a bad attitude about economics.

"Stephanie told me a little about you," Russell said. His voice had changed somewhat, and his eyes darted from this thing to that. I was about to learn why I was invited on this luncheon cruise.

"Didn't realize Stephanie knew anything about me to tell."

"I guess your friend Hank filled her in." Russell cleared his throat. "She said you work on people's phobias."

I nodded. "That's right."

"Free-lance?"

"No. I work in conjunction with a licensed therapist in the city. She refers clients to me when she feels she's done all she can on the couch."

"Then you take them out onto the field of battle?"

"That's the idea."

Russell broke off a piece of salmon and put it in his mouth. "I've got a phobia of my own. Maybe you can help me out one of these days."

"Depends on what it is."

Russell attempted to smile. The tentative grin stayed reluctantly on his lips as if prodded from behind by a bayonet. "Sounds ridiculous coming from a sailor, but I have a fear of deep water."

"Not so ridiculous," I said. "A friend of mine has a lobster business in Maine and the way he tells it, half the fishermen who work for him can't even tread water."

Russell put down his drink and ran both hands upward across his face and into his hair. "See . . . with me it's kind of strange. My ability to swim depends on how deep

201

the water is. Put me in a pool and I can swim laps all day, but take me out there . . ." He pointed to the dark blue water beyond the Golden Gate Bridge. "The thought of a mile of cold, dark water below me . . . I'm paralyzed. It's such an irrational fear. There's no reason for it at all."

"That's the definition of an irrational fear."

"I'm the same way in an airplane. The higher up I get, the worse it is. You can almost measure it. I'm three times more frightened at thirty thousand feet than I am at ten thousand feet." He laughed a short, nervous laugh. "Pretty crazy, hunh?"

"Not that crazy," I said. "There's a guy at the St. Francis Hotel who does nothing but wash coins and iron dollar bills."

Russell flinched, barely. I wouldn't have even seen it if I hadn't been looking for a flinch. Mention of the St. Francis had disoriented him for a moment. A tiny electrode to the central nervous system. Then he recovered.

"How'd you know that about the St. Francis?" Russell asked. He was all smiles and benign curiosity, but his gaze was a little harder than before. The ice-blue polygraph eyes were all over me.

"I'm a student of San Francisco esoterica," I said. "Kind of a hobby with me."

Russell just kept staring and nodding. Then he exhaled and reached for the bottle of wine. "Anyway," he said. "I might call you about this phobia thing some day. I want to race in the Trans-Pacific this year, so be thinking of ways you might cure me."

"I will."

"Good!" Russell smiled. "In the meantime, *I'm* a student of smoked salmon esoterica. Let's eat."

And we ate the rest of our meal in relative silence. Then Russell lifted anchor and we sailed the not-too-deep waters back to Sausalito.

13

"Let me get this straight," Hank said. He was in bed, puffy-lipped, sipping tea through a straw. Carol sat next to him, at the edge of the pillow. Hank set the cup on the tray beside him and held out his right hand in front of me and began counting off fingers.

"Marty got his head blown off, I got the living bejesus pounded out of me, you were dangled over the edge of a cliff, and you just went off sailing in the deep blue sea with the guy who is probably responsible for all of it?"

"Correct."

"Why make it so complicated?" Hank said. He was trying not to yell. "Let's do it this way. When Matty gets home from his friend's house I'll have him get his fingerpaints and he can smear a big, bright bull's-eye in the middle of your forehead!"

I sat at the foot of the bed. "You know me, Hank. I've never been able to say no to smoked salmon."

Hank's face turned a brighter shade of red. Carol put her hand on his shoulder.

"Take it easy, honey," she said. "You'll tear your stitches."

After Russell and I had said our good-byes I thought it was only right to swing by Hank and Carol's and tell them everything. About my meeting with Meredith, what I'd seen in Russell's office, and the afternoon sail to Angel Island with Russell's proposal that I help him overcome his fear of deep water.

"Trust me on this, Hank," I said. "I'm not going to do anything stupid. Inhaling and exhaling are two of my favorite things. Besides, what does Russell Axton have to gain by harming me?"

"Who the hell knows?" Hank said, coming up out of the bed another inch or two. "The rest of us will give that question a lot of thought when your body washes ashore."

"Sit down, Hank," Carol said sternly. "That's the last time I'm going to warn you."

"You're exaggerating the danger, Hank."

"Am I?" Hank smirked. "Guess who called Carol late last night?"

"Who?"

"Our old friend Bongo. Seems those anonymous buyers have been leaning on him a little harder."

"How so?"

"He didn't go into details," Carol said

softly. "All he said was 'harder.' And their offer for the property just dropped to two hundred thousand."

"Did you tell Bongo what happened to Hank at the Holy City Zoo?"

"Damn right she did," Hank said.

I kept my eyes on Carol. "And?"

"Bongo said that we should be very, very careful," Carol said. "He said he thought these people could be dangerous."

"Even better," Hank said, still off on his own tangent. "Maybe you and Russell can go scuba diving together. Sure, why not? Way, way down, where it's dark and cold. Five bucks says he's got a fear of that, too. I'm sure he'd be more than happy to loan you his extra-heavy weight belt."

I turned from Carol and gave Hank my gritty, Sergeant Rock look. "I'm a phobia therapist," I said melodramatically. "No ocean too deep, no mountain too high. It's my job."

Hank's face turned bright red again and Carol stood and cupped her hand under my arm. "That's it," she said. "I'm going to have to separate you two."

She ushered me out of the room and closed the door to Hank's high-pitched protests.

"You do that very well," I said.

"I get a lot of practice."

We went into the living room and I watched while Carol picked up some scattered toys. "Now it's your turn to tell me I'm crazy," I said. "You don't have any stitches so you have permission to shout as loud as you want."

"I'm not going to shout about anything," Carol said. "Do whatever you want."

Carol got down on all fours and reached way under the couch for a stray wiffle ball.

"You don't seem too concerned," I said.

"I'm not," Carol said, her voice muffled by the edge of the couch. "Because in two days it won't be a problem for any of us."

"Come again?"

Carol straightened back up and looked me in the face. "When Mr. Brambley or Bongo or whatever he calls himself phoned last night I told him that was it. We wanted out. I gave him instructions to start digging for that loophole you were talking about at Mel's. This morning he found one. In fact, I'd just hung up the phone not ten minutes before you stopped by. The game's over, Quinn. Over." She turned and headed down the hallway and I was right on her heels.

"Whoa!" I said. "What are you talking about? What loophole?"

Carol went into the kids' bedroom and I trailed her in. She knelt and opened the toy chest beneath the bunk beds and tossed in the toys.

"We can't sell it or lease it or long-term rent it," Carol said flatly, "but there is one thing we *can* do. We can just turn our backs and walk away from it."

"Walk away?"

Carol smiled and flicked her hand like Tinker Bell discarding some excess stardust. "One signature. All gone."

"You're not serious?"

Carol's expression hardened. Her smile evaporated. "I'm deadly serious, pardon the expression. It's a simple process of just transferring the title with no money changing hands. Mr. Brambley said there was nothing whatsoever in the will to prevent Hank from doing that."

"This was just a minor detail Marty overlooked?"

"Don't get that tone of voice, Quinn. Mr. Brambley said that in an unusual will like Marty's the restriction of title transfer was usually implied. But he also said that Jamaica was Jamaica and in the Third World one could . . . work around things."

"I bet. Especially if a couple of thugs start applying the pressure."

"Give it up, Quinn. We're going to do what we're going to do." Carol eased into the lower bunk bed and stretched out. Her feet dangled off the edge. "No wonder kids don't like to sleep on the bottom. It's like being locked in the trunk of a car."

"The property is worth at least two million dollars, Carol."

"Staring up at a boxspring all night long . . ."

"Two million, minimum. Probably more like four or five."

Carol crawled out from under the bunk bed and sat on the edge of the mattress. "Two million dollars?"

"That's right."

She nodded her head as if actually thinking it over, but I knew she wasn't. This was a show for Quinn. "Of course, that's just gross," she said. "You're forgetting to deduct the associated expenses. Intensive care and emergency room bills. Funeral costs."

"Carol . . ."

"Why are you doing this, anyway?" she asked suddenly, as though it had just occurred to her. "This is *our* problem. Hank's and mine. And don't tell me it's the two million or one million or however many million because I know you, Quinn. It's something else."

An electric silence filled the room. I leaned up against the wall and took a deep breath.

"Do you believe in ghosts?"

Carol's whole head moved when she said, "What?"

"Bongo believes in ghosts."

"Oh, Quinn . . ."

"Bongo said that in Jamaica a dead man's ghost comes back to 'ride' the living. It sounds strange, but I almost feel like Marty's ghost is riding me. I can't just write it off and move to the next thing."

Carol stood abruptly. "Well, I can. And I don't believe in ghosts. And I don't care about the money. We didn't have two million dollars before and we can do without two million dollars now. I want our lives to get back to normal. I used to hate normal. Now I *love* normal. Normal's my favorite thing in the world!" Carol was getting worked up. Her cheeks were flushed with color. "Look what they did to you, Quinn! Look what they did to Hank and Marty. Who's next? Cort? Matty? Unh-unh. They can have the damn waterfalls."

I exhaled and looked out the window. "I thought the good guys were supposed to fight the bad guys."

"This is the real world," Carol said, walking out of the room. "Sometimes the bad guys win. Sometimes you throw in the towel and let the bad guys win."

I lingered for a second, alone in the room. Stared down at He-Man shoved sideways in the toy box, his terrible swift sword bent in half against a bag of marbles, useless. Sometimes the bad guys win. When I was a boy that wasn't the way things worked. When I worshipped before the shrine of Saturday Matinees such a notion was unthinkable. The bad guys *never* won. Evil was a bumbling, hopeless entity that was easily dispensed with. John Wayne leaping into a World War II bunker and blasting fifty inept Nazis to smithereens before number fifty-one would sneak in a lucky, cowardly shot and superficially wound him.

But of course Carol was right. Real evil wasn't like that. Real evil was harrowingly competent. They'd manipulated Marty's land and his life, ruined people, hurt people, showed utter disdain for generational pride, and now were about to walk off with the whole thing without working up a sweat. He-Man and Superman and Batman were right where they belonged. Gathering dust at the bottom of a toy box.

Carol was back in Hank's room, sitting on the edge of the bed. I came in and sat down. Neither one of them would really look at me.

"I'd love to stick around," I said. "But

211

there are some puppies back at the apartment that need to be drowned . . ."

Silence.

"And you know how much I like to drown puppies . . ."

Silence.

"Especially blind ones . . . cute little fluffy blind puppies . . ."

Carol's eyes narrowed. "Respect our decision, Quinn."

I crossed my legs and licked my lips. "Can I ask you a personal question?"

"Why not?" Carol said. "You're going to ask it anyway."

"Why did you pick Marty to be the godfather of your first son?"

Carol shrugged. "It was Hank's decision. I never even met the man till he stopped by last . . . whatever it was. April."

"Yet you trusted Hank enough to allow him to ask a complete stranger to be the godfather to your first child?"

"Yes."

"Why?"

"What's your point?" Carol asked. She knew what the point was and her voice was losing its force.

I looked over at Hank. "My point is that on the flight back from Jamaica Hank told me about Marty. He said that Marty always symbolized the ideals he respected. That you *both* respected. You said it yourself, Hank, how he was a throwback to a better time. Incorruptible. A man with principles."

Hank wouldn't look at me. He turned his attention back to his tea.

"Stephanie took me aside at Russell's party," I said. "She told me how important it was to Marty that the land be passed down to his godson. He put his life on the line to see that it happened. What we're talking about here isn't just some dirt and sand and water. We're talking about the most important thing in Martin Greene's life. Something that a long line of strong people guarded and protected and fought for, and I just think we're rolling over at the first sign of pressure."

In the silence that followed I felt a little foolish. Jimmy Stewart would play my role in the movie, Frank Capra directing, and in the end I'd stagger off to sustained applause and they'd put my virtue under glass and charge people a dollar to walk by and gaze upon it.

"We understand everything you're saying, Quinn," Carol said gently. "But we're not changing our minds. That's that."

"Then how about this?" I said. "You can give the property away, right?"

213

Carol looked at Hank and Hank looked at me and they looked at each other warily.

"Right?" I said again.

"Right," Hank said cautiously.

"Then give it to *me!*"

Hank's one good eye opened wide. "What?"

"Why not? You give it to me, you're off the hook. The worst that happens is they huff and puff some more and I eventually buckle under and settle for the original two hundred fifty thousand they offered. I'd give you the money, of course, but in the meantime the danger would be diverted from the Wilkie household."

Hank peered at me. The idea sounded too good. There had to be a flaw. Carol saw that I'd gotten through to Hank and her back stiffened.

"No," she said. "We're giving it straight to the people who want it."

"Quarter of a million . . ." Hank said dreamily. Then he snapped alert and gave me a dirty look. "Wait a minute. What about the big speech you just gave about principle and the sanctity of land?"

I smiled. "In the immortal words of Jesse Unruh, sometimes we must rise above principle. And if they ask Bongo what the hell's going on we can have him say that you

214

couldn't afford the upkeep. You know, the taxes and insurance and everything. So you gave it to me."

"Hmmm," Hank said. What came over Carol when Hank said "hmmm" was what killed the dinosaurs. Ice. Two feet thick. She stood and glared at me.

"Didn't you have some puppies to drown?"

She walked me out of the bedroom and we stood together in the hallway.

"You don't want to talk about it?" I said.

"No," Carol said calmly. "I have a feeling Hank and I are about to engage in an animated discussion now, and I'd hate for you to get hit by the flying debris."

"Fair enough. I have to get ready for my date tonight anyway."

That got her attention. "Date?"

"That's right."

"With who?"

"Stephanie Greene."

"You mean like an actual 'date' date?"

"Yep. I'm going to put on cologne and everything."

"I didn't know that you were . . . interested in her."

"I'm interested in finding out if her brother really does have a phobia about deep water. Despite overwhelming evidence to the contrary, I'm not stupid."

"I see." Carol nodded. "Dinner?"

"Of course."

"Restaurant, or . . ."

"Restaurant."

Carol kept nodding. "Which one?"

"Don't know yet."

Carol and I go back a long way. Knew her before I knew Hank. We had circled each other in the old days, exposing ourselves to well-known aphrodisiacs like popcorn and *Casablanca* and midnight beach walks to see if there might not be a spark between us. There was, but not the kind that ignites. Then one afternoon I introduced her to Hank and that was that. But the circling had curiously continued on through her married life, her kids, her new domesticity. I squelched the occasional daydream of what might have been, and she did her best to curb an otherwise morbid interest in my love life.

"Hank tells me Stephanie is fairly attractive," Carol said.

I laughed.

"What's so funny?" Carol said.

"Calling Stephanie Greene 'fairly' attractive is like saying Leon Spinks could use a 'little' dental work."

Carol made a disgusted sound. "Slut . . ."

I smiled, clicked my heels, and performed

a short little Germanic bow from the waist. "Thank you."

"And now if you'll excuse me," Carol said. "I have some business to finish up with my husband." She stood at the door waving good-bye to me, wiggling each finger of her right hand. I turned to leave and then she stepped back into the bedroom and the door slammed with enough force to shake the windows.

14

Stephanie's apartment was actually a cozy, one-bedroom cottage on the leafy eastern side of Telegraph Hill, where the average monthly rent could send a child in Peru through four years of college. You had to park down on Montgomery Street and climb a winding set of stairs, past the Shadows Restaurant, and up.

The apartment itself was a curious blend of California Modern, West Africa Primitive, and I'm Not Unpacked Yet. Stereos and wires and native masks and half-opened boxes were strewn across the floor, and Stephanie bustled back and forth among them while I stood waiting in the middle of the living room.

"I'm a last-minute person," she said, brushing past me and fastening on an earring. "Sorry."

"No problem," I said. "Plenty of time."

She stopped in front of the living-room mirror and worked on the other ear.

"Great place," I said. "Everybody in the city wants to live up here."

Stephanie shrugged. "I didn't have much choice in the matter. Russell had it rented for me before I even got here. There's supposedly a six-year waiting list, but he pulled strings, blah blah blah. Typical Russell. You look really nice, by the way," she said.

"Thanks."

I had on my one good suit. Left to my own devices, I am the type of man who would wear plaid pants with a striped shirt and think I was on the very cutting edge of fashion. Several years ago I resolved the problem once and for all by having a ladyfriend of excellent taste take me downtown and select an outfit. This shirt, this tie, these cufflinks, these shoes. That way I knew if I kept them all in the same corner of the closet I'd never have to worry.

"I was surprised you called," Stephanie said.

"So was I."

"After ten years of marriage it kind of felt like being asked out on a date."

"Did I do okay?"

"I said yes, didn't I?"

I leaned against the couch and crossed my ankles. "The whole process terrifies me."

"Why?"

"I don't know. It was one of those rites of passage I was never very good at. In

219

high school I remember trying to get up the courage to ask Debbie Gallagher for a date, just staring at the telephone, wishing I'd been born in New Guinea."

Stephanie squinted at me in the mirror. "New Guinea?"

"At least there you had your ritual circumcision with a dull knife and then it was over."

Stephanie smiled and shook her head and grabbed her coat from the back of the couch. "Did Debbie Gallagher say yes?"

"As a matter of fact, she did."

"Well, you're two for two."

While Stephanie spoke she adjusted my tie, did something to the shoulders of my jacket, gave my sleeves a little tug, buttoned one button on my suit and unbuttoned another. There was a confused intimacy in her attention to my clothes, the pressure of her fingers against my neck and shoulders and chest. I stood rigid and self-conscious before the focused attention. Then she bit her lower lip, took two steps back, and nodded.

"There," she said. "That's better."

"Just when I thought I'd finally learned how to dress myself."

"Don't knock yourself," Stephanie said. "Most men don't have anything near your taste in clothes."

"Thank you," I said.

Shameless.

We walked over to Scoma's on Fisherman's Wharf. For reasons of honor, pride, and mental health I try to avoid the wharf at all costs. But Stephanie wanted to have good seafood and look out on the bay while she ate and not bother with taking the car out of the garage, so Scoma's on the wharf was the logical choice.

We took our time, strolling through Ghirardelli Square, watching the tourists line up to buy souvenir T-shirts and ashtrays, turning their backs on the silky fog of San Francisco Bay to gaze at coming attractions at a wax museum.

We got to Scoma's at eight o'clock, scooted up to a corner table near the water, ordered our drinks, and spent a half-hour engaging in standard break-the-ice conversation. What we'd done. What we hoped to do. Stephanie did most of the talking. Her youth had followed fairly predictable lines. Wealth. Privilege. A mother and father acutely aware of how important it was for her to build her pedigree. Private schools. New England summer camps where they spoke French and played lacrosse. It was a social climate monitored as carefully as the incubated air of a premature baby, and Stephanie resisted it.

Not fervently. Just enough to be considered "spirited" by the country-club set. As much as they kept pointing her in the direction of Johannes Brahms, Stephanie Axton felt the insistent tug of Aretha Franklin.

She told me a little about Russell and was surprised when I mentioned that I'd gone sailing with him earlier in the day.

"He just called you up?" she said.

"He felt he owed me an apology."

"An apology for what?"

I briefly recapped my encounter with Gary, toning it down so that it was merely a hand on the lapel rather than a Wallenda act over three hundred feet of jagged rock. Stephanie slumped back in her chair, shook her head, and looked exasperated.

"I don't know why Russell just doesn't fire him," Stephanie said.

"You know how loyalty is. College buddies . . ."

"It's more than that," Stephanie said. "If it wasn't Gary it would be somebody just like Gary. Russell . . . he can be very immature about a lot of things. He's my brother. I love him and all that, but he's got this terribly infantile notion of what his image should be. He hooks up with a girl like Meredith because she flaunts her sexuality in public and he thinks that everybody envies him because he's the one she sleeps with. A trophy from the trophy case. And Gary, he's just the male version of Meredith."

"Tough guy?"

"Exactly. Russell always liked to run with these macho moron types, from the time he was in prep school. Even when he came to Jamaica. All of these great things to do there, right? Interesting expatriates, snorkeling, quiet time to lie in the hammock and read a good book. No. Russell's spending half his time down at the police station."

"In Priest River?" I said.

"Yes."

"You mean that little station that fronts the main plaza?"

"Yes," Stephanie said again. She looked at me curiously. "Have you been there?"

"Only briefly. Go on."

Stephanie shrugged. "Nothing more to say. I think Russell probably kept the cops well-stocked in booze and they in turn would let him hang around. Target practice with the guns. One time I was in town and I saw Russell riding around in the Land Rover with the police chief. They were wearing the same reflector sunglasses . . . embarrassing. Know what it reminded me of?"

"What?"

"When the firemen let a little boy ride

around in the big shiny engine and ring the bells." Stephanie shook her head and looked into the depths of her drink. Then she blinked and brought her head up quickly as though someone had just snapped a flashbulb in her face. "Stop it!" she commanded herself with a smile. "Tonight's for fun."

I toasted her resolve to put problems aside and nursed my drink and acted like I had no further interest in her brother. We ordered another round and silently watched the lights on the bay for a couple of minutes.

"Hank told me you and Marty lived in Montana for a while."

Stephanie shook her head while she swallowed. "Idaho."

"For how long?"

"Three years." Stephanie smiled. "Marty used to call it 'the thousand days.'"

"Why did you leave?"

Stephanie took a sip of her drink. "Combination of things. Marty didn't like teaching as much as he thought he would. Had no idea of the politics involved. The academic infighting. Disinterested students. Low pay. He was just about ready to look for a new career when his mother died. Marty didn't have any other family so the property in Jamaica passed to him. We sat down one night and talked about it and decided to make the move. Shake up our lives."

"I have a hard time picturing you in Idaho."

"So did I," she said. "And in a way, I never really fit in. The men all worked hard and played softball and the women sat around the potato salad, talking about their children . . . I don't know. I always felt like an outsider, and it made me sad. Not for them. They were really nice people. Decent people, happy with their lives. A world full of them and there wouldn't be mass murderers."

"The world is full of people like them," I said, "and there are lots of mass murderers."

Stephanie nodded, held my gaze for a moment. "Suppose you're right." She twirled her drink, watching the olive spin around at the bottom, and a slow smile spread across her face. "Anyway . . . I should have known how it was going to go. About two weeks after we arrived I was lying in bed with Marty, in the dark, staring up at the ceiling, and I started crying. I couldn't stop. Marty woke up and rolled over and asked me what was the matter. I stopped sobbing long enough to blurt out that I didn't think I could live in a place that had 'Famous Potatoes!' on its license plates. Marty laughed so hard I thought he'd fall out of bed. Then I started laughing too. It sounded so ridiculous . . ."

I began to laugh myself and it triggered Stephanie, and for a minute we sat like idiots at the corner table of Scoma's with our shoulders shaking, laughing out loud, ignoring our martinis. The waiter suddenly appeared at our table with a scowl on his face.

"Let me tell you about our specials tonight . . ." he said solemnly, and we suppressed our mirth as he went through his joyless incantation of salmon and swordfish, capers and dills and sauces.

"See that," I said to Stephanie as he walked away. "There are famous potatoes wherever you go."

After dinner we walked back through North Beach. I picked up a bag of pastry from my favorite late-night Italian bakery and we climbed the arduous steps back up Telegraph Hill to Stephanie's cottage. She kicked off her heels and walked around the kitchen in her nylons, putting half-full boxes of kitchen utensils away. I sat at the table and drank coffee and ate pastry.

"I'm compulsive," she said.

"Compulse away."

She worked and I sipped coffee and after the last of the bowls had been unwrapped we went into the living room. Stephanie turned the lights off and stretched out on one couch and I stretched out on the other, and we stared up at the dark ceiling and talked to each other as if we were camping out and gazing up at the stars after the fire dies down.

"It feels strange living alone," Stephanie said.

"I can imagine."

"When Dad died a couple of years ago my mother used to talk about how terribly lonely it was. At night especially. And when you first wake up in the morning. Those were the two times that really tore her up. Back then I just sort of patted her on the shoulder, but now I know what she meant. God, do I know." Stephanie paused. "Have you ever been married?"

"No."

"Close?"

"Once."

"Didn't work out?"

"Nope."

"Any reason?"

I exhaled and gazed at the ceiling. "Mady felt that she needed to find herself. I was in the strike radius of her finding herself."

"Do you still think about her?"

"Occasionally."

"Regrets?"

I shook my head. "Not really. I just wonder

sometimes what she's like now. Who she's with. What she's doing."

"Love is hard," Stephanie said.

"It's also timing and luck. If the timing had been a little different Mady and I might have gone somewhere. But it's tough, you're right. You and Marty were lucky."

A long silence followed. I heard Stephanie shift her nyloned legs on the other couch. More silence. Then she abruptly said, "Marty and I were going to get a divorce."

A few awkward seconds passed.

"I didn't know," I said. "Hank, he made it sound like — "

"Don't apologize. Except for Russell you're the only person I've ever told. I . . . I don't even know why I'm talking about it now."

"What happened?"

Stephanie sighed deeply. "I can hardly remember. My life with Marty, when I try to think back to it now . . . You know when buildings don't have a thirteenth floor? How the numbers on the elevator skip from twelve to fourteen?"

"Yes."

"That's what my marriage to Marty feels like now. There, but not there."

I kept silent and Stephanie began to talk. Slowly at first, with hesitation and awkward gaps, but then she warmed to it. The floodgates opened, and God, did she talk. A stream-of-consciousness ramble that wove in and out of the past, present, and future. There was no pattern, no logical progression. Just haphazard fragments of random information that suddenly seemed important enough to share. She'd spent five years at the end of a crushed seashell driveway watching her marriage erode. Five years of maintaining a steady-as-you-go public face while they gradually drifted apart. Stephanie with her classes in Kingston. Marty spending more and more time at his telescope, lost somewhere among the rings of Saturn. Now it was over. Marty was gone. There were no more bowls to unwrap or reasons to pretend. She needed to talk.

"Until the very end I still clung to the belief that we could salvage it," Stephanie said. "I believed in Marty. I believed in our marriage. I just couldn't accept that my original impulse about him so many years ago could have been so wrong."

"The original impulse was probably great, Stephanie. Things go wrong for all sorts of reasons."

"I know that in my head," she said. "But I don't *feel* it."

"Do you think if you'd had more time you might have worked things out?"

"No," Stephanie said.

"Why not?"

Stephanie was silent. Then she said, "Marty was having an affair."

"Did he tell you this?"

"No."

"How did you know?"

"I knew, that's all. A woman doesn't have to find a strange negligee draped across the shower to know her man is being unfaithful." Stephanie's voice was suddenly thick with emotion. A distant siren from North Beach wailed in the night. "A woman knows."

"I'm sorry," I said.

"You know what really hurts?"

"What?"

"Whoever it was . . . she'd been with Marty the weekend he was killed. I wasn't the last woman to share — "

"Wait a minute," I said. "The woman was there in the house when Marty died?"

"Yes. When I came back from Kingston the police went up to the bedroom with me and I could tell. One look at the bed and I could tell."

I felt a small burst of adrenaline. A quickening of the pulse. "Did you tell the police this?"

"What for?"

"Their investigation."

Stephanie laughed a sharp, bitter laugh. "Investigation? Did you see the Priest River police?"

"As a matter of fact, I did."

"Then you know. The Priest River police are four fat men who wear smelly uniforms and take bribes and sit around the station all day drinking rum. So no . . . I didn't tell the police."

I sat in the dark, thinking, piecing it together.

"Anyway," Stephanie said, "that was it. The final blow. I read once that funeral homes give the corpse a shot of some chemical before they bury it. It's so you can't make a mistake and bury someone alive. That's what Marty's affair was to me. A shot of embalming fluid, so that even the possibility of waking up in the grave was crushed, finally."

She rolled on her side, and I could feel her looking at me from across the shadowy room.

"You know, Quinn. What I can't bear is that Marty was yanked from me before we had a chance to understand what had happened. Why we had once worked, and why we had failed. I feel like I could accept anything if I only knew that. It wasn't fair that he died. That we never even had a chance to say good-bye."

I could feel Stephanie fighting back the tears. For almost a minute we sat quietly in the talked-out dark. Then I heard her stand and there was sudden pressure at the edge of my cushion. She was sitting next to me, silhouetted against the window. Her hand went to my chest and I held it there.

The muted light of the city shone on her face. Her cheeks were wet. She lowered her face and rested her lips heavily on mine. Her fragrance was lovely, her skin very, very soft. I touched her breasts through the fabric of her blouse, gently, peripherally. She didn't stop me.

What man among us doesn't harbor the secret belief that he has the touch of Aladdin? That there is no pain so deep, no emotion so atrophied that it cannot be dispelled and put to flight by the sensual brushing away of dust, the mumbling of magic words.

Stephanie pulled off her clothes as though they were on fire. When I tried to slow her down, to coax her back into some tenderness, she resisted. Fought it. So I grew still and allowed her to do what she needed to do.

In Mexico, at outdoor cafés, you will sometimes see a man walk from table to table with an electric box and two wires. For a quarter you can hold on to the wires while the man gradually turns up the juice. Whoever can hold on the longest before letting go of the scorching wires is the winner.

I was reminded of that while making love to Stephanie. It was full of a strange violence. I held on to her and the electricity increased and finally we could hold on to each other no longer and we fell away. There was more pain than pleasure, and she lay on the floor and silently wept.

I eased down onto the floor next to her and held her from behind for a long, long time. I could feel the moisture of her tears through her fragrant hair, the gradual steadying of her breath.

"It's late," Stephanie said at last. "You'd better go."

"Don't you want me to stay the night?"

"No." She turned to face me, resting her head on my chest.

"Are you sure?"

"I'm sure."

"But I thought you said the nights were the most difficult times of all. That they tore you up."

Stephanie cradled my chin in both hands and softly kissed me on the lips. "They do," she said. "Good-bye."

I walked home, breathing the cold and indifferent air of Union Street. Near the top of Russian Hill I caught up with a young couple who weaved slowly in front of me, laughing, intimate. They were intoxicated by love or lust or alcohol or some blend of the three. As I drew near the woman came to a halt and pointed to a van parked on the side of the road.

"The desert!" she cried to her companion. "The desert, vast and cruel!"

I looked at the vehicle. It was one of those customized vans that have elaborate paintings on the side. This one was the Sahara at midnight. Full moon in an ink-blue sky, sand dunes, camels.

The woman was silly drunk, and she grew more and more theatrical. "All my life I've wanted to be kissed under African skies!" she cried, and dropped to her knees on the sidewalk next to the van. The man laughed hesitantly, then went over to the van and got down on his knees next to her.

"Kiss me!" she said. "Kiss me beneath the African stars!"

The man leaned drunkenly forward and they put their faces right up close to the side of the van and kissed.

I kept striding up the street past them, toward home, and they stretched the kiss out for as long as they could beneath the false glow of the painted-on moon.

15

Three days passed. Three days of Quinn Parker folding up his Traveling Emotional Turbulence Show and giving it a rest. I spent most of the time in the confines of my apartment, listening to music, plowing through a four-inch-thick Russian novel, waiting for something to happen. But things were oddly quiet. Russell didn't contact me about his phobia therapy. Meredith didn't try to lure me once again into her satin sheets at the St. Francis. There was complete silence from Stephanie's end, and Hank and Carol didn't ask me to come by and discuss further this notion of me taking on ownership of Seven Altars.

On the fourth morning I broke down and phoned Bill Prescott, my now-and-then stockbroker. I told him that I was thinking of investing some money in Axton Enterprises and could he check it out. Bill said he'd have an opinion for me by three in the afternoon, and that I should stop by the office.

I called Bill because an inconsistency that

needed clearing up had been nagging at me through a thousand pages of Russian strife and intrigue. Given the pile of money Russell was apparently sitting on, and given how crucial Seven Altars was to his resort plans, why didn't he just momentarily put aside his plate of smoked salmon, dig down with his left hand, and grab an extra million from the bulging stack? Despite my speech at Hank's bedside, the preservation of the land was not really an issue. If Marty wanted his godson to be able to afford Harvard, then clearly the land had to be converted to cash one day anyway. Hank had expressly conveyed to Bongo that he would be more than happy to sell it for a reasonable price. What need was there for Gary and his strong-arm tactics? For the two thugs who roughed up Hank? It didn't seem logical that a guy like Russell Axton would start nickel and diming when so much was at stake.

I'd no sooner hung up from my conversation with Bill when Hank called. It was a little before noon, and he told me to come on over. Kids were in school, Carol was working. He was lonely and hungry. I was instructed to bring food and I would be rewarded.

I swung by a take-out Mexican place on Van Ness and ate a taco while driving out to Woodland Avenue, spilling shredded cheese everywhere. Hank had energy enough to answer the doorbell, but that was it. He staggered back to the bed and collapsed and I tossed the sack of food on the bedside table.

"Fast food?" he said.

"Tacos, burritos, chicken fajitas. Four of each."

Hank grunted at my choice and cleared out a place on the bedside tray. I set out the food and stuck straws in the soft-drink cups.

"What's new?" I said.

"Funny," Hank said. "I was just going to ask you that. How did the date with Stephanie go?"

"It went fine."

"Where'd you eat?"

"Scoma's."

Hank nodded. "I approve. Trust you were gentleman enough to settle for a goodnight peck on the cheek?"

I pulled my soft drink cup closer and began sucking on the straw. Kept my eyes down.

Hank lowered his head so he could look up at me. "You *did* settle for a peck on the cheek, right?"

"I'm sure there must have been a cheek-peck in there somewhere."

Hank kept staring at me and a look of disbelief came over his face. "You slept with her, didn't you? First night out of the blocks and you put another notch on the old wooden headboard!"

"I don't have a headboard, and even if I did I wouldn't put notches in it." I paused. "It wasn't how you're thinking anyway, Hank. She practically forced me."

I knew before I said it that it was going to sound stupid, but until the words were out there in the open air I didn't realize *how* stupid.

"Forced you?" Hank said sarcastically. "Forced you?"

"Let's drop it, okay?"

Hank straightened up and went back to picking at his lunch. "She forced you. That's a good one. Poor reluctant Quinn. There's this Italian proverb Carol's grandfather always quotes. 'Below the navel there is neither religion nor truth.' Forced you . . ." Hank muttered, shaking his head. "I bet you were hardly even able to perform."

"Enough, Hank."

"Hope your orgasm didn't leave an exit wound . . ."

"Enough!"

We ate our tacos silently awhile. I finished first and wiped the hot sauce off with a napkin. "Question. When you and Marty went drinking at the Cliff House, did he mention anything about a divorce?"

"What divorce?"

"His divorce."

Hank's mouth was full of food. He shook his head and swallowed. "I already told you, Quinn. Their marriage was going gangbusters."

"Stephanie told me that she and Marty were planning to get divorced."

Hank stopped chewing and watched me very closely. "For real?"

"For real."

He shrugged and resumed his chewing. "News to me. Like I said before, the way Marty told it they were happy as the day they met. Divorce, huh?"

"That's what Stephanie said. The information wasn't out there for public consumption. According to her, Russell was the only one who knew. The only one she told."

"Just Russell?"

"Nobody else."

Hank nodded. "I see your thinking. Russell would have known that Seven Altars was going to slip out of the family and maybe the timetable for Marty's demise needed to be accelerated."

"Exactly."

Hank exhaled and shook his head. "Incredible if true. Make your sister a widow over a stupid piece of land."

"There's another thing bothering me," I said. "Russell's no diabolical genius, let's face it. From what I can gather he sits on his boat and drinks expensive white wine and that seems to be the extent of it. He's not the kind of sinister force you send James Bond after."

"So?"

"So to have someone killed from thousands of miles away requires a certain degree of competence. Competence and balls. I'm not certain Russell has either."

Hank shrugged. "All it took to kill Marty was someone to pull a trigger. You can hire guys like that anywhere. *Especially* in Priest River."

"There's another thing," I said. "Stephanie said that Marty was having an affair at the end, and she's pretty sure the woman had been in the house the weekend of the murder."

"Witness?"

"Possibly, or maybe even someone who was involved with the murder. Bongo might know something. Or the guy with the ponytail. Norman. There was also that maid who was around. The one who took down the mirrors. Maybe they'd have an idea. They seemed to be a lot more tuned in to goings-on in Priest River than Stephanie. Wouldn't hurt to ask around."

"Ask around?" Hank said.

"Right."

"Bongo and Norman and the maid are all in Jamaica," Hank explained.

"I know that," I said.

"Jamaica is thousands of miles away, over great expanses of land and water."

"A plane leaves every day."

Hank looked dubious. "That's a long ways to go to ask a couple questions."

"They're important questions. I'd also like to check the public records down there. See who has been buying what around Seven Altars. Just a quick round trip."

"Look . . . as far as Marty's affair goes, it was probably one of the thousands of single women who land on Jamaica's shores every year looking for fun and romance. Or more likely still, Stephanie's imagination ran away with her. Marriage hits the skids and you start seeing things that aren't really there. I bet what happened was the maid wore a different perfume that day and automatically there's this mystery woman." Hank shook his head and began digging through the paper bag. "A long shot, Quinn."

"Might be worth investigating anyway. I'd also like to talk to Bongo about these anonymous buyers who are pestering him."

Hank pulled out a fajita, took a bite, then took another look at it. "Is it just my imagination," he said, "or do all of these Mexican 'specialties' taste exactly the same?"

"Hank . . ."

"I'm serious." Hank pointed at the various wrappers. "The only thing that distinguishes these things is the shape. Why bother with this 'taco' and 'burrito' stuff? Just do it by shape. Say, 'I'll take a semicircle no sauce, one cylinder extra crispy, and two of those trapezoids, heavy on the onion.' "

I closed my eyes. Slowly opened them. "Are you finished?"

Hank thought about it for a second. "Yeah, I'm finished."

"Good. You said on the phone you'd reward me if I brought you all these edible shapes. If I have to listen to you bitch, the least you can do is give me my reward."

"Ah, yes," Hank said. "Your reward." He picked up an envelope from the bedside table and tossed it to me.

"What's in here?" I said.

"You're two signatures away from having the title to Seven Altars transferred from Henry Ellsworth Wilkie to Quinn Parker."

242

Hank went back to his fajita. "Oh, well. My villa was nice while it lasted."

"What two signatures?"

"Yours as the new owner, and Bongo's as the executor of Marty's estate."

"Carol went along with this?"

"After you left the other day Carol and I had the absolute worst, knock-down, drag-out fight of our married life." Hank pushed aside the food and looked me in the eyes. For the first time in a long time he was dead serious. "Do you think this is the smart thing to do, Quinn? If they came after me you can be damn sure they'll come after you."

"I don't know."

"Whether they'll come after you?"

"No," I said. "Whether I'm being smart."

"I mean, I argued for your side," Hank said. "What you said made sense. But Carol made a real good case for just giving the damn thing away. Screw it. Pretend none of this ever happened."

"Carol wants to protect her family." I held up the envelope. "This is one way to protect them."

"I hope you're right," Hank said.

I began slowly gathering the fast-food wrappers, crumpling them into small balls, consolidating them in the takeout bag. "Besides, somebody has to stop the bully who extorts lunch money."

Hank shook his head. "First of all, I always had the policy throughout my school career of appeasing sandlot bullies."

"Why doesn't that surprise me?"

"Second of all, standing up to a lunch-money bully meant maybe a bloody nose. With these people in Jamaica you end up dead, and dead is a much more permanent condition." Hank stretched out the sore arm, wincing as he flexed the bruised muscle. He nodded at the legal papers with his chin. "Anyway, it's done. Enjoy it in good health. Just promise that if you look like you're going to get killed you'll just give these people the land, no questions asked."

"I promise."

"Good," Hank said. "Now that that's settled I'm going to draw a steaming hot bath and pull the water up over my shoulders and just lie there."

"Sorry you and Carol are battling over this."

"We'll get over it. Besides, there's a worse crisis facing the Wilkie household these days."

"What could possibly be worse than this?"

"High-level negotiations are currently under way with Matty's first-grade teacher. Seems he took his slingshot to school when he shouldn't have and it got tossed in the Gone-Till-June Box."

"What's that?"

Hank was aghast at my ignorance. "The Gone-Till-June Box? It's only the worst thing that can possibly befall a first grader. All other punishments pale before it. An item consigned to the Gone-Till-June Box might just as well have been tossed down a yawning crack in the earth."

"But he'll get his slingshot back in June, right?"

"That's eight months, Quinn."

I shrugged. "Not that long."

"One-ninth of his life . . ."

That stopped me for a second. I paused to briefly calculate how long one-ninth of *my* life was. "Hadn't thought of it that way."

"And it's his slingshot," Hank said gravely. "You don't understand about Matty and his slingshot. The first time he held it in his hands . . . it was one of those moments, Quinn. I wish you could have been there. A marrying of two things that were meant to be together. Peanut butter discovering jelly. Hepburn laying eyes on Tracy. Believe me, the Gone-Till-June Box is a crisis."

I filled the bathtub for Hank. He declined my offer to scrub his nooks and crannies for him, so I tucked the envelope into my pocket, locked the front door behind me, and pointed my van downtown.

Bill Prescott keeps a modest office on the tenth floor of a big, squat, no-frills office building on Sutter Street. I was introduced to Bill shortly after my accident with the power drill when I found myself with several hundred thousand dollars in cash and not the foggiest idea of what to do with it.

Our first meeting had sealed the relationship. I'm not a fisherman, but Bill invited me aboard his boat for a trip up into the delta to catch some steelhead. Get acquainted. Talk. Drink some beer. I was in a what-the-hell mood that day, so I joined him and we motored forty miles up into the hot, humid delta and I sat on the deck while Bill cast for steelhead and explained his economic theories.

It became immediately apparent that Bill Prescott was not your stereotypical stock-broker, moving money around from one thing to the next simply because he needed the commission. Bill felt you should know how to work the hog futures market when it was falling, but it was equally important to know how to raise, feed, and slaughter an actual hog. The doctrine of self-sufficiency. Not that survivalist nonsense, barricaded on a hilltop with an M16 and five years' worth of canned food. Nope. If things came to that, who'd want to hang around anyway? Bill simply understood that financial peace of mind was more than the accumulation of money. Economic history had shown time and time again that currency occasionally becomes worthless overnight. So, yes — use all the cunning you can to squeeze another half percent out of your money, but grow vegetables and know how to fish, too. I sat on the boat and watched the whiz and plunk of the fishing tackle, and by the time we motored back to San Francisco I knew I'd found my stockbroker.

I took the elevator up to the tenth floor and futzed around the waiting room while the receptionist buzzed for him. A minute later Bill came out of his glass cubicle to greet me, hand extended, smile as big as the whole New York Stock Exchange. He was a large man — about my size, but with thirty extra pounds of padding. He was perhaps forty years old — blond and big-boned and jowly, with fair skin and pale blue eyes.

"Gosh darn it, Quinn," he said, pumping my hand. "How come you don't stop by anymore?"

"Don't need to. You already made me a millionaire."

"A million ain't what it used to be," Bill winked. "A man of vision's gotta be thinking about two million."

We went into his office and he waved his hand at a coffee machine in the corner. "Help yourself."

I did, and while I stirred in the cream and sugar Bill settled his bulky frame down at his desk, put on a pair of glasses, and began scanning computer printouts, humming "Getting to Know You." His desk was littered with framed photos of his wife, Connie, and their three daughters.

"So how much were you going to put into Axton Enterprises?" Bill said, still looking at the printout.

"Neighborhood of twenty thousand."

Bill kept nodding. "Any particular reason?"

"Heard it was an interesting company. San Francisco–based." I smiled and shrugged my shoulders. "Be true to your school."

Bill set the printout down, leaned back in his chair, and took off his glasses. "Be true to your *solvent* school. Doctor Bill just saved you twenty grand. Keep your money under your mattress."

"Why?"

"The only interesting thing about Axton Enterprises is the speed with which it's crashing to earth. If this company doesn't go Chapter 11 inside a year I'll eat my tackle box."

"Bankrupt?"

"Complete washout."

I frowned. "That's strange. I heard it was a profitable company."

Bill shrugged and fiddled with his wedding ring. "It's like this. They're primarily in telecommunications, which is good and bad. The good is it's a lucrative field to be in. The bad is lucrative fields tend to attract a lot of competition. Axton Enterprises had it good for a long, long time. Found their own little corner of the market that nobody else wanted to bother with. But then the big boys decided it was worth the bother after all and moved in. And as for the stuff about being profitable, hell . . . half the companies in the United States are turning a profit when they belly-up."

"How does that work?"

"Quinn . . . in this world profits come and profits go, but there's only one cash flow. Take a look at this." Bill pushed the computerized printout toward me and I picked it up.

"What is it?"

"Cash flow statement for Axton Enterprises. Correction. The we-ain't-got-no-cash flow statement for Axton Enterprises.

See" — Bill pointed at a figure midway down the column — "they started getting into trouble right about . . . here. That was five years ago. That's how come they went public to begin with. Strictly a family business up till then. Okay, so they went public and the transfusion of new capital helped for about two years, but the same old problems were there. They didn't go away. Bathtub starts overflowing, you don't keep bailing water. You turn off the faucet. Now they've got zilch. Everything's been depreciated to dust. All intangible assets written down. Nothing left to amortize . . . it's a disaster." Bill leaned back and smiled. "Someday you'll have to give me the name of the genius who gave you this hot tip."

I smiled. "You know I'd never desert you, Bill. It's just that I saw Russell Axton's name in the paper the other day and he was referred to as a millionaire."

Bill shrugged. "Some people think he's a millionaire."

"You don't?"

"Quinn . . . I'm a real simple guy. The tip of my tongue sticks out when I add and subtract. But in my book, if you got twenty million dollars and owe thirty million dollars, you're not a millionaire."

I steepled my fingers under my chin and

gave the impression of befuddlement. "I don't get it, Bill. If they're so strapped for cash, how could they be planning a resort in the Caribbean?"

Bill wrinkled up his nose. "Planning what?"

"A resort. I think in Jamaica. At least that's the rumor. Very large scope. Condos, tennis, marina. Eighteen-hole golf course."

Bill shook his head. "They're not planning any resort."

"Are you sure?"

"Positive." Bill swept his hand over all the paperwork. "Axton Enterprises doesn't have an international portfolio at all. Nothing. Strictly a domestic outfit. Besides, they don't have the cash to build a caddyshack, let alone a golf course. Man oh man! I better put a freeze on your money so you don't go doing something stupid when I'm on vacation."

There was nothing more to talk about, so I stood and walked toward the door and Bill walked with me, his big paw draped across my back. His oldest girl, Christine, was graduating from high school midterm and I was invited to the party. He was proud as hell, and leaned against the office door for a couple of minutes telling me about her college plans. She'd been accepted to a music school back East. Bill wasn't so sure about the music game, how it was going to pan out as a way to make a living, but hell. Kid's got to give a dream a shot, right? Can't just hunker in right off the bat and live your life with only the utility bill in mind, right? I nodded. Right.

Bill was in the mood to chat about his daughter, so I relaxed and leaned against the wall and listened. He talked about her dream to study music. Her nervousness at leaving home. The conflict she had breaking up with her boyfriend. The more we talked, the more Christine started to sound like a faint echo of the seventeen-year-old Quinn Parker, and it was pleasant to stand and remember what it was like when all the risks were still out waiting for you, when your soul was right at the surface. One shallow scoop and you had it in your hands, squirming and slippery and thrashing for life.

Then Bill's secretary interrupted him with some business and he slapped me on the back and reiterated his advice to stay away from Axton Enterprises. There were plenty of other investment possibilities out there. We should get the old boat out of mothballs again and head out to the delta and talk about it. Maybe I might even learn to fish, in which case he'd waive his commission.

We laughed again and said good-bye and

I took the elevator down. There was something basic and solid about Bill that always picked me up. A guy out there doing his job, providing for his family, trying to do the right thing. I felt a twinge of irritation, remembering Marty and his glib reference to the mythical dentist from Toledo. Something told me that a good portion of the dentists in Toledo, Ohio, were probably very much like Bill Prescott.

And in my book that was just fine.

16

When I got back to the apartment I sat down and called Stephanie. Three days had passed and I figured it was time to stop pretending that nothing had happened between us. She answered on the third ring, and her initial upbeat "Hello" suddenly retracted when she heard my voice, the way your attitude changes when you realize a phone call is from a salesman.

"Do you like paella?" I said.

"Paella?"

"It's my one and only cooking specialty. Flexible ingredients and a huge margin for error. Why don't you come over and share the experience."

"I'm not sure whether I should."

"Why not?"

"Well . . ."

I took a deep breath and adjusted the phone on my shoulder. "Can I say something about what happened the other night at your apartment, Stephanie?"

Hesitation. "All right."

"First, I enjoyed it very much. I don't

think it was a ghastly mistake. I see no need for morning-after apologies, and I'd be a hypocrite if I said I wished it would never, ever happen again."

Silence on the other end. I cleared my throat.

"Second," I said, "if you're afraid I'm going to start assuming things, relax. You will not be plagued with neurotic phone calls at three in the morning. I'm not going to tear your clothes off or vow undying love, and I haven't been out pricing wood-paneled station wagons so we can have a vehicle to take our imminent brood to future PTA meetings. Okay?"

The ice at the other end finally started to break up. She chuckled softly. "Okay."

"So how about that paella?"

"What can I bring?"

"Just yourself."

"I'm on my way."

She arrived exactly thirty minutes later. At the sound of the buzzer I went down the fifty-four stairs and opened the door. She stood there with a look on her face that reminded me of some homeless waif out of Charles Dickens, about to ask for a crust of bread. She was holding a grocery bag.

"I'm glad you came," I said, and leaned over the bag to give her a kiss.

"Brought some Chianti," she said. "And some artichoke hearts. I didn't know if you liked artichoke hearts in your paella. I had it once that way in Madrid and it was really nice."

"Never tried it before."

"You don't mind, do you?"

"Of course not," I said. "My paella is like the universe. Constantly expanding."

"I mean, I know this is your dinner and all, and I'm the guest and you're the cook, but I just thought — "

I took the grocery bag out of her arms and looked into her eyes. "Can I ask a very, very personal question?"

Stephanie smiled uncomfortably. "Down here? At the bottom of the stairs?"

"Down here at the bottom of the stairs."

"Sure. Go ahead."

"You didn't conduct very many illicit affairs during your marriage to Marty, did you?"

"Affairs?" Her eyebrows went up. "Of course not. Never. I was completely faithful to Marty."

I smiled and kissed her again. "It shows. You have the most refreshing lack of ease about all of this."

"I guess I'll take that as a compliment," she said.

"It was meant as one."

Stephanie followed me up the stairs and I gave her the standard tour of the apartment. Once she realized that I had told her the truth on the phone and was not going to transform into a snorting rhino about to ram home the fevered appendage, she relaxed. I pointed out the two bedrooms, Oscar's room, the study, the bathroom with the nude Rubenesque wallpaper.

Out in the kitchen I popped one of the Chianti bottles and poured out two glasses. I put the Metropolitan Opera's version of *Carmen* on the stereo for additional Spanish flavoring, then came back into the kitchen and filled a large bowl with shrimp and we both rolled up sleeves and began peeling.

"Do you really like opera?" Stephanie said. "Or is this just to impress me?"

"A little of both. Mostly it's because I really like opera."

"I used to go all the time in New York," Stephanie said, tossing a freshly peeled shrimp into the pan. "It was one of those things I missed living in Idaho and Jamaica, but I had a hard time telling people that because they thought I was just being a snob."

"Matty was over here the other day — "

"Hank's son?"

"Right. His mother dropped him off here

for an hour while she went off to do something, and he was sitting around playing the Nintendo in the living room and I had *Madame Butterfly* on the stereo. I was just futzing around, not paying much attention, but Matty really started to get into the music. He actually turned off the video game and came over and sat next to me and wanted to know the story. What was happening."

"Did you tell him?"

"Of course. I'll explain anything to any kid who willingly puts aside his video game. So we sat down together in the living room and I recapped the whole thing. Told him Madame Butterfly was very upset because she had fallen in love with an American sailor and they had had a baby together but now the American sailor had gone away."

"Did Matty understand why the American sailor went away?"

"I'm not sure. I tried to explain about racism and how difficult it was to mix cultures back in those days and Matty sat there with his big wide eyes, chewing on his thumb."

"Do you think he grasped what you were telling him?" Stephanie said.

"I don't think so."

"Why not?"

"When my explanation was all over he sat there a minute, digested the whole thing, then turned and said, 'Uncle Quinn?' 'Yes?' I said. 'This American sailor . . .' he said, real serious. 'Was it Popeye?' "

Stephanie put down the shrimp she was peeling and started laughing.

"Don't laugh," I said, starting to laugh myself. "The poor kid was in deadly earnest. Popeye! That was the only American sailor he knew. I could barely keep a straight face."

"Popeye and Madame Butterfly in bed together!" Stephanie said. "What an image!"

"Can you picture what their child would have looked like?"

"Ouch!" Stephanie said.

We laughed some more and I topped off our glasses with Chianti and we moved from peeling shrimp to scrubbing clams. The preparation work was wrapped up in twenty minutes and we put the huge bowl of food on simmer and took our wine up to the roof and waited for the flavors to have a chance to hunker in and get to know each other.

The roof at 1464A Union Street isn't much. No weight rooms or Jacuzzis or manicured sunbathing areas with umbrellas and backgammon boards. It's just a funky, normal roof with tar and gravel and a narrow boardwalk that leads to a postage-stamp deck. But it's mine, all mine, and has a view good enough to bite down on. We sat in the two flimsy deck chairs and looked out across the rooftops of the marina to the foggy bay beyond.

"How did you ever find this apartment?" Stephanie said.

"Pure luck. About six years ago a friend who lived here said a spot was opening up. I wasn't crazy about sharing an apartment with three other people, but I was broke at the time and the rent back then was reasonable so I came over and took a look. It was love at first sight. Then when I came into the money from my accident I bought the other roommates out."

Stephanie nodded. "You said the room next to the parrot was your office."

"That's right."

"What is it you do, exactly?"

"I thought Hank already filled you in."

"All he said was you work on people's phobias."

I shrugged. "That about covers it. A friend of mine downtown is a professional therapist. Angie Lohr. She refers clients to me when the couchside stuff is finished."

"Couchside stuff?"

"Simple example. A guy's afraid of flying, Angie sits him down and they talk and eventually she gets him to where he understands his fear. To where he's ready to do something about it. Then he and I get on an airplane."

"That simple?"

"Sometimes simpler. Angie had a client once who walked around in absolute morbid fear of having his appendix burst. This fellow wouldn't venture more than ten or fifteen miles from a hospital. Every time he got a little indigestion he'd call an ambulance and get rushed to emergency. All the statistical evidence in the world couldn't get a ruptured appendix out of this guy's mind."

"So what did you do?" Stephanie said.

"I told him to check into a hospital and have the goddamn thing cut out once and for all."

"Did he?"

"Yep. End of problem."

Stephanie smiled and shook her head. "Wild."

"Of course, it doesn't always work out that way. Most of the time it's complicated as hell. Take the appendix out of a true phobic personality and he'll find another organ of the body that's on the verge of exploding."

"How did you get into this line of work?"

"The money from my power tool accident gave me the freedom to pick and choose. One day I was sitting around doing nothing when Angie called me. She was upset. Crying. One of her clients who had had a problem with being assertive suddenly decided that Angie had cured him and he went out and got assertive with the wrong person. Something ridiculous. Who was ahead of who in line at a movie. The other person took out a gun and shot him. That's when Angie decided that couchside solutions weren't enough. What she needed was a flesh-and-blood halfway house for people who want to see if they're really cured or not. I've had some training in the field so I volunteered my services."

Stephanie nodded and thought of what I'd said. I watched her closely while she sipped from her wineglass.

"Did you know your brother approached me about some therapy?"

Stephanie's head snapped up so fast I could almost hear the vertebrae pop. "Russell?"

I nodded. "Out on his boat, the day after the party."

Stephanie woodenly put her glass of wine down on the deck. "What did he say? Or is that confidential?"

"I'm not his therapist and he's not my patient, so there's nothing confidential about it. Russell said he was afraid of deep water. That it was hindering his wishes to be more of a sailor."

"That's all?"

"That was it."

Stephanie seemed slightly relieved. She nodded her head and clasped both hands around her right knee. "It's true, you know. Russell's been afraid of deep water his whole life. In Jamaica he'd never go sailing out past the reefs with Marty. Only in close, next to the shore."

"Tell me a little about Russell."

"Why?"

I shrugged. "He might be serious about wanting me to help him. The more I know about his personality, the better chance I have to effect some good."

Stephanie cradled her wineglass and looked out toward the water. "You have to understand something about Russell," she said. "His father — *our* father — was a very strong man. In every way. Physically. Professionally. An incredibly virile man. He expected nothing less from his family, business associates, friends. Do you know what I'm saying?"

"Sure. That Russell had lots of pressure put on him early."

Stephanie nodded. "It's what we talked about at Scoma's. Why he latches on to a girl like Meredith, or surrounds himself with tough guys like Gary. The big parties, the flashy cars. It's all his way of trying to compensate. This sounds like Introduction to Psychology 101, but that's how it is."

"I understand."

"This Horatio Alger stuff is going to sound silly coming from me," Stephanie said, "but I think my parents did Russell a great disservice by not allowing him to struggle on his own. They gave him everything."

"Killed his ambition?"

"Maybe," Stephanie said. "My father loved his work. The money he got from work was almost an afterthought. A bonus. In the early days he used to go out in the field with the workers and I can remember sitting at the dinner table as a young girl and noticing the construction dust in his eyebrows. The powder from the concrete. My mother used to say that my father would be happier losing money to a packed house than turning a profit with a small clientele. In a way, it showed the artist at work. But Russell wasn't like that. He wanted to be chairman of the board from the start."

I nodded and concentrated on my wine. "How often did Russell come to visit you in Jamaica?"

"In Jamaica?" She seemed puzzled by the question. "I don't know. Two or three times a year, maybe. Often enough."

"Did he have any friends down there?"

"No," Stephanie said. "Why?"

"Did he ever talk about wanting to live down there?"

"In Priest River?"

I nodded.

"God, no!" Stephanie said. "Emphatically not. Most people did. Most people who came to visit us, that's all they talked about. Turning their backs on their old lives and getting their beach shack at Priest River. But not Russell. He needs the bright lights. The comforts of home."

"Microphones down the cliff."

Stephanie halfway laughed and sipped from her wine. "Exactly. Microphones down the cliff."

"Come on," I said, standing. "I think the paella's ready."

We went below and ate the paella and polished off the second bottle of Chianti. Outside, the world turned dark and the fog rolled in. After dinner we sat in the living room in front of a fire and I tried to gracefully steer the conversation in the direction of Russell. There were still some blanks to be filled, some questions to be answered. But Stephanie would never take the bait for long. Somehow things always seemed to come back around to Marty. There were demons yet to be purged.

We made love. Stephanie's talk of Marty had worked as a curious aphrodisiac, just as it had in her cottage that first night. God knows why. Maybe the eroticism was spurred by the memory of a man who had shared her body for so long. Or maybe the motives had a darker source. A mixed-up, post-humous revenge on Marty for his unfaith-fulness. I wasn't sure what it was, but when events took us into the bedroom and we fell into each other's arms, the lovemaking — impassioned as it was — was still imbued with that-which-went-before. It was less communication than it was a plea for ex-planation.

She insisted on returning to her cottage, so while she got dressed I brewed some coffee and brought it to her. She sat on the edge of the bed and sipped.

"Stephanie," I said, sitting next to her on the bed. "I think you should know that Hank has signed over ownership of Seven Altars to me."

Stephanie's coffee cup stopped at her lips. She was suddenly as still as a photograph. "He did?"

"This afternoon. Bongo has to sign the papers. I'm probably going to go back to

Jamaica and have it done there."

"When?"

"Tomorrow."

Stephanie nodded, scanning the information in her head, reading between the lines. "Why did Hank give you the property?"

"Couldn't afford the upkeep. Insurance, taxes, maintenance. All the associated costs."

"It isn't that much," she said. "Five or six thousand a year at the most."

"Hank doesn't have the five or six thousand."

"Then I'll set aside a trust," Stephanie said. Her voice was rising, her manner agitated. "That property belongs to Marty's godson. Marty wanted it that way and that's the way it's going to be!"

"Relax," I said, putting a hand on her knee. "It's okay. I'm going to have Bongo put the property into an iron-clad trust, with Matty as the beneficiary. Nobody's going to be able to touch it for the next dozen years, not even me. That way I can graciously take care of the upkeep and Hank's kids will still reap the benefits."

Stephanie thought about it for a moment. "But why not just give the maintenance money to Hank each year?" she said. "Isn't that easier?"

I shook my head. "Hank would never go

for it. He has the stubborn pride of the truly destitute."

Stephanie nodded in a distracted manner. I could detect no particular worry in her face at the new development. But there were a few tenuous lifelines she was holding on to, and one of them was that out of Marty's death his godson was going to have opportunities he'd never had. That could not be threatened. That could not be violated or amended.

I walked Stephanie down to the street. It had turned into a very foggy night. Already little dewdrops of condensation were collecting in Stephanie's hair. She turned up the collar of her coat and hugged herself.

"Where's your car?" I said.

"I walked."

"Then I'll walk you home."

Stephanie shook her head. "No," she said, "I'd just as soon have a little time alone."

"Okay."

We stood together on the sidewalk for an awkward moment or two.

"Will you be going to the house?" she said at last. "Marty's house?"

"Maybe."

She nodded. Her face showed no emotion at all.

"Can I bring back a souvenir from the

islands?" I said.

Stephanie smiled a melancholy smile and looked me straight in the eyes. "I just spent the last couple of weeks getting rid of all my souvenirs." Pause. "When will you be seeing Bongo?"

"Day after tomorrow."

"Give him my love, and tell him I miss him."

"Will do."

"And Quinn . . ."

"Yes?"

She leaned up and put soft, warm lips against mine. When she drew back her eyes were troubled. "Be careful."

"Don't worry."

She nodded, gave me another kiss, and then turned and walked through the gusting fog of Union Street.

17

I got into Montego Bay at one in the afternoon, took a Cessna-for-hire over to Turnbull House, and checked in. The five hundred bucks a night stung mightily, but I didn't want to have to learn the ropes all over again this trip. Why not slide through grooves that had already been cut? Besides, I was going to need a car, and since Hank and I had already broken in the baby-blue BMW . . . what the hell? Keep it simple.

After a quick shower I hopped in the car and headed off to Priest River. My itinerary was vague. I'd called Bongo from San Francisco the night before and wasn't scheduled to meet with him until the next morning, but I felt like talking to him anyway so I swung by his office first. The door was locked. Nobody home. I left the car and set out on foot in search of the municipal building.

It was a single-story wooden building not far from the main square. Shiny white floors, air conditioning. The receptionist pointed me toward one window, and the woman in that window pointed me toward another window, and a woman in that window pointed me to yet another window. Bureaucracy in the United States may now and then test the limits of one's patience, but dealing with a government institution in the Third World would coax a fistfight out of Mother Teresa.

After twenty minutes of getting the run-around from a variety of low-level tyrants, I at last found a pleasant young woman who was obviously new to the job, sitting at a desk. She smiled and seemed reasonably efficient and was actually interested in helping me. We walked together down a dusty aisle to where they kept the Official Registry of Property Transactions. She tapped the oversized book on its spine with a long, bloodred fingernail. I thanked her and she smiled and went back to her desk.

The book itself was roughly the size and weight of a squared-off manhole cover. I eased it off the shelf, lugged it over to a remote corner, and settled in.

I found the regional map I needed and strained to remember the general boundaries of the architectural mock-up Meredith had shown me in Russell's office. Five years ago the landowners holding property around Seven Altars were actual people with actual names. James Simpson, Roger and Virginia

271

Wiley, Phillip Simon. Then one by one the names sold their land, and the human owners gave way to acronyms. JJY Corporation. T-III Enterprises. EHK Associates. All of the acronyms had their corporate headquarters in San Francisco. Different post office boxes in different zip codes, but all in the same city. No surprises there.

What *did* get my attention was the dramatic drop in the purchase price of the land in and around Priest River. The first parcel — a bluff at the north end of the bay — had sold five years earlier for a fairly high price. The next, less than reasonable. The next was a bargain. And so on and so on, each dramatically lower than the one that went before, till the final transaction — completed only three months earlier — amounted to little more than a flat-out giveaway. I made my notations and shut the book.

I was restless and unwilling to spend a long and lonely night at Turnbull House, so I took a chance and asked a boy who was leaning against a bicycle if he knew where Norman lived. The white man with the ponytail. The boy nodded in an exaggerated fashion. Sure, he knew where the man with the ponytail lived. He would show me himself. It was on his way home, and all I needed to do was follow.

I brought the car around and followed at ten miles per hour as the boy wobbled his bicycle along the rutted paved street out of town. We were going in the direction of Seven Altars, but several hundred yards before the turnoff to Marty's house the boy looked back at me and gestured down another dirt road that branched off to the right. I waved my thanks and he continued on his way home.

The driveway was practically a carbon copy of the entrance to Seven Altars. I motored slowly down the narrow passage, instinctively ducking beneath the occasional low branch. Then I was suddenly out of it, in bright, late-afternoon sunshine. A funky little beach house sat all by itself on a small, man-made knoll at the edge of the sea. There was no sign of life. I pulled up close to the house, cut the engine, and got out.

Norman's place was not so much a house as it was a glorified beach hut. It had a thatched roof and bamboo walls and a minimum of square footage. The man-made knoll it sat on tapered gradually down about twenty or thirty yards to the edge of the sea. A two-man skiff was on the shore, tilted sideways like a dead animal, bleaching in the powerful sun. A beautifully kept-up Chris-Craft was moored to a dock that extended out into the choppy surf. To my right an elaborate white Yucatan hammock hung between two palms, and just beyond the hammock was a serious-looking horseshoe pit. To the left an ancient automobile was in the final stages of pushed-to-the-side neglect. Weeds grew around the flattened tires, and a thick layer of dust covered the rusted body from top to bottom. Off to the west, across a mile of blue water, I could see Marty's house and the boat ramp and the stretch of beach trail that led to Seven Altars.

"I *thought* I heard something!"

I turned in the direction of the voice. Norman was wandering up from the jungle beyond the horseshoe pit, shirtless, a big smile on his face. His hands were filthy and a streak of engine oil bisected his muscular, hairy chest. He had a piece of machinery in one hand and a tool in the other. He drew nearer, blinked his nervous blink, and then pulled up short twenty feet away. He squinted and slow recognition crept over his features. "Wait a second," he said. "I know you . . ."

"Quinn Parker," I said. "I was here with — "

Norman snapped his fingers. "Sure! You and that other guy. The one who's got Marty's property. We all went up to the waterfalls."

"That's right."

Norman nodded, halfway smiled, then a new puzzle presented itself. "But I thought you said you were going back to Frisco."

"I did."

"You went and came back already?"

"It's a long story."

Norman shook his head wearily. "Man, I can't handle long stories without something to quench the thirst. Sit down on the porch. Relax."

Norman disappeared into the house and came back two minutes later with a bottle of bourbon. He put it down in front of me but I refrained.

"Go ahead," he said. "Have a blast."

"Maybe in a minute. How's Jana?"

Norman reached for the neglected bourbon, unscrewed the cap, and took a healthy swig. He pushed it again in my direction but I shook my head.

"How's who?" he said.

"Jana."

"Oh, her." Norman shrugged. "She's fine. Off at cheerleader practice, probably."

He laughed and I laughed with him. "So what's going on with you?" he went on. "How come you're back so soon?"

"Complications with Seven Altars."

"What sorta complications?" Norman said.

"The terms of the will were kind of unusual. Hank can't sell the place for another dozen years, but in the meantime he can't afford the upkeep, either."

"I hear that," Norman nodded. He took another gulp of bourbon and wiped his lips with the back of his hand. "Upkeep. That was Marty's big complaint, too. Said it cost him seven hundred bucks a month just for maintenance. And with all the crime around here it's only gonna get worse. Your buddy Hank, does he plan to move in?"

"No."

"Then he better figure in another five hundred a month to hire a couple of round-the-clock guards. Word gets out that house is just sitting, it'll be looted down to nothing. Zilch. There won't even be any nails left in the floor."

We were silent a moment.

"Can I ask you a couple of questions?" I said.

"Fire away."

"You own this property, right?"

"Right."

"Has anybody ever approached you about buying it?"

Norman blinked, smiled, and wiped the greasy sweat from his brow. "Why? You interested?"

"No. Not me. But has anybody else made overtures?"

Norman thought for a moment. Took another shot from the bourbon bottle. "As a matter of fact, somebody did. About a year ago."

"Know who it was?"

"Nope. Some asshole from the States. Wall Street type. Drove up in a nice car, wearing a suit. A suit! You imagine a fucking suit in this weather? I blew him off."

"You didn't want to sell?"

"Not then," Norman said. "Now's a different story, but I didn't want to sell back then. Anyway, this jerk was going to give me, like, fifteen cents on the dollar. Something like that. This isn't exactly prime real estate so I guess he thought he could throw a little chickenfeed my way and I'd grab it up. I politely told him to go fuck himself."

"And he never came back?"

"Nope. Nobody ever came back." Norman shook his head. "Maybe that guy knew something I didn't. All the bullshit going on in Priest River now, I probably should've jumped all over his piss-poor offer."

"It's a nice piece of property," I said. "Why do you say it isn't?"

Norman winked. "Come here and take a look at this."

We stood and walked down toward the

edge of the water, past the leaning two-man skiff. "Bad part about this property is it doesn't have much beach. Only this little bit right here where I keep my boat. That's what I mean when I say it isn't primo for the real estate market. It's kind of a strange-shaped lot, long and narrow, most of it going straight back toward the highway. But here's a nice little side benefit. See that out there?"

Norman pointed off to the right. Two hundred yards away was a small outcropping of rocks. Beyond the rocks was a shallow bay, fringed with white sand.

"The cove?" I said.

Norman nodded. "Locals call it Los Rodriguez. Who the hell knows why. Maybe the Rodriguez brothers lived out there back in the days of the Spanish conquerors. Anyway, there's a little dirt road from Priest River that goes right to it. It's a public beach. But you could sit right here all day with your binoculars and never, ever see another soul put foot on that sand. You know why?"

"Why?"

"The fucking duppy! The ghost!"

"I don't get it."

"Look. Every new moon this ghost pops up on the road to Los Rodriguez. Towns-people figure this beach is cursed, so ev-

278

erybody stays away. It's a public beach, but fact is it's more like an extension of my property." Norman smiled and squinted into the sun. "The other day I was thinking there might be a business opportunity here. Rent-a-Ghost. Ensure total beachfront privacy for you and your family."

We laughed and stood there looking out at the cove for a moment or two. "How much do you know about Marty's private life?" I said.

Norman shrugged. "Some. I mean, you can't live in a little place like this and not get to know your neighbor pretty well. Why?"

I crouched down, picked up a stick, and began absentmindedly drawing a circle in the sand. "Stephanie said Marty was having an affair at the end."

"No kidding?"

"That's what she said."

Norman crouched next to me, nodded his head, and looked out to sea and thought about it. "Yeah," he said. "Maybe. It could've happened."

"But it was nothing you knew about?"

"Marty was discreet. His family was British and he still had a lot of that close-to-the-vest stuff in his blood. Didn't take a genius to see that things weren't all that sensational in the marriage, and Stephanie was out of town half the time going to college. Sure. It could've happened. Why does it matter now? Marty's dead."

"Stephanie said this woman had been at the house the weekend Marty died."

Norman stayed in his crouch and concentrated on the circle I was drawing. "I get your drift. A witness."

"That, or if Marty was framed, somebody who was in on it."

Norman kept nodding, pinching his lower lip with his thumb and forefinger, concentrating on the circle.

"Do you know who it might have been?" I said.

"No."

"No ideas at all?"

"Unh-unh."

I erased the circle and started scrawling a new one. A better one. A rounder one. "It would've been someone neither the killers nor police knew about. Someone whose presence was only detected by Stephanie."

Norman leaned back and rested on his elbows. "Jesus . . . I don't know. Gordon, he's the chief of police, he questioned everybody."

"How hard did he question?"

Norman gave me a look. "Hard. Most of the gringos here — Stephanie included —

they think he's just this fat cop getting drunk all day, but he's not. Gordon's tough. The locals know how tough he is. Ask anybody. There's a saying in Priest River that if Chief Gordon really put his mind to it he could extract information from a corpse. No . . . if Marty was having an affair with a local woman, Gordon would've dug it out."

I stood and wiped the dirt from my hands. "Oh, well. Long shot."

"You know who it probably was," Norman said. "It was probably some secretary from Chicago down on vacation. Port Antonio's only a little ways up the road. Wall to wall women, on vacation, looking for a fling. Negril's the same way. Montego Bay. Shit, man . . . Jamaica's one of those places where people come to get tan and get laid. That's what it probably was. An impulse thing."

"Nobody local?"

Norman shook his head. "Doubt it. Marty was too sharp a guy to start up an affair with a woman who was going to be hanging around a lot. I bet it was just a weekend thing, him blowing off steam."

We stood and strolled back to the house and Norman took another swig from the bottle. "You staying at the house?" he said.

"Hotel."

"Got an extra bed here if you want."

"Already checked in and put some miles on the BMW. But thanks."

Norman smiled sadly and leaned against the side of the beach hut. "I'll give this place another year, maximum. Already making plans to beat it. Too many islands in the blue, blue sea to spend time getting fucked here. Don't have to hit Norman Tollinger over the head with a two-by-four to wake him up."

"Where will you go? Spain?"

Norman's smile lost its melancholy tint. "Naw. Changed my mind about that. I'd rather stay in this part of the world. Martinique."

"Why there?"

"Heard an ugly rumor the girls go topless on the beaches." Norman winked. "You know how the French are. Thought I'd better go check it out. Natives aren't so restless. It's more live and let live."

"Jamaica's not like that?"

Norman shook his head and stared sadly out in the direction of his boat. A fish broke the surface of the water, and from the jungle behind us a monkey screeched and clattered through the trees. "People here don't have any trouble with the 'live' part," Norman said at last. "Living is no problem at all. It's the 'let live' aspect that hangs everybody up, Quinn. That's the whaddayacallit? The fly in the ointment. Nobody wants to 'let live.' "

Twilight was thickening. I said good-bye to Norman and wheeled on out to the highway and headed back to Turnbull House. The road was filled with people walking home from a long day in the fields. Heads hanging. Bone tired. I hadn't swung a machete in my life, but I knew what they felt like. My eyes burned and my head ached. I ran my free hand through my hair and sped down the road.

Halfway to Turnbull House I noticed the Land Rover. It was coasting a comfortable distance behind me, neither gaining nor losing ground. It was too dark to make out a driver. Too dark even to see if there were others in the vehicle. I gently accelerated and the Land Rover stayed with me. Then I downshifted and the Land Rover slowed to maintain the same distance. Okay.

It was dark when I finally tooled the BMW into the long, sweeping oval driveway leading to the front gates of Turnbull House. The tall, gangly valet came trotting out from beneath his fancy white canopy. He was tall and thin with very short hair and from a distance looked a lot like Michael Jordan. I kept my eye on the highway. Ten seconds passed, and then the Land Rover gently coasted by. It didn't pull in and it didn't slow down. It just continued on without hesitation, a Sunday drive in the country. I was still too far away to see the driver.

"Evening, sir," the valet said.

"Good evening," I said, and handed him the keys. "Listen, could you do me a favor?"

"No problem, sir."

"Good." I took a ten-dollar bill out of my wallet and handed it to him. The valet didn't take it. He looked at it suspiciously.

"What that for?"

"If a light brown Land Rover comes up the driveway, could you let me know? I'll be in the bar for an hour or so, then in my room. Room 108."

"Light brown Land Rover?" the valet repeated.

"That's right."

"It follow you?"

"I think so."

The valet looked concerned. "That be Chief Gordon, y'know. Police chief."

"I know."

"You in trouble?"

"I haven't done anything wrong, if that's what you mean."

The valet nodded, thought about it, tossed

the car keys in the air and caught them overhand. "First the bar, then Room 108?"

"That's right." I pushed the ten-dollar bill at him and he shook his head and pushed it back.

"Whatever I can do to trouble Chief Gordon" — the valet smiled, getting into the car — "me do free of charge."

He wheeled the car toward the garage and I went into the lounge and ordered a Scotch. Five minutes later my friend the valet was suddenly standing by my side. He leaned down low and whispered in my ear.

"Land Rover come, sir."

"Is it Chief Gordon?"

He nodded. "But him nuh come to the door. Him jes sit there. Not do nothing."

The valet gestured for me to follow and I did. He took me up a flight of marble stairs to a second-floor veranda where I was able to look out over the grounds in relative seclusion. The night was alive with crickets. Moonlight dappled the hills in the distance. The grounds of Turnbull House were lit by discreet and muted floodlights, and behind me I could hear the dark waves of the warm Caribbean breaking gently on the smooth and carefully raked sand.

"There." The valet pointed out toward the highway. Parked at the entrance to

Turnbull House, half-sheltered by an enormous palm tree, was the Land Rover. The floodlights cast curious shadows, but I could make out the vague silhouette of a single person sitting in the driver's seat.

"Thanks," I said. "I'm going to go back down to the lobby. Let me know if he starts to come in."

The valet shook his head. "Chief Gordon no fock wit you in dis place. Is like an embassy, Turnbull House, y'know? Hands off. Owner of dis place, mon . . . him have Chief Gordon for breakfast, there be trouble here."

I went back down to the lounge and sat at a table by myself and gave Chief Gordon some thought. There was a lot to think about. His reputation. The propensity for violence that I had seen firsthand. His effortless accessibility to both weapons and ganja, and his convenient role as chief investigator of Marty's murder.

Then I put Chief Gordon to one side and thought of Stephanie. How she'd shaken her head over dinner at Scoma's, telling me of Russell and his vicarious love of things macho. Little rich boy hanging around the Priest River police station, slumming with the badasses, shooting their guns, wearing their *Cool Hand Luke* sunglasses, buddying up to the head honcho with the baby teeth who was rumored to be able to extract information from a corpse.

Okay, the connection was there. So what? So what if Chief Gordon was Russell's long-distance muscle Hank and I had been wondering about back in San Francisco? That did nothing but confuse Bongo's role in everything. With Chief Gordon pulling the strings the "anonymous" buyers would not have been so anonymous. And Bongo would certainly have had a clue as to the goings-on in Gordon's personal fiefdom. Virtually all of the information received in San Francisco had come from Bongo and Bongo alone, and we'd accepted it without question. There were plans to develop Seven Altars. Bongo had all ten fingers in the legal pie, and Chief Gordon had the local machinery to keep forensic zeal to a minimum.

My thinking was making me nervous, so I finished off my drink and went to my room. I didn't bother to check if the Land Rover was still parked outside. It either was or it wasn't, and me peeking out from the top of the second floor veranda wasn't going to change things.

I got into bed and lay in the dark for a long time without being able to sleep. I tried to organize the pieces of the puzzle, grouping the various parts together by color and shape and plausibility. Bongo, and the ease with which he'd found the bargain basement loophole. The mystery woman who'd spent the last night with Marty. Eyeless, pockmarked Gary. How twelve bullets to the face could chip away recognizable facial features, one by one. Russell's convenient fear of deep, lonely waters, and how Stephanie had backed up the story.

I tossed and turned, got up for a drink of water, then came back to bed determined to shelve all speculation until I had a chance to talk with Bongo in the morning. To induce sleep I decided instead to think of the waterfalls themselves. Seven Altars. And as I began to drift into sleep I found myself thinking of the story Stephanie had told me in Russell's Seacliff studio of how, swimming alone at the top pool, she had been startled by Marty's sudden reflection next to her. I could almost feel the moment. Could hear the screech of the monkeys, feel the cool of the shaded jungle, see the rays of sun slanting down into the moist, green cathedral.

What had it been? What had occurred that afternoon at the top of the canyon while she swam alone in the emerald water, attempting to wash the grief away? The mind playing tricks? Optical illusion? Magic? Or was it something else?

Were there mirrors in this world the maid can't unhook from the wall and carry away?

18

I woke early the next morning from a deep and dreamless sleep and drove immediately back into Priest River. There wasn't a Land Rover in sight. First stop was 57 Livingston Road, Suite III, but Bongo's office had a little handwritten note on the outside door saying, "Back in thirty minutes."

I waited on the front porch awhile, then strolled the two blocks back to the main square and plunked down on a bench near the fancy gazebo. Winston, the retarded boy who'd shined my shoes the previous trip, came shuffling up, kit in hand. He had the same goofy smile on his face, and he gestured at my feet.

"No thanks," I said. "Tennis shoes this time." I held my right foot up. "See? Tennis shoes."

Winston nodded and dug around in his shoeshine kit and held out a bottle of white polish. "Tennis shoe !" he exclaimed proudly. "Reebok!"

"No," I said. "It'll ruin them."

"Ruin them!" he said.

I exhaled, thought about the replacement cost for a new pair of sneakers, then gave Winston the go-ahead. What the hell? Enthusiasm and industriousness were rare commodities these days, and one should reward them when possible. When he was finished he started in with the exaggerated winking again and asked for five dollars. I slipped him a buck and he went on his way, beaming.

The day was already blistering hot. Humid. Sticky. I walked back to Bongo's office, but the note was still there. The rum shop next door looked cool and shadowy, so I decided to wait for Bongo in a little bit of comfort.

The place was pretty much empty. Two listless fans twirled from the ceiling. There was no bar to belly up to, just a counter with a wall full of bottles behind it, three rickety metal tables with the emblem of a cigarette brand on the top of each, and a half-dozen fold-out metal chairs like you used to sit on in school assembly back in junior high. The walls were cinderblock.

I looked at my watch. The note on the door said thirty minutes. If Jamaica time was anything like Mexico time, that could mean anywhere from one to five hours. A young woman in heels and a tight-fitting dress swept the floor. She looked like Jimi Hendrix, and if it was possible to be in the

291

throes of a towering snit, she was in one. The woman swept right past me, almost brushing the tops of my newly shined sneakers, and disappeared through the back with an unnecessarily violent slam of the screen door. Up close I saw why she resembled Jimi Hendrix. The she was a he. Not a bad wig, and the high-heels were sharp, but the five o'clock shadow ruined everything.

To the right a couple of silver-haired men were hunched over a table, playing dominos. Above them hung a faded picture of Queen Victoria, and next to the picture a desk fan had been bolted into the wall, and it was blowing vigorously down on the table where the men sat.

"Morning," I said.

One of the men looked up at me, watery-eyed, expressionless. Then he glanced around the bar. "Where Mona?"

"Mona?" I said.

The man made a gesture of one sweeping.

"Oh." I pointed to the back screen door. "She went out that way."

The old man shook his head and painfully pushed his way up from the table and went behind the dilapidated counter and put a shot glass in front of me. I hadn't intended to drink, but his prolonged, arthritic effort changed my mind.

"Rum?" he said.

"Well . . ."

He selected an unlabeled bottle from a shelf on the wall behind him and poured it out with a trembling hand. I smiled my thanks but he just stood there, frozen, holding out the uncapped bottle. I took the hint and killed the first shot. It was a tough thing to kill at ten in the morning. The old man immediately poured out a second shot and waited, poised to lay on the third.

"Let's leave it at two," I said.

The old man nodded and screwed the cap back on.

"Listen," I said. "Do you have any idea where Bongo might have gone?"

The old man looked up at me with his watery eyes. "Bongo?"

I hooked my thumb at the office next door. "Bongo. The lawyer."

"Bongo there," the old man said. "I jes hear him."

"You did? How long ago?"

He held up his hand and spread his bony, callused fingers. "Five minute."

I paid him and went back out into the street and up onto Bongo's front porch. I banged on the door. The door gave to the pressure of my knuckles and swung slowly open before thumping gently into something and easing back. I paused, took a breath, and pushed the door open again. The thing it had bumped into was the globe of the Earth Bongo had had sitting on his desk. Only now it was on the floor, on its side, with a crack that went from Great Britain all the way down the Atlantic to Brazil.

I stepped into the room and surveyed the damage. There is a shock that comes with seeing the savage destruction of property that is as visceral and sickening and mind-numbing as the viewing of a mutilated corpse. You can see it in the anguished faces of strangers who inch by a car wreck long after the victims have been hauled away. The twisted metal is enough. The shattered glass has its own terrible eloquence.

Papers were strewn everywhere. Folders, envelopes, packets. The two file cabinets had been pried open and ransacked. Everything that had been on the wall — diplomas, art-work, framed photographs — had been torn down and smashed on the floor. Slash marks zigzagged the windowshades. I called Bongo's name. Nothing.

I edged around the desk and the broken glass crunched beneath my feet. I wasn't breathing. Wasn't making a sound. Dreading to find what I was sure I would find. But there was no blood, no body. I checked the two rooms in back just to be sure, but that was it. The house was empty.

I went back out onto the front porch and closed the door behind me. The heat was overwhelming, and I regretted the two rums I'd put away under the guise of being polite. I took a moment to collect and organize my thoughts. Was Bongo aware yet of what had happened? Was it Bongo the old man had heard five minutes earlier, coming back to discover the chaos, or had it been someone else?

Bongo's porch was not the place to mull these questions over, so I climbed down the three steps to the street and began walking up the block to where I'd parked the car. As I passed by the rum shop I noticed Mona was out on the front porch. She was sitting in a chair, head down, sobbing, the broomstick propped to the side. When I passed she lunged up from her grief to look at me, eyes wide, nostrils flaring, as a swimmer who has almost drowned gasps for air when breaking the surface of the water. Tears had streaked her mascara. The eyes were smeared with black, and the wig hung from an odd angle. There were wicked stepsisters somewhere in Mona's life, and her anguished gaze seemed to be scanning me for spare glass slippers. I picked up my pace.

I got back on the two-lane highway going east and, keeping my eyes on the rear-view minor, accelerated out of town. Priest River had finally gotten to me. Ghosts and heat and rum and offices trashed. Retarded shoe-shine boys. Brokenhearted transvestites. Brutal police with reflector sunglasses and their boot heels propped up in the typewriter keys. If Franz Kafka had known about this place he would have run for mayor. I needed the fresh sea breeze on my face. Smell the salt water. Figure out what the hell to do next. When I came up on the unmarked turnoff to Seven Altars I instinctively turned right.

I didn't have to jump to a conclusion. The conclusion jumped at me. Word had filtered from San Francisco to Priest River that the elusive deed of title to Seven Altars had gone from Hank Wilkie to Quinn Parker. Somebody decided it was time to go into Bongo's office and have a look at the documentation, up close and personal. Except why wreck the place? Why go to the trouble of breaking the diplomas? Were they unable to find what they wanted? Or were they sending a message to Bongo the way the last eleven bullets entering Marty's brain had been a message?

I maneuvered the long and tangled private driveway and parked in the empty seashell driveway in front of the house. I sat there for a moment waiting for the dust to settle. All was still and quiet. Nobody had followed me.

I opened the front door with the key Hank had given me, went through the living room and out onto the deck where the barbecue had been held. The lounge chairs were still out on the deck, along with a half-full bag of charcoal and some snorkeling gear and even Marty's expensive 112th Street telescope, tilted upward, pointing at the stars.

I stretched out on the lounge chair, leaned my head back, and closed my eyes to the harsh light glinting off the Caribbean. On what planet did your paranoia lie, Martin Greene? Who was it you saw closing in?

There was a pause in the breaking of the waves and in that pause I thought I heard something. A crunching sound. Not close by. Medium distance.

I went back into the house and cracked the front door and peeked outside, and my body went cold. A car. It was parked at the spot where the overgrown single-lane entrance to Seven Altars met the open seashell parking area. It was still back in the tree cover, and if I hadn't been looking I probably wouldn't have seen it. Two young black men got out of the car and left the doors open.

One wore a red beret, the other had on a white and black polo shirt. They stood about fifty yards from the house, and I could see the man with the beret lean close to the other one and whisper something. The man in the polo shirt nodded. Then they quickly and quietly left the car where it was and began walking toward the front porch.

As they drew closer I felt a small shock of recognition. The man in the red beret was the same man I'd seen flee from Chief Gordon that first morning in the town plaza. The other fellow I'd never seen before. Neither man bothered with the pretense of concealed weapons. The pistols they loosely carried were in full view. As the men neared the house they branched off, one to each side, sealing off the escape routes north and south, surrounding me.

I moved silently from the door and went back out onto the rear deck. I held my breath and catapulted up and over the guardrail and down onto the beach fifteen feet below, landing hard, rolling twice and then springing immediately to my feet. There wasn't a sound in the world.

I moved carefully at first, skirting the edge of the jungle, heading west toward the jungle trail that led to the waterfalls. I only glanced over my shoulder once, saw nothing. It was important to keep going. Quickly. Silently. No wasted activity. One foot in front of the other. Faster. Faster.

Then there were shouts. I whirled and saw the man in the beret up on the deck, pointing in my direction. For a precious moment I thought that I might be okay. That I had a chance to open up enough of a gap between us so that I might disappear into the jungle, emerge on the road, and flee. But in the next instant the hope was choked off. The man on the terrace was yelling to his partner, and I suddenly saw in one horrifying moment that the second man had already been making his way down the jungly beach. At the shout he snapped alert, saw me, and broke into a run.

I turned and ran. Ran as fast as I could, ducking beneath the low-leaning palms, dodging the coconuts that littered the sand like bleached bowling balls. Up ahead was the little green sign pointing the way to Seven Altars. I tried to think as I ran. I would pull out the sign and take it with me. Without the sign they wouldn't know exactly where to turn. The trail to the waterfalls looked just like any other animal trail. I'd be safe. They'd never find me.

I reached the sign and leaned to pull it out. I yanked and it stuck fast and I yanked again, harder, and as I did something whispered past my ear. It was warm and hummed like a tuning fork. I turned around and the man with the polo shirt was very close to me, no more than twenty yards away, silhouetted against the sea. He stood in a semicrouch, legs spread wide apart, flexed at the knees, gun held out before him with both hands. There were three spurts of light from the end of the gun and I instinctively raised my hands to shield my face. The tree behind me spit out chunks of bark, and searing pain ripped across my face like the brisk slash of a riding crop. I put my hand to my cheek and came back with fingertips bloody.

I was shot. Or was I? The blood was there, but my body was fine. It was only a piece from the splintered tree. The man in the polo shirt lowered his gun for a moment. He saw the blood on my face and was waiting for me to drop. I lurched the sign from where it had been hammered in the earth and bolted inland, toward the waterfalls.

There was more shouting and I moved quickly to the first pool. There was no way I could survive unarmed against two men with weapons. My only chance was to somehow disable the first man, get his gun, and take my chances with the second.

There was a shelf of rock just to the left of the first pool. I tucked myself behind it, back flat up against the moist green covering. I gripped the end of the wooden sign. Lifted it into striking position. Waited.

I was having trouble breathing. Mist from the waterfalls drifted through the air. Monkeys screeched in the trees above like berserk telephone wires. The blood pounded hot in my ears. Then I heard him coming.

I couldn't tell if he was alone or with his partner, but it made no difference. I had to do what I had to do. My fingers gripped the wooden sign. I told myself to concentrate. I'd have one shot. Look for the spot. The bridge of his nose. Locate it quickly and swing hard. No hesitation. Forget that it's a human face. Swing as hard as you can. The bridge of the nose.

The leaves rustled and parted and suddenly Polo Shirt was right there before me. I was expecting him and he wasn't expecting me, and that was the difference. Before he could bring his gun up I concentrated on the bridge of his nose and swung the sign with all my strength.

Polo Shirt was almost fast enough. He backed away but the edge of the sign caught him solidly in the throat and I heard the cartilage give way. He made no sound.

301

Showed no undue alarm. The hands made a brief, spasmodic attempt to reach up to the crushed larynx, but that was it. The eyes went strangulation wide and he pitched backward into the thigh-deep waters of the emerald pool and was utterly still.

I dropped the sign and fell to my knees at the side of the pool. The gun had gone backward with him. I could see it at the bottom. Black, lethal, useless. I didn't know much about guns. If I fished it out would it still work? Then I heard the rustle of the leaves down the trail. No time! I sprung to my feet and scrambled up the large smooth boulders, toward the top of the waterfalls.

I only looked back once, between the third and fourth pool, and I saw Beret closing ground. He hadn't lingered to grieve over his companion.

The seventh and last pool waited just above me. I was hyperventilating. The memory was dim, but all I could remember about the top pool was that it was fed by a waterfall that cascaded over a solid, twenty-foot-high rock face. I didn't know for certain what was beyond, but at some point the jungly hill had to level out and work its way down to the highway on the other side. But how to get past the rock face? There must be a way. A tree to climb. Footholds in the cliff. Anything.

I pulled myself up, bleeding and exhausted, to the top pool and stared at my own death. The rock face was before me, water rushing swiftly over the top. No trees to climb. No miraculous toeholds hacked out of the side of the granite tomb. It was over. I had nowhere to go.

Beret saw my dilemma and came to a halt. He stood thirty feet below me, at the edge of the sixth pool, and a smile crossed his face. He was breathing heavily. Sweat darkened his shirt. He held the gun casually in his right hand. I kept my eyes on him and reached down to pick up a baseball-sized rock. Beret looked at the rock in my hand and slowly shook his head.

"Die with dignity, mon," he said. "Die with dignity."

He brought his weapon up and then there was movement to my left, and three sharp explosions reverberated off the canyon walls. Beret spun completely around twice and went down in a heap in the rocks sloping off to the right of the pool.

Bongo stood next to me. He stared down at Beret and methodically put the safety back on his weapon, tucking the gun in his pants pocket. Then Bongo looked over at me and pointed a finger at his cheek.

"Are you shot?" he said.

"No."

"Your face . . ." he said. "I thought you had been shot."

I began to come out of my shock. "How . . . how did you get here? How did you know?"

"I didn't know." Bongo took a deep breath. "I told you before, this is the place where I come to think. I came here to think."

"With a loaded gun?"

"When my office is destroyed I prefer to think in the company of a loaded gun."

Bongo clambered down the rocks to the sixth pool and stood over the man he'd just shot. The beret had come off, and there was a small hole in the side of the man's head. The blood seeping out was the consistency of a milkshake, thick enough to hold up a straw.

Bongo looked at the man's face and slowly shook his head.

"I've seen this guy before," I said. "My first day here, while you and Hank were signing the legal papers. He was in the plaza with another guy. The cops pulled up and he ran away."

Bongo nodded distractedly. I wasn't telling him anything new.

"Do you know him?" I asked.

"Yes."

"There's another one down at the bottom."

Bongo looked up with surprise. "Another one?"

"I hit him with the sign. I think he's dead, too."

"Show me."

It was difficult going down. My legs were weak and unsteady. Bongo moved on ahead of me, strong, confident. Forget the dreadlocks. Forget the nice-and-easy ganja-smoking persona and forget the affable law student just back from UCLA. The grim, terse, methodical nature in the face of such violence revealed a whole other side of Bongo's nature. He hadn't come to understand suffering through song lyrics, and he didn't learn trouble from the brain trust at Paramount Pictures.

By the time I caught up with Bongo he had already waded into the pond and was standing waist-deep next to the floating body. He gently lifted the head, took one look, then let it drop back into the water.

"Ta rass!" he hissed. "Shit!"

"What?"

Bongo just stood there in the water, hands on hips, staring out into the leafy jungle. "You brought your car?"

"Yes."

Bongo stood there, took a very deep breath,

and exhaled slowly. "Okay. Go to the car and wait for me."

"What about the bodies?"

"I'll handle it."

"But they're — "

"I said I'll handle it!" Bongo shouted. "Now go wait at the car!"

I didn't say another word. I maneuvered past the pool with the body and parted the first heavy leaves of the jungle path. Before descending I sneaked a quick look back. Bongo still stood in the water, his dreadlocks hanging low. The body floated next to him. Bongo just stood there, staring down at the lifeless corpse, a burnt and ragged priest at some terrible baptism. Then I turned and hurried back to the car and didn't look back again.

19

Twenty minutes later Bongo came back to the house. He was breathing hard, and his eyes were grim and determined.

"Are you okay?" he asked in a remarkably calm voice.

"I think so."

He signaled me to come around with him to the front porch. We went out to the white car, put the vehicle in neutral, and together pushed it out of the way. Then we got in the BMW, Bongo driving, and headed back out the driveway, toward the main road.

"What did you do with the bodies?" I said.

Bongo shook his head. "Not your problem."

We were silent a moment. Bongo reached the main road and made a tire-squealing left, back toward Priest River.

"Where are we going?" I said.

Bongo shook his head. "Find someone."

"Goddamn it, Bongo! They tried to kill me! I'm not in the mood for twenty questions! Now where the hell are we going?"

Bongo turned, looked at me, thought about

307

it. "I'm going to find my best friend."

"Your best friend?"

"Yes."

I leaned back in the passenger seat and rubbed my face. "Look, Bongo. I told you, the guy with the beret I've seen before. He was in the plaza with another man. A short guy. Muscular. Wore a white headband. Chief Gordon beat him up and cut off his dreadlocks."

"Archie?" Bongo said.

The name struck a responsive chord. "Yes! That was it! Archie! One of the cops called him Archie. If we could find him . . . shit, I don't know. Maybe he could tell us something. It's worth a shot."

Bongo didn't answer. He kept slamming the gears of the BMW, driving furiously through the chaos of dust and shadow. Then he abruptly said, "Archie Barrett is the one who tried to have you killed."

Silence.

"He what?" I mumbled.

"Archie Barrett is the one who tried to have you killed."

I stared at Bongo's profile as he drove. "You . . . you know that? As a fact?"

Bongo took a deep breath and let it out. "The men at the waterfalls work for Archie Barrett," he said with strained patience.

"They would not have come after you without his instructions."

I turned completely sideways in my seat and faced Bongo. "Then why in the hell are we looking for your best friend?"

"Because Archie *is* my best friend!" Bongo snapped. "That's why!"

That silenced me. Ten seconds passed. Bongo gave me a side-glance, shook his head, and took a deep breath.

"No quick way to tell the story, mon," he said.

"Try."

Bongo relaxed for a moment. Sighed and slowed the BMW down from its breakneck speed.

"Archie . . ." Bongo said as though the name had just come up for the first time. "Archie Barrett is Robin Hood."

"Robin Hood?"

"Archie is the man who lives in the forest. Comes out to fight other people's battles." Bongo's face softened for a moment. "Me and Archie, we were like Tom Sawyer and Huck Finn. When I read that book in college I thought, yes mon. Paint them black and put them in the islands, you have Bongo and Archie."

"What happened?"

"Archie went bad," Bongo said. "That's

what happened. Archie never knows when to turn and walk away, live to fight another day. The beating you talked of . . . where they cut his hair . . ."

I nodded.

"Archie changed after that. Something broke inside. Made him a little crazy." Bongo pointed at his eyes. "You look in there, you can see it. A year ago if you asked me could Archie kill somebody, I would have said no. But now . . . I don't know. I think Archie has become dangerous. He isn't a folk hero anymore."

I watched the trees fly by as we neared the town of Priest River. "But why would Archie want me dead?"

Bongo shook his head. "I don't know. Somebody hired him."

"Who?"

Bongo shifted gears and the BMW entered town. "That is what we are going to find out, Quinn. We are going to find out right now."

Conversation stopped as we sped through town, angling along the southern edge of the main square. I recognized Norman sitting on a bench near the gazebo. He was getting his shoes shined by Winston. When he glanced up and saw us, his face became a mask of surprise. Then he smiled broadly

310

and waved frantically for us to stop, but Bongo kept right on driving. No time for chitchat.

We followed the paved road for as long as it went, then nosed down off the concrete onto a heavily rutted dirt street. This was a section of Priest River I hadn't seen before. The last decrepit outpost of civilization before the jungle itself. The air was warm and lush and you could feel the thick, humid weight of the Tropics press down on you. Thatched houses. Cattle wandering about. Naked children stood on the side of the road and watched us drive by with a kind of hostile curiosity.

We drove in silence for another five minutes, then Bongo suddenly swerved to the left and came to a halt in front of a corrugated tin building.

"He's here," Bongo said. "That's his moped."

A Vespa was sitting out front, hitched up to a post like a horse in the Old West.

"You want to come in or stay here?" he said.

"I'm going wherever you're going."

"Then let's do it."

We got out of the car and walked in. The building housed a one-room bar, about twenty feet wide and maybe fifty feet long.

The door opened to a row of stools that bunched up close to a varnished, chest-high bar. A half-dozen tables filled the room as it stretched to our left, and a surprisingly nice jukebox was pushed up against the far wall. Two of the tables were filled with men drinking beer. A solitary figure sat on the furthest barstool, bottle of rum and shot glass before him. It was the man I'd seen in Chief Gordon's police station getting his garden shears haircut. Archie Barrett.

A very heavy woman with Hindu features stood behind the bar. She was strong rather than fat, and you could tell that once upon a time, twenty years and a hundred pounds ago, she had been a very beautiful woman.

"Afternoon, Margarita," Bongo said. He was talking to the woman behind the bar, but his eyes were fixed unwaveringly on Archie.

"I no want no trouble, Bongo," Margarita said.

Bongo shook his head. "The trouble already happened, Margarita. There won't be any more."

Margarita didn't look terribly comforted. Bongo leaned on the varnished bar and kept staring at the man on the barstool.

"Hello, Archie."

Archie turned from the contemplation of

his rum glass and gazed at Bongo. He was short, solid, deeply suspicious. The tree-trunk legs and powerful arms brought to mind a miniature Joe Frazier, and his stubby, rutted face carried the scars of many a streetfight. After the incident with Chief Gordon he only had the beginnings of dreadlocks — "nubbies," Bongo had once called them — little twisted spires of hair that sprang two inches out of his head in all directions. The large and terrible scar from the garden shear haircut slashed across the top of his scalp, and the nubbies grew in confused tangles around it. Archie's eyes were the kind of bloodshot that doesn't come from hangovers and late-night television. This red was permanent. Burst capillaries. Another one of the scars he carried with him from the last beating. The red lent some heat to his eyes, and I could feel the burn of his glare across my face, ears, and shoulders.

Archie slowly pushed himself off the barstool and hobbled over to the jukebox in the corner. He put in a coin, punched in his selection, and hobbled back toward his chair. An electric silence filled the room as the music started. The song was "Burnin' and Lootin'."

"Who your fren?" Archie said. His voice was old and tough and crusted over, like something that had fallen off the back of a cement truck.

"Surprised he's still alive?" Bongo said. "You think him dead right now, don't you. You think maybe now this town's got two duppies instead of one?"

"What you talkin' about?" Archie said.

"Why did you do it?"

"Do what?"

"Try to kill this man here?"

"Kill this mon?" Archie looked at me and smiled. "How I kill a mon when I be sittin' here drinkin' rum inna rum bar, eh?"

"Don't fock with me!" Bongo slammed his fist on the bar. Archie flinched, lost his smile for a moment, then retrieved it. "Don't treat me like I'm a fockin' idiot!" Bongo said. "Those men at the waterfalls worked for you! I see Reggie waving a gun at my friend here, mon! What Reggie doing there if you don't send him?"

Archie listened very carefully, gently stroking his left arm with his right hand, softly, softly, as though counting the individual hairs. "Reggie . . . him deader?"

"Yes, mon! Reggie deader! And the other one I don't know the name of, him deader too! Now you tell me quick-quick who put you on us or I see you go to jail! I don't care what anybody says!"

The silence in the room was almost palpable. Archie's smile broadened, and some softness crept into the harsh, red eyes. "Bongo Brambley gonna tek me a jail, eh? Mistah Rasta lawyer gonna tek the rude boy an put him inna Babylon cell, eh? Do Chief Gordon job for him?"

Bongo exhaled deeply. He turned around a complete three-sixty and looked around as if trying to figure out an angle to take. "Come on, Archie," he said in a softer voice. "Tell me now. I'm your friend. Who paid you to do this? What happened to you, Archie. You lost your brains? You fock with your friends because the price is good?"

Archie quit smiling. "I didn't know them come for you. If I know that, I not let it happen."

Bongo leaned very close. His voice dropped low, almost to a whisper. "Who hired you, Archie?"

"I can't tell that, mon. How I can tell that an' survive still?"

"Only way *for* you to survive!" Bongo yelled.

Archie stared at him unwaveringly, and for the first time I could see that glint of insanity. More than mere facial features had begun to melt away under the hard clubs of endless police onslaughts. The broken nose, the thickening scar tissue, the teeth loosening and falling from his mouth one by one. Used to be a folk hero, Bongo had said. Robin Hood. Huck Finn. Ethan Allen with his Green Mountain Boys. Only people don't want their Robin Hoods to look like they just went through a sausage grinder. They don't want a visual reminder of what eventually happens to you if you fight the system too much. And now Archie was starting to lose it. The toeholds of sanity were cracking out from underneath him one by one, and there wasn't much left.

I went back out onto the front porch to get some air and leave Bongo to talk to Archie in private. Make it look less like an inquisition by committee. A small crowd had begun to gather in the street. They milled around in front of the bar, pretending that they weren't gathering. There weren't many secrets in Priest River. Word had gotten around that Bongo and Archie were going to have it out.

I'd only been outside a few minutes when I heard a low rumbling on the horizon. The two dozen or so people who had gathered in the street got out of the way and the police Land Rover suddenly appeared around the corner. The four cops I'd seen during my first visit were in the vehicle, with Chief

Gordon riding in the passenger seat up front. Shit! In the wake of the Land Rover another fifteen or twenty people hurried to the scene. The prospect of trouble swelled the crowd.

I went back inside the rum shop and tapped Bongo on the shoulder. He broke off his argument with Archie and glared at me. "What do you want?"

I hooked my thumb at the door. "Problems."

Before Bongo could say another word the door swung open. Chief Gordon stood there a moment, surveying the room, then casually sauntered in. One other cop came in with him. Just as thick, just as cocky, wearing the same reflector sunglasses. Gordon Junior. Bongo and Archie fell silent. The whole bar went silent. All we could hear was the scratchy music from Archie's song on the jukebox.

Chief Gordon and Junior went up to the bar and heaved their beefy hindsides up onto the barstools.

"Two Red Stripe, Margarita," Gordon said.

"I tell you what I tell Bongo," Margarita said. "No trouble in my bar. You want fe mek trouble, you tek it in the street. Why you don't tek trouble elsewhere?"

Chief Gordon ignored her. Instead, he turned on his barstool and pretended to notice the three of us for the first time. "Hey! Look who here! Is Archibald. How come you so bald, Archeee-bald? Where you dreadlocks?"

Archie glared at the two cops. Bongo put his hand on Archie's shoulder.

"Let's go talk outside, eh?"

Archie didn't respond. He just sat and glowered and watched Chief Gordon put his fat lips around the bottle and drink.

"Let's go," Bongo repeated.

"No, mon," Archie said. "I not put up wit such blood-clot fockery. I and I talk right here."

Bongo leaned close to Archie and spoke through clenched teeth. "Don't be stupid. Use your brains. Gordon here waiting for you to do something."

Chief Gordon drained his beer and ordered another one. He shifted his butt on the barstool and looked over at Junior. "What that song say on the jukebox there?"

Junior shrugged. "Burnin' something. Lootin' something."

"Burning and looting?" Chief Gordon said with surprise in his voice. "This bar be a place fe promote burning and looting?"

The silence in the bar thickened.

"We can't have that," Chief Gordon said. He pushed himself off the barstool and walked slowly to the jukebox, yanked it six inches away from the wall, leaned down, and pulled the plug. The song ground to a slow, thick halt. Chief Gordon walked back to the bar and settled in.

"There," he said. "Much better."

"What you do with my jukebox!" Margarita screamed. "Is a new jukebox!"

I watched Archie. His hand was a balled fist, the red in his eyes suddenly molten. He stood up. Bongo tried to hold him down but Archie shrugged him off. Archie hobbled to the jukebox and plugged the machine back in. An automatic mechanism caused the song to quit and the needle to go back to its spot. Archie dug deep for another coin, inserted it, and punched in the numbers on the panel. Ten seconds passed, then the song started again. The same one. "Burning and looting tonight . . . burning all illusion tonight . . ." Archie didn't come back to his seat. He stood at the jukebox, legs planted, arms folded defiantly across his chest.

Chief Gordon paused a moment, then did a long, drawn-out, theatrical double take from his barstool.

"Archeee-bald," he said, tsk-tsk style. "You must not heard me. What you be doin' here playing this rude-boy music?"

Junior leaned close to Chief Gordon. "Maybe

he didn't see you unplug the machine."

"That what happen?" Gordon asked Archie. "You no see me unplug the machine?"

"Ta rass," Archie mumbled.

Chief Gordon and Junior looked at each other and smiled sad, wistful smiles. "Him still not know his manners," Junior said.

Chief Gordon stared at Bongo with a fixed, malignant grin on his lips. "Your hair gettin' wild again, rude boy. Think it be gettin' time for another trim."

Junior laughed as they both reached for their rubber truncheons at the same time.

"He's done nothing wrong," Bongo said to Gordon. "Leave him alone. Let it be." Then, to Archie. "Turn the fockin' song off, Archie! Now!"

"You best be quiet, Bongo," Chief Gordon said calmly, his eyes firmly on Archie. "This not concern you."

Junior slid off his stool and took a step toward the jukebox. Archie never changed his expression. He matter-of-factly removed a gun from his inside shirt pocket, pointed it with care and precision, and fired one bullet after another into the two policemen until there weren't any bullets left.

The noise shook my teeth and jaw. Junior went straight down without a sound, but Chief Gordon staggered back, smashed into

320

the bar, and took both barstools and a bottle of beer with him as he crashed solidly to the floor. It was all over in five seconds. There were no screams, no shouts. In the traumatized aftermath there was only the song playing on the jukebox, the smell of sulphur, and Chief Gordon's bottle of Red Stripe rolling along the wooden floorboards, spilling beer as it bumped and rolled down the slope of the floor toward the entrance to the street.

"My God!" Bongo breathed.

Gordon and Junior lay absolutely dead motionless. There wasn't so much as a leg twitch left in either one of them. Gordon's reflector sunglasses had come off and he was staring frozen-eyed at the ceiling, little rounded baby teeth bared, lip curled in the rigor-mortis snarl of a dog hit in the road and left in the sun.

Then Margarita started screaming. The shrieks seemed to ripple the air in the bar like heat waves on pavement. I looked at Archie. He was leaning against the jukebox, one foot crossed over the other, reloading the pistol with the deliberate calm of a man stringing laces through new shoes.

"Archie!" Bongo shouted. "What have you done?"

The door to the bar suddenly burst open

and the other two cops rushed in, weapons drawn, looking this way and that. They didn't look at the jukebox in time and Archie leveled his reloaded gun and fired again and again and again, and another cop went backward and down. The fourth fired one wild shot in Archie's general direction and then fled back toward the Land Rover. Archie calmly walked to the door and followed him out.

The second wave of violence jolted everyone from their collective stupor. There was a sudden surge of frantic shouts and panicked movement. I felt a hand roughly grab my upper arm. Bongo. He yanked me out the back door and together we half-fell, half-ran through a tangled thicket that skirted the rum bar and rejoined the road further up.

"What about the car . . ." I said.

Bongo shook his head. "We come for it later. There's a shortcut back to town. Follow me!"

Bongo headed off into the dense jungle and waved for me to follow. But as I turned to go I looked back at the bar and dirt road and saw an astonishing sight. It was Archie, running down the street without a trace of limp, redeeming pistol held high above his head like an Olympic torch, firing an occasional volley at the veering Land Rover and the one policeman left who was trying desperately to drive away. The people who had gathered on the street did not try to stop Archie. They did not impede his progress or beg him to come to his senses. No. Instead, they parted to let Archie run cleanly between them, as though he were a long-distance runner on the last leg of a grueling marathon, dashing toward the tape, the flashing cameras, and the cheering crowds. Toward the glory that immortalizes.

20

A soft hand was nudging my shoulder. I didn't want it to nudge me. I didn't want it to nudge me because I was ahead on the count, three and one, and I knew the pitcher was going to groove a fastball right down the middle and I was going to hit a frozen rope right out of the park over the left-center field fence. I was concentrating on my swing, on where the ball was going to be. I had my spot. I knew how I was going to do it. All I needed to do was concentrate.

The pitcher wound and served it up and I swung as hard as I could. But the ball didn't go anywhere. There wasn't a ball anymore, just the pitcher, and as I swung his eyes went wide with horror and disbelief and his neck snapped backward and I could feel his life come to an end all the way down the varnished wood of the bat, up into my fingertips.

My eyes jerked open and the stewardess quit nudging me. She leaned down close and smiled her perfect smile.

"We've landed, sir," she said.

"What?"

"We've landed. We're in San Francisco."

I pushed myself up straight in my seat and glanced around at the empty aircraft. The stewardess softly laughed. "You were really out. Not many people can nap all the way through a landing."

I tried to rub my face awake. "I . . . I haven't had much sleep."

She winked a knowing wink and went back to checking the overhead compartments. "A lot of our passengers on the Montego Bay flight come back a little short of sleep."

I wandered the airport in a semitrance, doing the things that needed to be done. Baggage. Customs. Declaration of goods. Then I retrieved my van from long-term parking and drove up to the kid sitting in a little booth at the exit gate. Jagged metal claws loomed up from the pavement before me, and to the side was a sign warning of severe tire damage should I try to sneak past. I paid the boy some money and he pushed a button next to the register. The steel jaws retracted back into the earth. I watched them slide away, and then I drove over the suddenly smooth road. Give the man some money and the nasty blades go away. Maybe that's all it took. Maybe things weren't any more complicated than that.

Bongo had hustled me out of Jamaica. All hell was breaking loose and there was nothing to be gained by me catching a stray bullet between the eyes. When the dust settled he would be in touch. I'd nodded, climbed into the single-engine Cessna, and watched Bongo turn back in the direction of Priest River. Back into the madness.

It was late afternoon in San Francisco and traffic on the Bayshore Freeway was very fast and very heavy. Seventy miles per hour, bumper-to-bumper. It got my attention. Cleared the cobwebs. I thought of the wino who several years back had wandered up onto the Santa Monica Freeway in Los Angeles and was run over by two hundred automobiles before someone's Mercedes finally flipped what was left of him over the side. There was no time to dwell on Jamaica. I clutched the steering wheel and concentrated on the job at hand.

I found myself driving toward Hank and Carol's house. It wasn't a conscious decision. It just seemed the place to go.

Carol answered the door and my presence startled her. "Quinn!"

I leaned down and gave her a kiss and she pulled her face away with concern. She held my arms with both hands, up close to my elbows. I felt something weaken inside me, something starting to crumble that was not going to stop crumbling.

"What happened, Quinn?" she said. "Did you go to Jamaica?"

"Yes."

Cartoon voices drifted in from the living room. I stood in the entrance and took a deep breath to steady myself.

"Quinn." She put her hands under my chin and forced me to look at her. "What happened? Tell me."

I looked down into Carol's troubled face. "It's good to see you," I said.

"What?"

"We should've made love way back when, you know that? We really should have."

The concern in Carol's expression deepened. What had weakened inside me were tears. I felt the sting in my eyes and I closed them, closed them hard, and Carol was holding me with her head pressed against my chest.

"Oh, Quinn . . ."

We held each other tightly, rocking slowly together in the foyer. Thirty seconds passed. A minute. When we let go and I opened my eyes I saw a single tear trailing down Carol's cheek. She had no idea why I was upset. Not a clue. The simple fact that I was in pain was enough. While we looked into each other's faces, Cort appeared around the corner from the living room and stood there for a moment, nibbling on his finger.

"Mommy . . ."

Carol turned her face sideways on my chest. "Not now, honey. Wait a minute."

Cort stood there and looked at us. "Is Uncle Quinn crying?"

"Yes, honey," Carol said. "He is."

"How come?"

"Because he's sad."

"How come he's sad?"

"I'll tell you later," Carol said. "Now go back in the other room."

Cort did as he was told. Carol held on to me for another minute and then I gently eased her off.

"I'm okay now," I said. "Don't know what came over me."

"I'll echo Cort's question," she said. "How come you're sad?"

I held her hand and shook my head. "I'll tell you in a minute. Is Hank here?"

Carol nodded. "He's in the backyard."

"I need to talk to him."

We walked together down the hallway and through the kitchen to the back patio. Hank was out in the far end of the yard. A hoe was in his hands, and he was hacking away at a square patch of ground.

"What's he doing?" I asked.

"Gardening."

There is a school of psychology that says the quickest way to overcome a great emotional shock is to experience another shock of equal magnitude. It is the theory behind shouting "boo!" at a person who has the hiccups. Applied on a more profound level, it is argued that parents who lose a child are often incapable of mending the heartache until they experience the birth of another baby. I never subscribed wholeheartedly to this doctrine until I walked out onto the patio with Carol and saw Hank Wilkie attempting to till the earth. The stark and horrifying images of Jamaica evaporated before it like smoke in a storm.

"Is he sick?" I said to Carol.

She shrugged. "He suddenly wants a garden."

"Maybe those two thugs in the alley kicked something loose upstairs."

Carol shook her head. "It was the trip to Jamaica. Hank got a glimpse of what real poverty was like, and what might happen if suddenly all our affluence in this country got turned upside down."

"So he's growing his own food?"

Carol looked up at me with long-suffering

eyes. "That's not the worst of it. Look at this."

She went back into the kitchen and re-emerged ten seconds later with a book. One of those oversized paperback guides you find in supermarket magazine racks. *Plumbing Made Easy*.

"You've got to be kidding . . ."

Carol shook her head. "Apparently after the apocalypse there aren't going to be any plumbers, either. Can you imagine what would happen if Hank was turned loose with a leaky faucet and a wrench?"

"The mind recoils."

"You know how mechanical Hank is? A light bulb change requires a hardhat and industrial goggles. He starts worrying in mid-February because Daylight Savings Time is only a few weeks away and then he's going to have to sit down and learn how to adjust his digital watch." Carol sighed and folded her arms across her chest. "There's nothing to do except let him get it out of his system."

I laughed and walked down into the yard and up to where Hank was hoeing away. He still hadn't seen me. Sweat had darkened the back of his shirt, and as I drew near I could hear him swearing softly under his breath. They were formidable swear-words, weighing in at five to ten syllables each, suffix piled upon suffix, and I suspected Hank's bold march into self-sufficiency was already winding down.

"I'm proud of you, Hank," I said. "This is the kind of thing that made this country great."

Hank didn't act the least bit alarmed. He simply turned slowly, leaning heavily on the hoe, and looked me up and down.

"You're back."

"I'm back."

"I thought you were going to spend a few more days."

"Didn't work out that way." I looked down at the patch of garden. "When do you expect your first bumper crop?"

"Go ahead and joke, but don't come running to me for tomatoes when the food trucks stop running." Hank tossed the hoe to the side and flexed his fingers. "Jesus . . . farming is hard work."

"Farming is what you do with tractors," I said. "What you're doing is gardening. By the way, your face looks better. Almost back to normal."

"Thanks."

Hank walked back up to the patio and I followed. We scooted the two deck chairs into the little wedge of late-afternoon sun that was left and turned our faces to the warmth. The shadows were deepening, and a breeze was kicking up off the Pacific Ocean a few miles to the west.

"So how did it go?" Hank said. "Plane flight was probably perfect, right? No two-thousand-foot nosedives?"

"All the turbulence of a parking lot speed bump. Hardly knew we were in the air."

"Naturally." Hank yawned and inspected his hands for blisters. "What about the legal stuff? All the papers get signed?"

"I don't know."

Hank looked up. "What does that mean?"

"It means Bongo's office was ransacked and I never had a chance to talk to him about it."

"Ransacked?"

"That's right."

Hank cleared his throat. "Okay. Why don't you back up and tell me what happened."

"Carol should be out here, too."

Hank went into the house and got Carol and when they settled in I told them the whole story, from the research in the municipal building to the final, violent chapter in the life of Archibald Barrett.

The tone was somber when I finished. The wedge of sunlight had slid off the patio and was dying in the leaves of the overhanging trees.

"What are you going to do now?" Carol said.

"I'm waiting to hear from Bongo. But if they tried to kill me once it's reasonable to assume they'll try to kill me again. I'll hold my ground as long as I can, but that's it. There are a great number of things worth dying for in this world, but Martin Greene's beach house in Jamaica is not one of them."

"I'm glad to hear you say that," Carol said.

There was the sound of a car pulling up in front of the house and we could hear a door chunk shut and a child's voice. Carol stood and carried her chair back inside.

"Matty's home from T-ball," she said. "I've got to get dinner going."

She went back into the house and Hank and I sat in the chilly twilight and listened to the sound of pots and pans banging around.

"Forgot to tell you I saw Norman again."

"Norman?"

"The guy with the ponytail and nervous blink."

Hank thought for a moment. "The one at the waterfall with the naked girl?"

"And you call me a slut . . ."

"Sure," Hank said. "I remember Norman. Wall to wall chest hair. What about him?"

"After I checked the transaction records

I went out to his place and we sat around and shot the bull awhile and right in the middle of it he said something that may have inadvertently hit the nail on the head. We were talking about the ghost that keeps popping up in town. Norman said that ghost was the best thing that ever happened to him because it scared people away from his beach. Kept things private. He said a guy could probably make money that way. Rent-a-Ghost, he called it."

Hank looked at me blankly. "I'm not following."

"Why *not* Rent-a-Ghost?" I said. "Of course, that would just be a subsidiary of the parent organization, Rent-a-Panic."

Hank closed his eyes slowly and opened them just as slowly. "This conversation would be greatly facilitated if you would start speaking English."

"Picture it going something like this. Five years ago Russell took over Axton Enterprises from his father. The old man was pushing seventy, time to step down. Changing of the guard. The transition had the company executives a little jittery because up to this point the most grueling endeavor Russell ever attempted was trying to put more topspin on his overhand lob. Ineffectual. The family joke. But now he's at the helm of this big organization, feeling bullish, ready to show the world how wrong they've been. He goes to visit sister Stephanie and her husband Marty and sees Seven Altars for the first time. He's knocked out. Russell didn't understand about telecommunications and marketing, but he *did* understand about resorts. Christ, he was practically reared in a resort of one kind or another his entire life. So here was a chance to do something big. Here was something special."

Hank was reluctantly following my train of thought. "So he starts buying up land?"

"Yes. According to the records in Priest River, the first purchase was made five years ago this month. It's that bluff at the northern end of the bay that you can see from Marty's terrace. Paid top dollar. He sees the resort going from one end of the bay to the other, with Seven Altars right in the middle, the crowning jewel. All the purchases were made by dummy corporations with post office boxes in San Francisco. It's there in black and white."

Hank rubbed his chin and mulled it over. "But I thought your stockbroker friend said that Axton Enterprises was broke."

"It wasn't then. It was just *going* broke. The father died and competition moved in for the kill and Russell wasn't up to the task. A squadron of accountants moved figures from here to there and bought the company a couple more years, but that was it. As we sit here on this porch, the Good Ship Axton is about to go glug."

"I'm still not following," Hank said. "What does the Priest River ghost have to do with this?"

I leaned forward in my chair. "I checked the records, Hank. Within two months of Axton Enterprises going public, Priest River changed. Dramatically. Just like Bongo said it did. The town went from being a sleepy little paradise to having the largest concentration of weapons and violent crime, per capita, of anyplace else on the island. Anywhere! Worse than West Kingston!"

"Hold it," Hank winced. "Are you trying to tell me that Russell Axton is somehow responsible for Priest River's crime wave?"

"Why not? With Chief Gordon there to make it happen? A million-dollar mansion is only one Molotov cocktail away from being garage-sale material. I saw the same thing happen when I did my Peace Corps stint in Guatemala years ago. As the violence escalated the upper classes unloaded their vacation properties for a song. They took whatever they could get and beat it to their condos in Miami. Norman said some guy came by a while back and offered him fifteen cents on the dollar for his property. He turned it down then, but he'd beg for it now." I paused and leaned back in my chair. "Can't you see? It's the Rent-a-Ghost theory Norman was joking about, only on a larger scale."

Hank shook his head and went back to examining his hands. "I don't know, Quinn . . ."

"Look. Russell discovers he doesn't have the cash flow to buy any more property in Priest River. At least not at Jamaican beachfront prices. He's screwed that up like he's screwed up everything else in his life. So he needs to make the rest of the property affordable. If you can't raise the money to meet the price, you've got to drag the price down to meet the available money. Nothing complicated there. What's to prevent him from flooding the area with weapons and throwing a sheet over somebody and calling him a ghost. Arrange for a couple of nasty incidents. All of a sudden people are bailing out of Priest River like it's the fall of Saigon. Are you with me?"

Hank nodded. "Keep going."

"Fine. So now Russell can turn the panic on and off like a faucet. When he finally has the entire bay — including, of course, Seven Altars — safely in his hip pocket, the supply of weapons miraculously dries up. The shootings stop. You can't find a ghost for a hundred miles. An anonymous donation beefs up the local police force, they give the gazebo a fresh coat of paint, and peace is restored. Now you can't touch beachfront property in Priest River for less than a million, and Russell's resort is the talk of the Caribbean."

"Possible," Hank said. "With Marty being the stumbling block. He wouldn't sell, and he wouldn't scare."

"Exactly. But he *could* die, and since he was married into the Axton family himself, Seven Altars would fall into place at the most reasonable price of all. Free. The grieving widow would hand it over and return to the United States to make a new life for herself."

"You know what this means?" Hank said.

"What?"

"It means that Russell consciously and willingly made his sister a widow."

I took a deep breath and thought for a second. "I suppose you're right."

"You munched smoked salmon with him. Do you think he's capable of that?"

"I don't know. I really don't. But I *do* know that Russell was already far too committed to the Resort at Seven Altars to let

338

it fall through. This was going to be the eleventh-hour coup that would save the day. Who knows? Maybe Russell was going to give Marty more time to think about it. But when Stephanie confided in Russell that a divorce was in the air . . . the timetable had to be accelerated."

Hank nodded and pulled at his lower lip. "Do you think Archie and his hired guns did Marty?"

"Possible. They tried to do me."

Hank shook his head and kept playing with his lower lip. "No good."

"What's no good?"

"Your scenario. It doesn't work."

"Why not?"

Hank leaned forward on his chair and worked his hands together as if molding a snowball. "Russell and this Chief Gordon were pals, right?"

"Right."

"And you think that Gordon was Russell's man down there. The one tossing, as it were, the symbolic Molotov cocktails into million-dollar mansions?"

I nodded. "That's right."

Hank frowned. "Yet Archie and Chief Gordon appear to be on opposite sides of the fence."

I sighed. "Given that Chief Gordon dug

339

a canal in Archie Barrett's skull with garden shears and Archie, in turn, emptied his revolver into Chief Gordon's stomach . . . Yes. One could painstakingly arrive at the conclusion that there was some mild antipathy between the two men."

"Don't be sarcastic," Hank said. "I'm simply drawing on my algebraic background to figure this thing out."

"Your what?"

Hank held up three fingers. "Look, Quinn. You've got Russell, Gordon, and Archie, right? A, B, and C. It's a basic principle of math that if A equals B, and A also equals C, then B equals C."

Hank finished with a flourish and leaned back in his chair. He'd staggered himself by his own powers of logic.

"I'd lay off the gardening if I were you," I said. "I think you accidentally inhaled some fertilizer."

"Okay, Quinn, fast and simple. If Archie and Gordon were at war with each other, they both couldn't have been working for Russell. Whose team was Archie on? Whose orders was he obeying?"

I looked off to the side and thought about it for a moment. "I don't know. Maybe he was in it for himself."

"Well," Hank said, throwing up his arms,

"we'll never know now, so let's not worry about it. In the meantime, what's next?"

I came back out of my thoughts. Refocused on Hank. "Next? I guess Stephanie is next. I'm seeing her tomorrow night."

"Are you going to tell her any of this?"

"I don't see how I can't."

Matty, the six-year-old, came thundering out onto the back porch with a big smile on his face. He hugged me, then hugged Hank, then looked out at the patch of garden.

"When's food gonna come up?" he said.

"When I plant seeds," Hank said.

Matty nodded and turned on his heels and raced back into the house.

"Happy kid," I said.

"That's because while you were gone we had a successful conclusion to the Gone-Till-June Box deliberations. The slingshot's due to be released from Golden Gate Elementary any day now."

We laughed and shook our heads, and Hank gazed down at a spot near my left wrist. "Other than the body count, what was it like being back in Jamaica?"

"Uh-oh," I said.

"What?"

"You've got that road-of-excess look in your eyes again."

"Does it show?" Hank said.

"I thought being wrapped around a toilet bowl for half a day would have cured your love of exoticism."

Hank was smiling to himself, not really listening to me. "We're taking the kids to see Carol's great-aunt tonight, over in Daly City. She's blind and doesn't always wear sunglasses, so I was trying to prepare the kids for the fact that, you know, Aunt Mary was going to look a little odd. That they shouldn't be scared. You know what Cort said when I told him Aunt Mary was blind?"

"What?"

"He wanted to know if she'd been attacked by a spitting cobra. Isn't that great? Spitting cobra!" Hank smiled and shook his head. "Wouldn't it be fantastic to have that as your frame of reference. That when some-body goes blind a spitting cobra is the first thing you think of? What a wild way to approach the world."

I pushed myself up off the chair. "Speaking of approach, it's time I approached my apart-ment. Haven't even been back yet. Oscar's going to be pissed."

Hank nodded and stood with me, flexing his fingers. "I've got to put something on these hands. Shit. Three blisters already. Maybe what I ought to do instead of a garden is stock up on some canned food."

"Good thinking."

We wandered into the kitchen where Carol was rushing from one thing to the next.

"I'm off," I said.

Carol turned the heat down on a saucer full of onions, wiped off her hands with a towel from the refrigerator, and nodded with her chin at the oven. "Honey, could you keep stirring those so they don't burn?"

Hank nodded and took up his position at the stove. Carol linked her arm in mine and walked me to the door.

"Everything going to be okay?" she said.

"Sure. Why not?"

We stood in the entranceway and she gave me a curious look. "Quinn . . . you weren't serious earlier when you said how we should have made love back in the old days . . . were you?"

"I was under emotional strain."

Carol smiled. "Come on. Were you?"

"You'll never know, and I'll never tell." I made a gesture of zipping my mouth shut and clamped my lips tight.

Carol shook her head. "You're a real pain in the ass when you try to be coy."

"Sorry."

Ten seconds passed while I pulled on my jacket. We just stood there and looked at each other. Then Carol glanced back down the hallway in the direction of the kitchen and her head went sideways, like a puppy trying to isolate an unusual sound.

"Wanna stay for dinner?" she said.

I looked into her warm and friendly face. Smelled the aroma of sizzling garlic and onions. "I'd love to stay for dinner."

And I did.

21

"Welcome back!" Stephanie called from the foot of the stairs. I leaned over the bannister and looked down at her. She was carrying a full grocery bag and her face was bright and lively. "Jesus . . . I'd forgotten how cold San Francisco could get."

"What's all the food?" I said.

"Thought we'd continue in the fine paella tradition," she said, climbing the stairs. "Only this time I'm choosing the cuisine."

"Stephanie . . ."

She reached the top of the stairs, gave me a kiss, and then headed down the hallway toward the kitchen, talking over her shoulder as she walked. "You being such a Mexico fan I thought I'd try something south of the border. There was a recipe in the *Chronicle* today. *Chilis en nogada.* Ever had it before?"

"Yes."

Stephanie stopped for a moment, shook her head, then continued on. "Naturally. One of these days I'm actually going to give you a new experience and fall down with shock."

She disappeared around the corner and I

stood for a minute by the stairway. My stomach muscles were clenched tight. My head hurt. I took a deep breath and went down the hall. "Here," she said, putting the grocery bag down on the dining-room table. "Let me do this properly."

She linked her arms around me and gave me a strong, purposeful kiss on the lips. Her skin was still cold. Then she stepped back and stood in the sunset glow that streamed through the dining-room window. She wore jeans and very white tennis shoes and a light-blue flannel shirt with the sleeves rolled up and the top two buttons undone. In the golden air she was mesmerizingly beautiful. Her hair was loose and soft and framed a face that was just beginning to show signs of life. Of renewal. Of the setting aside of blind-side tragedy.

The knot in my stomach tightened. She was going to hate me in a few minutes. It was not going to be disappointment or wonder or confusion. She was going to hate me. She was going to experience a depth of loathing she'd never known before. It was inevitable. I was about to tell her that the brother she adored more than life itself had the blood of at least five people on his hands. That he'd doubtless made her a widow. That he'd tried to have me killed. The brightness was going to fade from Stephanie's face. It would start as disbelief, denial, then the evidence would begin to overwhelm her. And then she would hate me.

I looked at Stephanie and her head tilted an inch and she gave me a funny, puzzled smile. Curious at the intensity of my stare. Her brown eyes caressed me, and I let myself be caressed. She would never look that way at me again.

"So how was Jamaica?" she said.

"A long story."

"Good! You can tell me the whole thing and then we'll have an excuse to make it a long night."

Stephanie turned, went into the kitchen, and began opening drawers.

"What are you looking for?" I said.

"Something to shred cheese with."

"Bottom drawer on the left."

Stephanie found the shredder, took a block of cheese out of the bag, and began unwrapping it. "Since this is another theme dinner, what should we be sipping on? Tequila?"

"Stephanie . . . we need to talk."

"Talk?"

"Yes."

"You sound serious."

"I am."

Stephanie gave me a sideways look. A sideways smile. "I thought you said you weren't going to be pricing station wagons."

"This isn't a joke, Stephanie."

She put the cheese down and turned to face me straight on. The laughter had left her face. "What's the matter, Quinn?"

"I'm going to have to tell you something you're not going to like. But you have to know. I can't . . . I can't keep quiet about it anymore. Did you tell Russell that I was going back to Jamaica? That Seven Altars was being turned over to me?"

"Russell? What does he have to do — ?"

"Did you tell him?"

Stephanie's body seemed to solidify before my eyes. All the soft places grew hard. She folded her arms across her chest, straightened her back, tilted her head slightly backward from the neck. "Yes, I told him. What was wrong with that? Did something happen in Priest River?"

"Yes. Something happened in Priest River. But it's more than that. It's been happening for a long time in the Conference Room on the thirty-third floor of the Embarcadero One Building."

Stephanie paused a second, then a crooked smile fractured her face. It was the tentative, unwilling smile of someone who hasn't quite understood the more off-color aspect of a dirty joke.

"What's that supposed to mean?" she said.

"Why don't we go in the living room and sit down?"

"No." Stephanie stood her ground, tightened the fold of her arms across her chest the way you cinch a belt in another notch. "Why don't we talk about it right here, standing up. Russell's offices are on the thirty-third floor of the Embarcadero One Building."

"I know that."

"Then say what you're going to say. Point blank."

"Point blank?"

Stephanie nodded, and the tendons in her throat tightened. "Go ahead."

"All right. Did Russell ever talk to you about the possibility of making a resort out of Seven Altars?"

Stephanie seemed to have been braced for a different question. Her eyes lost their hardness and turned quizzical. "A resort?"

"That's right."

"Of course not," she said.

"Why do you say 'of course not'?"

"Russell's not in the resort business."

"In the Conference Room on the thirty-third floor of the Embarcadero One Building is an architectural mock-up of the Resort at Seven Altars. An Axton Enterprises Development. Marty's property is right in the middle of it."

"You're wrong," Stephanie said flatly.

"I've seen it with my own eyes, Stephanie."

Silence. Stephanie lowered her gaze and studied the half-unwrapped hunk of cheese on the drainboard. "You mean if we went down there right now you could show it to me?"

"Not now. After what just happened in Jamaica there's probably been some tidying up. There was a lot of secrecy around it. I doubt the mock-up still exists."

Stephanie kept her eyes on the cheese. "And you say you've seen this thing personally?"

"Yes."

"How?"

"Meredith showed it to me."

"Meredith?" Stephanie's eyes snapped up to meet mine. "When?"

"The day after the party."

Stephanie nodded. Assimilated the information. "If this was such a great secret, how did she know about it?"

"Russell took her up there one night when he was drunk. Wanted to show off or something. I don't know the exact details."

"How did this start?" Stephanie said de-

350

fensively. "You tracked Meredith down at the party and the subject of secret resorts just sort of happened to come up?"

"Stephanie . . ."

"What if I say I don't believe any of this?" Her voice was getting higher.

I took a deep breath. "Two men tried to kill me in Priest River. They both died. I killed one. Bongo killed the other. A man named Archie Barrett who used to be Bongo's friend was behind it. The Priest River police tried to take Archie in and he snapped. Flipped. Shot at least three of them — including Chief Gordon — and is probably dead himself right now. I'm not imagining things, Stephanie."

Stephanie closed her eyes, let her body drift backward a couple inches till it stopped against the drainboard.

"Are you okay?" I said.

She nodded a bewildered nod.

"You need to know this," I said. "I'm sorry. I truly am. But we can't keep pouring wine and laughing and having theme dinners and pretending nothing's happening. Russell is in a lot of trouble. I don't know how involved he is with any of this directly, but he's in trouble."

"Russell wouldn't do this," Stephanie said. Her voice was very weak, coming across miles of terrain and many, many years. "I know him. I love him."

"I know you do."

"You and Meredith can look at all the toy model resorts you want," Stephanie said. Her voice was gaining strength, tinged with indignation and outrage. "Russell is my brother and he could never kill anybody. Could never even be involved with killing. When he was twelve he accidentally killed a bird and he cried for two days."

I ran my fingers through my hair. "Goddamn it, Stephanie! Stop it! Russell's not twelve years old anymore."

Stephanie's pupils were suddenly the size of pinpricks. She pushed herself away from the drainboard, brushed past me, and grabbed her coat from the back of the couch.

"Don't go," I said. "I'm sorry."

"Day after the party . . ." Stephanie said tersely, pulling on her coat, thinking about it. "That meant you knew all this during our dinner at Scoma's."

"Not all of it, no."

"But enough."

"Yes," I said quietly. "Enough."

"And you just wined me and dined me and bought the pastry. Watched me unpack. Lay there in the dark and listened to me spill my stupid guts out and then made love to me without a second thought."

"It wasn't like that," I said. "You know it wasn't."

"Then why didn't you tell me any of this before?" Stephanie said with a sudden fierceness. "Afraid a little honesty might ruin a perfectly good chance to get laid?"

"Don't say that."

"Or was it the strong and powerful man syndrome? Protect the delicate sister who wouldn't be able to handle the truth?"

"I didn't want to jump to conclusions. I know much more now than I did then."

Stephanie pulled the collar of her coat up close to her soft brown hair. Her eyes were pinched tight with suppressed emotion. "Sorry about the dinner," she said. "But you've already had it before, right? Nothing new."

"Stephanie . . ."

"And just for your information, in many, many ways Russell is *still* twelve years old. I realize to a regular grown-up like you that doesn't mean much, but I mean it as a compliment. Twelve years old is a good age to be. More people should try it!"

Then she turned on her heels and walked quickly down the hall without looking back or saying good-bye.

I awoke to a sudden jangling of the telephone. At first I didn't recognize it for what it was. The sound was incorporated into the fabric of my dream, an electronic scream against an unseen enemy, and I had to fight my way out of sleep. I fumbled for the phone and glanced at the bedside clock. Ten after four.

The voice on the other line was breathless. "Quinn! Thank God you're there!"

"Wha? . . . Stephanie?"

"No! It's me! Meredith!"

I sat up quickly and rubbed my face. "Meredith?"

"I'm in trouble, Quinn." Her voice was strained, all high-pitched and whacked-off nerve endings. There was the sound of sporadic traffic in the background, a truck roaring past, like she was calling from a pay phone somewhere on the freeway. "I gotta talk to you right now!" she said.

"Hold on a second." I set the phone on the bed and reached to turn on the lamp. Oscar stirred slightly from the other room at the sudden commotion. A ruffle of feathers, nothing more.

I picked up the receiver. "Okay," I said. "Are you still there?"

"I've gotta see you right away!" Meredith practically shouted. "You gotta come right now!"

"Meredith . . . settle down. Take a deep breath."

She did, and in the silences between passing trucks I could hear what I thought were stifled sobs. But when she spoke again it was in a voice free of tears. "There's something I didn't tell you that other morning at the St. Francis. Something important."

I waited while a truck thundered by. "What was it, Meredith?"

"About me and Marty. We were having an affair. It wasn't no big deal, but I was there the weekend it happened. At the house, I mean. Stephanie, she was over in Kingston and — "

"Never mind that," I interrupted. "What's happening now, Meredith? Where the hell are you?"

"I ain't gonna talk about it here," she said. "It's more complicated than you think. More than just me and Marty together. I need you to come right now. This is freaking me out!"

"Are you in danger?"

"I think so."

I held the phone to my ear and thought for a moment. "Where are you now?"

"Gas station on 101, but I'm heading down to the boat. Russell's boat. My folks left today . . . I'm back living there. It's on the end of the pier just south of — "

"I know where it is," I interrupted. "Just go and wait and I'm on my way."

There was another pause. "You know which is his boat?"

"Yes," I said.

Silence. "How do you know that?"

"I'll explain later, Meredith. Now, please! Just go back to the boat and wait there."

"You're not one of them, are you?"

"No," I said. "Now go back to the boat and just wait!"

"Okay," she said. "But hurry!"

I drove across the Golden Gate Bridge in the early morning darkness and wheeled down Alexander Avenue to a strangely quiet and empty Sausalito. I parked at Flynn's Landing and walked carefully down the gangplank leading to Russell's boat. It was quarter to five. The night was clear and chilly, and a waxing moon cast pale light on the water. Not many people out. The occasional jogger, a few fishermen, an isolated car getting a jump on the bumper-to-bumper. Gusting wind rattled ropes and sails, and the boats creaked in the water.

Russell's boat was the only one on the pier that was lit. I got to within fifteen feet of it, stopped, and listened. No movement, no sound. The interior lights were on and the curtains were pulled.

"Meredith . . ."

No answer. Then, louder, "Meredith!"

Nothing.

I walked up to the edge of the boat, knelt down, and cupped my hands around my mouth. "It's me. Quinn."

I straightened up and took a deep breath to steady my nerves. Then I grabbed hold of the dock rope and pulled myself aboard.

I went down into the cabin and called for Meredith again. Everything was lit, the bed was made. All the signs of life, but no life. I went from room to room, cringing at what I might find as I opened the doors, but found nothing. The boat was empty.

I waited on the edge of the gangplank for fifteen minutes. There have been maybe five times in my whole life I ever thought about having a cigarette, and this was one of them. I stood in the early-morning darkness, alone, listening to the pilings groan beneath my feet, resisting the bulge and surge of the sea.

I didn't like the timing. I didn't like that I had finally told somebody other than Hank about Meredith and the thirty-third floor, and now Meredith was making hysterical calls from pay phones at four in the morning. What had Stephanie done when she'd left my apartment? Called Russell to confirm? Investigated the thirty-third-floor office herself? What? Whatever it had been, an alarm had been sounded and the spotlight had come on and everything had landed solidly on Meredith Nelson.

So it was Meredith who'd been with Marty that last weekend. Why not? Perfectly logical. Meredith lived nearby, she was more than willing, and she would have had ample reason to keep her mouth shut. And I remembered the look in her eyes when she opened the door to Russell's Conference Room.

The fifteen minutes came and went. I walked back to my van, crawled in, and rubbed the lack-of-sleep burn deeper into my eyes. Okay. Next step. What I'd do was drive back into the city. Go to my apartment. Call the St. Francis to see if by any chance Meredith Nelson was still registered there. She said she wasn't, but she'd gotten me out of a deep sleep at four in the morning and maybe I didn't hear right. Then I'd brew some coffee and watch the end of the late-late movie and wait for her to call me again.

I wheeled the van out onto Bridgeway and started south, following the curve of the bay. The sky was beginning to lighten beyond the hills of the East Bay. I could make out the shadowy outlines of Angel Island and Alcatraz, black shapes in a graying ocean.

Years back the city of Sausalito built a walking path that paralleled Bridgeway, skirting the edge of the water, right down among the mossy rocks. Even at this odd hour some people were strolling along it, bundled up, looking out at the bay and the magical lights of San Francisco in the distance.

I'd gone a half-mile down Bridgeway when I saw the woman who was about to scream. She was jogging toward me along the footpath, thirty yards away, and I could see the scream develop. She glanced out to sea once, twice, and on the third time held her glance. Her jog slowed and slowed until she was almost running in place. Then even that stopped, and she stood absolutely motionless gazing out at the water. Recognition slammed her body. Her arms flew up toward her mouth but stopped halfway as if they'd hit something and shuddered there chest-high like two quivering pieces of splintered wood. Her lips warped apart and the terrified silhouette was frozen for a split second. A tentative, momentary, caved-in silence.

Then she screamed.

She screamed like I've never heard anyone scream before. High-pitched, hysterical —

it spun end over end in a plummeting wail. Horrible. Not human. A man who'd been jogging lazily behind her accelerated and sprinted to the scene. He took her by the shoulders and shouted at her. She violently shook her head. He shouted again, and the woman pointed out at the water. The man looked and turned back in my direction, his face bright and vivid with shock.

I pulled the van to a stop on the wide divider of Bridgeway and yanked on the emergency brake.

"Police!" the man yelled at me. "Get the police!"

"What is it?" I yelled.

The man ignored me, but the screaming woman lunged back in the direction of the bay and pointed a wild finger out at the water. I followed the imaginary line.

Twenty yards into the bay, among the rocks along Bridgeway Avenue, is one of Sausalito's most famous landmarks — a life-sized, art-deco sculpture of a seal. Mounted on a flat boulder, the seal is completely submerged at high tide, only to gradually resurface as the tide goes out. A few years back a real seal came up and sat next to it and somebody took a picture, and now every gift shop in Sausalito has a postcard of the statue.

But what I now saw was not postcard

material. I saw what had made the woman scream. A body had washed up against the seal, snagged on the uplifted head, shifting in the swell of the sea. A crowd began to form around me. Cars pulling over. Jostling. Maneuvering for a better look. The body was white and swollen and in the pale gray dawn all I could make out was a splotch of red hair and the soaken remnants of a clinging, Ferrari-red velvet dress.

I backed away from the crowd. The woman who had been screaming was huddled on the ground, being comforted by the man who'd jogged up to her. All I could hear was low, thick gurgling, as if hysteria had turned her inside out and she was drowning in her own demented blood.

I got into the van and quietly eased it back out onto Bridgeway and continued on at precisely the speed limit. A police car with sirens wailing flew by me on the left and kept on going.

I swallowed hard. The morning fog was coming in as I drove across the Golden Gate Bridge toward San Francisco. Fast-moving, pale, diaphanous, like torn remnants of a shredded nightgown. It swept toward the wakening city from the dark curve of the ocean as though fleeing from something unimaginable.

22

I stopped at a motel coffee shop on Lombard Street and spent ninety minutes putting a dent in their coffee inventory. Then I got back in the van and headed toward Seacliff.

Russell Axton's street was a quiet one on non-party days. It was eight o'clock on a Tuesday morning, but there was no bustle of rush hour here. No movement of any kind. The houses had that boarded-up feel of Cape Cod beach homes in the dead of winter. Shades pulled, curtains drawn, humming electronic circuitry clicking on reading lights for nobody.

A uniformed Latin maid met me at the door, and after initial surprise and resistance, escorted me down into the living-room area. She asked me to wait and disappeared through the sliding glass doors onto the terrace where Eddie had once tended bar and warned me of how Early Wynn dealt with hitters who insisted on crowding the plate. The maid was back almost immediately, and she left the sliding-glass door open.

"Mr. Axton will see you on the terrace."

"Thank you."

I walked past her and heard the sliding-glass door rumble heavily shut behind me.

Russell was sitting at a table set for one, having breakfast. Linen and sterling silver utensils. A bowl of fruit and a pot of coffee and a sweeping, fresh-air view of the Golden Gate Bridge. He was wearing his tennis whites. They were so white it was painful to the eye. He didn't stand to greet me and he didn't say hello.

"Little early for visiting, isn't it, Quinn?"

"I was up early."

Russell pointed at a deck chair at the other end of the terrace. "Pull up a seat."

I got the chair and scooted it to the table.

"Just as well you came," he said. "I was going to call you later today anyway."

"Stephanie talked to you last night?"

Russell nodded. "Oh, did she ever. We had a long talk. An interesting talk."

"I can imagine."

"No," Russell said, dabbing his lips with his napkin. "I don't think you can imagine. You know what you remind me of, Quinn?"

"What?"

"One of those archaeologists who finds a two-inch bone in some cave and then proceeds to construct a ten-story-high dinosaur out of it. One percent fact, ninety-nine percent supposition."

"The mock-up in your office being the two-inch bone?"

"That's right."

"Sorry," I said. "We archaeologists can only work with what we've got."

Russell leaned back in his chair and steepled his slender fingers beneath his chin. A soft ocean breeze ruffled his light, sandy hair. There was an unblemished calm about him. Control. If he was the one who killed Meredith he was disguising it with a chilling thoroughness.

"What brought you to my Conference Room in the first place?" Russell asked.

"I thought Stephanie already talked to you."

"I want to hear it again. From the horse's mouth."

"Meredith took me there."

"Why?"

"She was angry with you."

Russell nodded. "Why was she angry?"

"The two of you would know that better than me."

"Cut the bullshit," Russell said. "Since you and Meredith seem to be so chummy she must have told you something. Why was she angry?"

"Why she was angry wasn't important.

What she showed me in the Conference Room was important."

"Come on," Russell said. "Humor me."

I sighed. "She said that on the night of the party you practically raped her."

Russell leaned forward in his chair, poised as though waiting for more, then laughed a short, single burst of laughter. "*Raped* her?"

"That's what she said."

"We've lived together almost two years, for Christ's sake!" Russell laughed again.

"Doesn't matter if you're celebrating your silver wedding anniversary," I said. "Shove the woman down in the cake and have your way against her will and it's rape."

Russell lost his smile. "Look. I'm not going to sit here and argue legal technicalities about rape. Meredith has a flair for dramatics, in case you haven't noticed by now. She was going to be a theater major in Houston. Did you know that?"

"No," I said. "I didn't know that."

"Well, she was. And anyway, I'm not the kind of man who needs to rape anyone, least of all her." Russell examined his thumbnail. His tone grew sober. "Not that it's any of your business, but Meredith and I have decided to separate on a trial basis."

Russell kept looking at his thumbnail. I watched him closely. His sorrow seemed genuine. For the first time I began to believe that he had no idea of Meredith's death. Nobody's blood runs that cold.

"Tell me about the Resort at Seven Altars," I said.

"Why should I do that?"

"If you don't I might be forced to construct another ten-story dinosaur, and this dinosaur I might put in a cage and take to the police."

Russell looked at me, took a deep breath, and nodded. "Okay. What do you want to know?"

"Why was it so secret?"

Russell shrugged. "Isn't it obvious?"

"Maybe," I said, "but now it's your turn to humor me."

"Okay, Quinn. I'll spell it out. The business world is a tough world. I read something once and I never forgot it. 'Whatever is not nailed down is mine, and whatever I can pry loose is not nailed down.' That's the business world, Quinn. That's why I kept Seven Altars nailed down in a place where it couldn't be pried loose. I know you think I'm a big joke, me and my yacht and my inheritance, but you're wrong. It never seems to occur to anybody around here that maybe I just might possibly have a little bit of business savvy up here." Russell tapped the side of his head with his finger.

"But Seven Altars didn't belong to you."

"I was planning to buy it from Marty. He and I talked about it a couple of times when I was in Jamaica visiting."

"And?"

"He was on the verge of selling when . . . when he got mixed up with that drug thing."

"What about Hank?" I said. "The property is his now. Why haven't you approached him about buying it?"

"For Christ's sake!" Russell flared. "Can't I let Marty's corpse cool before I start negotiating real estate deals?"

The fabricated indignation was getting to me. I stood and walked to the edge of the terrace. Looked down at the rocks far below that were wired for sound. Then I looked east, past the Golden Gate Bridge to the curve of bay where Meredith had snagged against the seal. My eyes burned for lack of sleep. They'd be attempting to identify the body by now. It wouldn't be long. A few more hours, perhaps, and Russell's doorbell would be ringing.

"You're in trouble, Russell," I said.

"No. *You're* the one in trouble if this harassment continues. I haven't done a damn thing wrong. Nothing! I invite you to my party, I take you on my yacht, I let you come out here on the terrace and ruin my fucking breakfast so you can call me a rapist and a thief. In return for that what I get is my own sister suddenly looking at me like I might be a goddamn murderer! You got something to say you say it right now or get the hell out of my house! Come on, let's have it! Cards on the table!"

I turned and faced Russell. "You've already bought up the land surrounding Seven Altars, right?"

Russell held his hands out, palms to the sky. "What's illegal about that?" he practically yelled.

"You purchased the property for about a tenth of its appraised value."

"It's a volatile market! Prices are down!" Then Russell put on the brakes and stared at me warily. "What'd you do, anyway? Put a private investigator on me? How the hell do you know what I paid for things?"

"I just checked the records."

"What records?"

"In Priest River."

Russell stared at me a moment. His confidence wasn't quite what it was. Then he looked to the clouds and shook his head with exasperation. "Can't win. Can't fucking win. You know what kills me?"

"What?"

"What kills me is that if what's-his-name,

Donald Trump, if he did this, if he put the Seven Altars package together . . . shit! Everybody'd call him a financial genius. Brilliant. Shrewd. Need a guy like that in the White House. But when it's Russell Axton . . . unh-unh. Everybody all of a sudden says, hey, what's the catch? Who is he screwing?" Russell paused, took a deep breath. "Come on, Quinn. You're the one with all the theories. The master of psychology. Explain that one to me."

"It just seemed a little coincidental to me, that's all."

"What coincidence?"

"You decide to build a resort on a mile-long chunk of Caribbean coastline and presto, that mile-long chunk suddenly goes from being an expensive slice of paradise to having the worst crime rate in the country."

"This might really take you by surprise, Quinn," Russell said sarcastically. "But coincidences *do* happen. That's why we figured out a word to describe the phenomenon and put it in the dictionary."

"The dictionary is full of other words, too. Extortion. Terrorism. Manipulation."

"I think you'd better leave, now," Russell said.

"Did you know a man named Archie Barrett?"

369

"No." Russell wasn't really listening to me. "But I *do* know a man named Gary Rudd and I'm going to have him toss your ass out of here in about thirty seconds."

"I think you did know Archie Barrett."

Russell drummed his fingertips on the tablecloth. "Twenty seconds."

"Meredith was having an affair with Marty. She was at the house the day Marty was killed."

"That's it!" Russell said, standing up and moving toward the sliding-glass door. "You just lost your twenty seconds. Get the hell out of here!"

I stayed where I was. "You're in trouble, Russell. A lot of trouble."

"Of course I am! I mean, to hear Stephanie tell it I've killed — directly or indirectly — let's see . . ." Russell counted his fingers. "Marty, two strangers who tried to kill you, three police officers . . . who else?"

"Archie Barrett."

"Of course," Russell said, slapping his forehead. "Archie Barrett. Who could ever forget him, whoever he is. Am I forgetting anybody?"

"Yes."

"And who would that be?"

"Meredith."

Russell had his right hand on the sliding-glass door, and when I said Meredith's name the knuckles went white. The color drained from his face. Eyes vacant. It was like watching time-lapse photography of someone decaying right in front of you. He turned sideways, kind of in a dream state, and looked back in the direction of the flat, blue Pacific.

"What do you mean?" he said.

"I'm sorry, Russell. She's dead."

"No," he said. "She can't be."

"I doubt if the police have even identified her yet," I said. "That's why we need to talk now. You need to tell me what you know about Archie Barrett. You need to be prepared to give yourself up. It's all over, Russell. Do you understand what I'm saying? It's all over."

Russell wasn't with me. His breathing was fast and shallow and he was blinking hard. Only the sliding door kept him on his feet.

"You're lying!" he said. His pale face was suddenly flushed red. He quit leaning on the door. "You're doing this to me on purpose. What are you doing this for?"

"Russell . . ."

"Get out!"

"The police are going to — "

"Get out!!"

His scream shattered the morning air. Beyond the sliding-glass door I could see the maid briefly glance out at us, concerned, then duck back into the kitchen. Russell stood before me, feet planted wide apart, trembling with rage.

I wanted to talk, to calm him down, to cushion the blow and help him think straight so the hole he'd dug for himself wouldn't get any deeper. But Russell was still blind with rage and confusion and it suddenly occurred to me that the maid might be on her way to find Gary.

I left Russell standing on the terrace and walked quickly out of the house.

23

A reporter friend once told me that there are two baskets sitting atop the obituary desk at the *San Francisco Chronicle*. The Good Stiff Basket, and the Bad Stiff Basket. The distinction between the two baskets is not a complicated one. Good stiffs are newsworthy, bad stiffs aren't. My friend had always found it rather amusing until one morning he came to work and discovered his own father-in-law's obituary had been casually tossed into the Bad Stiff Basket.

For about thirty-six hours after the body was identified, Meredith Nelson was a good stiff. No, she was a *great* stiff. Her death had all the elements that Action News saliva is made of — wealth, decadence, mystery, the promise of lurid intrigue among the promiscuous and drug-loving super rich. Television reporters at the scene fought desperately for good camera position in front of the seal sculpture, and they intoned gravely about hints of foul play.

From Russell's house I had gone straight back to my apartment to wait out the inevitable phone call, the ring of the buzzer, the grim-faced men in uniform wanting honest answers to tough questions. Chess champions are said to lose ten pounds during the course of a three-hour match by doing nothing more than sitting and fretting and concentrating on the black-and-white board. I never understood how that could happen until the day Meredith's body was fished out of San Francisco Bay. I stayed in my apartment and waited. Sweated off the pounds.

But nothing happened. Nothing happened that day, and nothing happened halfway through the next. Russell Axton, the victim's high-profile playboy lover and number one suspect (I quote verbatim from the morning *Chronicle*), had disappeared. Apparently headed for the hills. Police estimated he probably had a six-hour head start, but they were optimistic about apprehending him.

Then, midway through the second day, the story that held so much promise began to weaken. Maybe it wasn't murder after all. Preliminary autopsy reports indicated that Meredith's blood alcohol readings at the time of her death were off the chart. Traces of cocaine. Russell Axton, the jealous lover who'd hit the high road, suddenly had an iron-clad alibi in absentia. The live-in maid claimed he'd never left the mansion the night of Meredith's death. Now it appeared Russell's curious flight was more panic than a running away from guilt. With each hour the whole affair began to look less like murder and more like a drugged-up girl who took an ill-advised drunken stroll on the slippery deck of a yacht at four in the morning. She fell. She hit her head. She rolled soundlessly over the side of the boat and into the water, just like Natalie Wood. Except Meredith Nelson wasn't Natalie Wood. When murder was taken out of the equation, Meredith turned out to be just another Bad Stiff after all.

Hank checked in once to see if I was aware of what was going on. I told him I was and left it at that and he refrained from asking awkward questions. The less the Wilkie family knew, the better.

Early in the afternoon of the second day I was just about to venture out and have a beer at the Bus Stop and think about next steps when the phone rang. Stephanie's voice took me by surprise. She was at Russell's house in Seacliff, maintaining a foolish vigil, waiting for him to return home. She asked if I could come over. She wouldn't blame me if I didn't, given the way she'd attacked me the other night, but she needed company. She needed very badly to talk.

I drove over and the same uniformed Latin

maid answered the door. There was a jolt of recognition in her brown eyes. Hesitation. Then Stephanie appeared behind her.

"Quinn . . ."

The maid grudgingly opened the door wide enough to let me in, then she turned and disappeared into the kitchen.

"I'm glad you came," Stephanie said.

"How are you holding up?" I said.

Stephanie managed a brave smile and gave her shoulders a small shrug. She didn't look good. Exhausted. Beat. The once-radiant Jamaican tan was starting to thin out. Weak coffee with too much cream. I stepped into the room and gave her a hug. At first she just stood there, arms straight down at her sides, letting herself be hugged like a reluctant kid in the arms of an overbearing uncle. Then her arms came up and linked around my back and we stood like that for a minute, embracing each other.

"Why did he leave, Quinn?" she said into my shoulder. "Why did he run away?"

"Scared, that's all."

Stephanie unlinked her hands behind my back and we stepped away from each other.

"But couldn't he see that this is just going to make it worse for him?" Stephanie said.

"I doubt he's thinking very clearly one way or the other right now."

Stephanie nodded, turned, and went into the kitchen. She came back in a moment with two glasses of lemonade and handed one to me without asking if I wanted it.

"Let's go upstairs," she said. "Not much privacy down here." Stephanie pointed at her ear and nodded her head toward the kitchen.

We went down the hall and up the spiral staircase and into Russell's private studio. It looked just as it had the night of the party when Stephanie had turned on the ocean speakers and told me of her vision of Marty in the reflected waters of Seven Altars. It seemed like years ago.

Stephanie eased herself down onto the couch, carefully, gently. All of her movements were cautious and controlled.

"You've been watching the news, I suppose?" she said.

"Yes."

"What do you think happened?"

I shook my head. "No idea, Stephanie."

"Do you think Russell did it?"

"No," I said.

"Why not?"

"Because I came over to talk to him yesterday morning. Early. He was sitting out on the terrace having his breakfast, ready for tennis. He wasn't behaving like someone who just killed somebody. And if he was going to be running, he would have been long gone by then, not pushing around cantaloupe with his fork."

"You came over yesterday?" Stephanie asked.

"That's right."

She took a deep breath, ran her tongue along the ridge of her upper lip. Then she stood and put her lemonade down and walked to the tinted window overlooking the Pacific.

"Aren't you going to ask me why I was over here?" I said.

Stephanie kept her back to me and shook her head. "No. I'm all out of questions. I'm exhausted. I don't want to know anything more about anything. All I want is for Russell to come home and put his life back in order. If he's in trouble he needs to know that I'm here for him." Stephanie paused and wandered over to the control panels. "Why doesn't he call? He could at least call."

"Autopsy report says Meredith was stinking drunk and coked to the eyeballs," I said. "Accidental death by drowning. That, along with the maid's alibi . . . when Russell gets near a TV or radio, he'll come back."

Stephanie wasn't really listening to me. She turned a couple of knobs on the control panel, and the room was filled with low-level static and confused ocean sounds. She turned the volume down and shook her head. "Great. Even the waves aren't working anymore."

"Need to adjust the equalizer," I said.

Stephanie turned and forced a smile. "How's your lemonade? Refill?"

"Sure."

Stephanie took both our glasses and went out of the room. I sat and listened to the malfunctioning version of the Pacific Ocean. White noise, lapping water, buzzing.

I picked up the heavy Goya book from the coffee table and set it on my lap and began absentmindedly looking through it. Happy-go-lucky type, Goya. Demons, nightmares, executions, monsters devouring their own children. While I flipped the pages the buzzing from the ocean microphones started to get on my nerves. I set the book aside and went over to the control panel to turn it off. But as I stood over the buttons and switches with my hands in my pockets the buzzing sound intensified. Then it backed off. Then it swelled again. It was a familiar sound. Not static. I tried to place it. From my past somewhere. What? Then it clicked.

I went down the spiral staircase and passed Stephanie as she was coming down the hall with the two lemonades in her hand.

"What's the matter?" she said.

379

"Nothing. Let's have these out on the terrace, okay?"

Stephanie looked confused, but shrugged her shoulders and turned around. "Okay."

On the terrace I went to the guardrail and looked down the cliff. It was not a sheer drop, but the bottom was obscured by a small bulge of rock that came out from the cliff about halfway down. The water was green and foamy and rough.

". . . in the cards, I guess," Stephanie said.

I turned and looked at her blankly. "What?"

"You didn't hear a thing I said, did you?" Stephanie smiled.

"Sorry. I was distracted."

"Aren't we all," Stephanie said.

"Is there a way to get down there?" I said.

"Down where?"

"The cliff. Down to the bottom."

Stephanie stared at me. "Why?"

"Is there?"

She nodded cautiously. "Sure. I mean . . . it's steep, but . . . What are you talking about, Quinn?"

"I think I know what's wrong with the microphones. Loose connection. I'll fix them for you."

Stephanie laughed, but I didn't laugh with her. "You're serious, aren't you?"

"How do I get down?"

Stephanie put her lemonade down on the guardrail. "Over here."

I followed as Stephanie led me to the far left side of the terrace. The guardrail unhooked and an animal trail switchbacked down the cliff.

"Just follow this," Stephanie said. "It's only hairy in one spot, and you'll see a cable to hold on to. Other than that it's safe. I used to do it lots of times when I was a girl."

"Okay." I smiled. "Be right back."

Stephanie shook her head at such foolishness and went back into the house.

Stephanie was right. It was not nearly as hard a descent as it looked to be from the terrace. A switchback trail had been hewn out of the mud and rock, and as I maneuvered down the cliff I saw why. There was a little patch of hidden beach directly below. Charred logs from a long-forgotten campfire were arranged in tepee fashion in the middle of the beach. People had probably been scrambling down to this spot for decades.

I was twenty feet from the base of the cliff when I saw the source of the insistent buzzing. Flies. Thousands of them. They were clustered over a swell of scree, boulders, and thick shrubbery that tapered out from the bottom of the cliff. Resting gently among the bushes was Russell Axton. He was at a forty-five-degree angle, upside down. Peaceful-looking. The tennis whites weren't as white as they'd been the day before, and a bright splinter of bone, sticky with blood and covered with ants, protruded from the torn flesh of his upper leg. The flies whirled in a furious tornado above the body, so frenzied by the serendipitous feast that they seemed unable to stop and settle down and revel in the pints of thick, blackened blood. Russell's left arm was tangled in the microphone wire, held out from his body, like a man in a sling in a hospital bed.

There was no need to climb any closer. I turned around and made my way back up the steep and rugged switchback.

Stephanie wasn't on the terrace when I finally pulled myself up the last few feet. I didn't go looking for her. Instead I went into the kitchen where the maid was washing dishes. She threw a quick glance my way, frowned, then went back to the dishes.

"Can I ask you a question?" I said.

She nodded her head. "What?"

"When I came to see Mr. Axton yesterday . . . after I left, what did he do?"

"Nothing."

"Nothing at all?"

"Nothing at all."

I took a deep breath and thought about it. The woman still didn't entirely trust me. "Do you mean he just stayed out on the terrace and finished his breakfast?"

"No." The maid concentrated harder on the dirty dishes. "Mr. Axton was very angry. You make him very angry."

"How do you know that?"

"He was yelling."

"I'm talking about *after* I left."

"Yes," the maid said. "Yelling."

"After I left?"

"Yes."

I thought for a second. "Yelling to himself?"

The maid shook her head and pointed toward the ceiling. "On the telephone. Upstairs."

I started to speak when the door opened and Stephanie came into the room.

"I thought I heard you in here." She smiled. "Microphones all fixed?"

I left the maid to her dishes and hooked my hand under Stephanie's arm and led her out of the kitchen. I sat her down in the sofa in the living room.

"What's the matter, Quinn?" she said.

There was no way to say it but quickly. "I found Russell."

A five-second pause. "You *what?*"

"He's down at the bottom of the cliff."

Stephanie was very still. She clasped her hands gently together and rested them in her lap. There was distance in her eyes . . . the look of someone politely waiting out a preacher's dull sermon.

"Did you hear me, Stephanie?"

"You saw him?"

"Yes."

"And he's dead?"

"Yes."

Stephanie nodded dreamily.

"I'm going to go upstairs and call the police," I said. "Are you going to be okay?"

She nodded. "I'm fine."

She wasn't fine, but I had to make the phone call. I walked briskly down the hall and up the spiral staircase and into the studio. The flies were still buzzing on the ocean speakers so I turned the system off. I was giving thought to what I was going to say to the police when they questioned me. How much I needed to tell them, and how much could remain unsaid.

I picked up the phone. It was an elaborate, high-tech instrument, with dials and buttons and various incomprehensible memories and an answering machine built right into the phone itself. There was a separate button for 911 and my finger went toward it. Then I stopped. My eyes scanned the function keys. Hold. Mute. Flash. Pause. Program. There was a button for speakerphone and a button for conference calls, and down at the bottom, all the way to the right, was another button. Redial.

I felt my heartbeat quicken, and my finger drifted away from the 911 button. Russell had come up here immediately after I'd left and he'd placed a call. An argument had ensued, an argument so violent that Russell's shouts could be heard by the maid on the ground floor. Then Russell ended up at the bottom of the cliff.

I returned the receiver to its cradle, turned on the speakerphone, and pushed the redial button. The touch tone went through its sequence. A lot of numbers. Long-distance. Two rings, and a man's voice came on.

"Hello?"

The connection was scratchy. "Is Tom there?" I said, thinking fast.

A few moments of sullen, windy silence came back to me across thousands of miles of telephone wire.

"Tom?" the man said. "Nope. No Tom

here, buddy. You got the wrong number."

"Sorry to bother you."

"No problem."

The man hung up. It wasn't much, but I knew the voice. It chilled the blood. Numbed the brain. I turned from the phone. Stephanie was standing at the entrance to the studio. She was deathly pale, and her eyes had a jerky, finger-in-the-socket look. She'd recognized the voice, too. It was Norman. The tanned and ponytailed Grease Monkey in paradise.

24

The paramedics brought the body up on a wooden skid, dragged up the side of the cliff by pulleys connected to an electrically powered hoist. Stephanie stood on the terrace and insisted on watching the procedure, despite my attempts to steer her elsewhere.

When they finally got what was left of Russell to the top, the paramedics unstrapped the body from the wooden skid and slid the broken remains into an olive-green plastic bag. During the transfer the body lay fully exposed for a half-dozen seconds.

I was standing next to Stephanie and tried to shield her, but I was too late. She looked down at her brother, and her face so twisted with horror that they mirrored each other, the brother and the sister, the one living and the one dead. Then the medical people brusquely hauled the body away and that was that. Stephanie stood where she was, frozen, encased in silence.

A tight-lipped and impatient lieutenant grilled me for a half-hour while I sat on the living-room couch. The way he asked the questions convinced me that they were thinking suicide all the way. Russell's fragile psyche was well documented. They knew of his hopeless devotion to Meredith, and the maid outlined in great detail Mr. Axton's excessive grief at her tragic death. The lieutenant also knew that Russell was at the helm of a financial empire about to go bankrupt. Mix all those things together and you have a prime candidate for suicide. People threw themselves off high buildings for a lot less.

Then the lieutenant shut his notebook and the flurry of official activity ended as abruptly as it had begun. Everyone filed out en masse, and Stephanie and I were left alone in the silent house.

"Norman killed Russell," Stephanie said suddenly. Saying it out loud brought the color back to her face. It cleared the glaze from her eyes.

"Norman's in Jamaica."

"You know what I mean," Stephanie said. "He had somebody else do it. Gary. He had Gary do it. Russell called Norman and then Norman called right back and told Gary to do it. To make it look like a suicide."

"Maybe," I said softly, putting my hands on her hands. She withdrew them instantly. She didn't want the purity of her emotion tainted by mercy or softness or patience.

388

"Norman killed Marty, too," she said. "Both of them. My husband and my brother."

"Take it easy, Stephanie," I said. "You've had a terrible shock. Tomorrow we'll — "

"He's not going to get away with this."

"Stephanie, listen to me. He's not going to get away with anything. But there are — "

"I'll take care of it myself if I have to."

I positioned myself directly in front of Stephanie and took hold of both of her shoulders. "You're not listening," I said. "This is a police matter. Just because Norman's in Jamaica doesn't mean he's immune. He can be extradited."

"Marty's death was a police matter, too," Stephanie said. "You see the good that did."

"This is different. This murder — if it *is* murder — happened on American soil. We don't have to deal with a Chief Gordon here."

Stephanie turned her head to the side so she wouldn't have to look at me. "Okay," she said. "You're right. We'll let the police handle it."

"Are you just saying that, or do you mean it?"

"I mean it."

"You're telling me the truth?"

Stephanie nodded.

"Okay," I said. "I believe you. First thing tomorrow we'll go down to the Hall of Justice and talk to some people. How does that sound?"

Stephanie nodded. "That sounds good."

"All right, then."

I let go of her shoulders and she took a deep, controlled breath. "Will you drive me home?"

"Of course."

"My car's parked out front . . ." She waved her hand in the general direction of the street. "I'd drive, but I don't feel — "

"Come on," I said, helping her up. "Let's go."

I drove Stephanie back to her apartment on Telegraph Hill. I parked in the garage down on Montgomery and walked her up the stairs to her cottage. A soft breeze rustled the trees, and the yellowish streetlights cast agitated shadows on the steps before us. Stephanie took out her keys and opened the door. Her hands were surprisingly steady.

"Do you want me to stay?" I said.

She shook her head. "No. I'd rather be alone."

"I'll be a perfect gentleman. No groping in the middle of the night."

"No," Stephanie said. "If you spent the night, I'd want you to grope. It's better that I just be alone for a while."

"Sure?"

"I'm not as shocked about this as you think, Quinn. The minute I heard on the news that Russell had disappeared, I knew he was dead. Way down deep, I knew it. Seeing his body out on the terrace there . . . I'd been bracing myself for something like that for hours. Really." She forced a smile. "I'm in better shape than you think. I'll be okay."

"I'll take your word for it," I said quietly. "What time do you want me to come by tomorrow?"

"Earlier the better."

"Eight o'clock?"

She nodded. "That's fine."

"You're not going to do anything foolish, are you?"

Stephanie looked directly at me. "Like what?"

"Like forming a one-woman posse. Like taking off into the sunset to right some wrongs."

"Of course not."

"Because if Norman is really behind all this, he's not going to hesitate to dispose of anybody else who's standing in his way. You. Me. Anybody."

Darkness fell across Stephanie's face again. Within that shadow nothing was excluded. I could see her eyes grow fond of the imagined retribution. The pain of it. The delicious, disquieting, payback pain of it.

"Get some sleep, Stephanie," I said.

"I will," she said.

"See you in the morning, then."

She nodded. "In the morning."

I drove home, fixed myself a nightcap, built a fire, and sat in the overstuffed armchair, watching the flames. A long-forgotten memory was coming to the surface and I couldn't for the life of me understand why.

Years ago, in Denver, I used to go to the dog races. To make the dogs run, a mechanical rabbit is attached to the inside railing of the track. The rabbit is called Rusty. "Here comes Rusty!" the announcer shouts, and the mechanical rabbit speeds around in front of the frenzied dogs. One night I bet all my money on a dog I was convinced could not lose. I'd seen it race before and, assuming a good start out of the gates, it was virtually unbeatable. This night it ran the race of its life. It exploded out of the starting gates and had a six-length lead on the field before the first turn. The lead was stretched to ten lengths at the halfway point and was twenty coming into the last turn. The dog could have slowed to a home-run trot and waltzed in for a victory. But instead it ran faster and faster. I was down close to the track, leaning against the chain-link fence, and I saw the dog's wild eyes as it closed in on Rusty. Then, just thirty yards from the finish line, the dog put on a final burst and caught up with the little metal rabbit and took a bite out of Rusty and electrocuted itself right there on the home stretch. The dog flipped head over heels, like a cartwheel, with sparks and flames shooting out from its rigid body. People screamed. The other dogs scattered in confusion. Rusty sizzled and smoked and all the overweight trainers hurried onto the track to round up their disoriented greyhounds.

I nursed my drink and continued to stare into the fire. I never went to another dog race after that and had actually forgotten the incident entirely. *Had* forgotten . . . until tonight. Tonight I saw something I hadn't seen since that long-ago evening in Denver. There was something in Stephanie's eyes that reminded me of that dog as it rocketed around the final turn. The same determination. The same sense of straining at the leash, of closing in on something that was just a little bit out of reach.

I drank half my drink and dumped the rest of it down the sink and tossed and turned for an hour before falling into a troubled and restless sleep.

When I got to Stephanie's apartment shortly before eight the next morning, I was tired. I leaned on her doorbell and yawned. Across the wooden lane a middle-aged woman came out of her cottage, locked her door, and checked her purse. She was dressed for a day at the office, fashionable yet functional, and she carried a thin and efficient-looking briefcase, embassy black. I smiled at her as she drew near and she smiled back.

"Nobody's home," she said.

"Pardon me?"

"You're looking for the new tenant? The woman?"

"That's right," I said.

"She left last night."

My stomach slowly rolled over. "Are you sure?"

"Am I ever!" The woman shook her head, swept back her bangs. "The taxi driver, bless his dear blue-collar, cigar-smoking heart, rang my doorbell in the middle of the night looking for her. So yes, I'm sure."

I pointed at Stephanie's door. "Did you actually see her leave?"

The woman nodded. "One-eighteen in the morning, with a suitcase. Believe me, I remember. Are you a friend?"

I nodded numbly.

"Then please give her some friendly advice," the woman said. "From now on when she calls a taxi make sure she gives the right directions. What we in the neighborhood usually do is meet taxis down on Montgomery. That way we avoid confusion, because the numbers *do* get screwy up here. Okay?"

I nodded okay and the woman tucked the briefcase up close to her side and walked on down the steps.

I drove my old white van as fast as I could to Hank and Carol's house. Carol was just out the door with Cort, taking him to day care, and she steered me in the direction of the Dry Eye Restaurant on Haight Street, Hank's new workplace. She wanted to know what was up and I told her I'd fill her in later and pulled away, watching her recede in the rear-view mirror, Cort standing next to her with his lunchbox, asking questions that she wasn't answering.

The Dry Eye was an undistinguished two-story building among a whole row of undistinguished two-story buildings on Haight Street, three or four blocks east of Golden Gate Park. I found some metered parking around the corner and went into the Dry Eye. If Carol hadn't assured me that it was a restaurant, I would have sworn that I had walked into the middle of an exceptionally busy laundromat. Noise and moist heat and people wishing they were elsewhere. I spotted Hank right away behind the grill at the far end of the restaurant. He was cooking side by side with a swarthy-looking character of Middle Eastern descent. Hank was trying to decipher an order hanging on the metal order wheel when he saw me. He said something to the swarthy man and came out from behind the grill area, undoing his apron as he walked.

"Hey!" the swarthy man yelled. "Whaddaya doin'?"

Hank turned around and made a gesture. "I said one minute, okay? Jesus . . ."

"Am I getting you in trouble?" I said.

Hank waved his hand. "The simple fact that I work here means I'm in trouble."

"Your boss?"

"That's Abdul. He's the owner," Hank said. "Know what he was doing this morning when I came in?"

"Never mind about that."

"No, listen. This'll give you some idea of what I'm going through."

I shut my eyes. "Okay. What was he doing?"

"He was in his office, sitting at his desk, and there was a box of hot dogs in front of him. Right on the desk! He was just sitting there, gazing at them. Last week he decided to upgrade the hot dogs. Order the premium brand. I stuck my head in the office this morning and he said to me, 'Hankie!' That's what he calls me. Hankie."

"Like the thing you blow your nose in."

"Right. So anyway, he says, 'Hey, Hankie! I got a treat for you this morning! Come over here and smell the Cadillac of hot dogs.' I'm not making this up. The Cadillac of hot dogs! What's next? The Aston-Martin of chicken nuggets?" Hank shook his head. "Anyway, I wouldn't smell them and he got really pissed. I mean, really, really pissed. Told me that if that was all I cared about the quality of hot dogs in the Dry Eye I was jeopardizing my ability to rise to assistant manager. So screw it. If I want to take two minutes off, I'll take two minutes off. What're you doing here?"

"I have to go to Jamaica today," I said.

Hank did a slow, mental count to five. "Do what?"

"Go to Jamaica."

"Correct me if I'm wrong," Hank said, "but didn't you just go to Jamaica?"

"Yes."

"Didn't you just go twice?"

"I've got to go again."

Hank looked off to the side and addressed

an imaginary third party. "Does a power drill ever blow up in my hands? No. I've got to catch hell for not smelling the Cadillac of hot dogs." Then Hank turned back to me, shaking his head. "I hope to hell you're at least on some sort of frequent flyer program. What's the problem now?"

"Russell."

"What about him?" he said. "No, let me guess. He's developed this phobia about making repeated trips to Jamaica and you're going to — "

"Russell's dead."

I suddenly had Hank's complete attention. "He's what?"

"Day before yesterday. A triple somersault off the top of his Seacliff terrace."

"Good God . . ." Hank slowly sank into a chair at the table. "Suicide?"

"I don't think so."

I gave it to him as quickly as I could. All of it. Meredith's phone call, my predawn trip to Sausalito, the argument with Russell on the terrace, the final phone call to Norman in Priest River, and now Stephanie's disappearance. When I finished Hank slowly nodded and looked off to the side, thinking it over.

"So Norman's behind it all . . ." Hank said.

"And I'm afraid Stephanie's gone down to settle the score."

"Maybe not," Hank said thoughtfully. "Just because she got in a taxi . . . She could have gone anywhere."

"Stephanie's on her way to Priest River, Hank. Trust me. She didn't leave a note or run off with a bottle of telltale tanning oil, but that's where she went."

"Even if she did . . . how do you expect to catch up with her?"

"I'm going to lease a private jet right now at the airport. If Stephanie flew commercial we should arrive at the same time, more or less."

"I'm coming with you," Hank suddenly announced.

"You're what?"

"This private jet, it has an extra seat, right?"

"Hank . . ."

Hank stood and began folding up his dirty apron. "If Stephanie's in trouble, I'm going to help. Two people can cover twice the ground twice as fast."

"That's not why I came by, Hank."

"Of course it's not," he said. "You came by to tell me to keep an eye on things back here in your absence. Feed the parrot. Check the answering machine. Am I right?"

I nodded.

"Well, forget it," Hank said. "Stephanie and Marty stuck their necks out for me and my family and that's the main reason all this trouble started. I'm going, Quinn. That's all there is."

"What about Carol?" I said.

"She'll understand."

"No she won't."

"Then she won't understand. Either way, doesn't matter. I'll hash it out with her later. Besides, I'm still in such deep shit at home over this Seven Altars business that a couple of extra shovelfuls on the dungheap won't make any difference. I figure once the feces level rises above your head it doesn't matter how much further you sink. Drowned is drowned. I'll call her from the airport."

"And the job?"

Hank pointed at the floor. "This job?"

There was nothing more to say. Hank placed his folded apron on the table and tucked in his shirt.

"Let's get going," he said. "I hate long, drawn-out good-byes, and Abdul's an emotional kind of guy."

25

The private driveway leading to Norman's beach house seemed more dark and over-grown than I remembered it, with slanting rays of late-afternoon sunlight filtering through the treetops. I drove halfway down the dirt road and came to a stop while we were still hidden from view and out of ear-shot. I cut the engine and Hank and I sat silently in the Turnbull House BMW, watch-ing the dust settle around us.

It was hot. Choke-collar humid. Elaborate spiderwebs shone in the dying light, and all around us tattered vines hung down from the tops of trees like abandoned ropes from ancient lynchings. The driveway ahead of us went straight for another thirty feet then swerved to the right and disappeared into the thicket.

"It's right around the bend," I said. "Last chance for us to conclude this is stupid and go back."

Hank nodded. He was thinking about it, and so was I. Phobia therapists and stand-up comics are poor candidates for SWAT team commandos.

401

"Recap for me why it's stupid," Hank said.

"He's probably armed and we're not. There are other stupid reasons, but that's the main one."

Hank nodded. We fell silent again, and gazed together down the winding, shadowy road.

The Lear jet had put us softly down at the Turnbull House runway three hours earlier, and so far the rescue mission had been an exercise in total frustration. The usual customs official at Turnbull House wasn't there and, despite not having a single piece of luggage between us, we had to wait thirty minutes for another immigration officer to arrive. When we were finally cleared we drove into Priest River only to find Bongo's office locked up and shut down. So we turned around and backtracked to Seven Altars on the off chance that Stephanie had gone there to think things out. She hadn't. The house was empty. I went out on the terrace and peered down the beach in the direction of the waterfalls. No. If we ran out of places to look I'd go there. But not until. There was no place left to go but the only place a vengeful Stephanie would have gone.

I drummed my fingertips on the steering wheel and we continued to gaze down the shadowy dirt road.

"He's probably not even here," Hank said.

"Why wouldn't he be?"

"All hell breaking loose like this, people dropping dead left and right . . . I'd be halfway around the world by now."

"Except Norman has no reason to think anybody's going to be coming after him. As far as he knew, there were only two problems left, Russell and Meredith, and now they're gone."

Hank nodded and took a deep, deep breath. "Okay, then," he said. "We've come this far. Let's go."

We left the car where it was, sliding out silently and leaving the doors open. Then we went quietly down the dirt road, moving in tentative slow motion, like children who've finally decided to enter the haunted forest they've been warned about all their lives.

As soon as the beach house came into view we stopped and crouched behind a tree and watched for a minute or two. All was still. No signs of life. Everything was just as I had remembered it from last time except for one thing. A light brown, late-model Nissan was parked over by the horseshoe pit. The car had a Hertz rental sticker on the back bumper. From beyond the corner of the house I could see something else that was different. Norman's boat was gone. His Chris-Craft wasn't there.

"Boat's gone," I whispered to Hank. "And that's a rental car."

"Not Norman's?"

I shook my head. "Stay here. I'm going to check the house."

I skirted along the edge of the tree cover till I was within twenty feet of the house. Then I ran, low to the ground, up to the wall facing west. There was a single window and I peeked in. The light wasn't good, but I could see enough to know that the place was empty. Norman wasn't around. We were too late. He'd left.

"Quinn!"

The voice wasn't Hank's, and it was directly behind me. I whirled and flattened myself against the wall. There was a rustling in the trees beyond and then Bongo came climbing out, brushing the dirt from his shoulders.

"Jesus, Bongo!" I said in a clenched whisper. "You scared the hell out of me!"

Hank had seen Bongo coming and was out from behind the tree cover, trotting toward us. Bongo was wearing his faded green bathing trunks and a white T-shirt, and he had his dreadlocks tucked up beneath a multicolored loose-knit beret. A sheen of sweat covered his face, and he was out of breath. "No one here," he said. "No need to whisper."

Hank came alongside and he and Bongo nodded to each other.

"I tried calling you from San Francisco," I said.

"My phone is still disconnected," Bongo said.

"Norman was the one behind all this," I said.

Bongo nodded. "I know."

"And I think Stephanie's come down to — "

"I know," Bongo interrupted. He pointed at the Nissan. "That's her car. I checked with the car company in Kingston. She rented it this morning."

All three of us looked at the abandoned car, then at the empty boat dock. "Let's go inside," Bongo said.

Norman's door was unlocked and we filed in. Packed boxes were stacked against the wall. The clothes closet was empty. The room smelled of imminent and hasty flight.

"Have you seen Stephanie?" I said.

Bongo shook his head. "No." He settled into a bamboo chair near the door. "First tell me what you know. See if we know the same things."

I did. While Bongo and Hank sat and listened I paced the darkened room and told them everything that had happened in the past few days. Bongo nodded through the whole thing, and when I was finished he stood and walked to the far window.

"Archie's dead," he said.

"I thought he probably was."

Bongo nodded. "Same day. He ran for the hills but they found him and shot him. Don't care how crazy he got, I still lost my best friend." Bongo took a deep breath. "After Archie was dead I talked to some people. Some people who would not talk about Archie when he was alive. His other friends from his other life. They told me about Norman."

"Why did they do that?"

"Norman set up Archie," Bongo said, looking me straight in the eyes. "Norman hired Archie to have you killed at the water-falls, and when it didn't happen and he knew I was involved, it was Norman who sent Chief Gordon to take care of Archie. Archie was going a little bit crazy. Archie might think friendship is more important than a hit job and tell me who was hiring him to do this fockery."

I nodded, remembering how we sped by Norman in the town square while he was getting his shoes shined by Winston. The shock on his face. "What else?" I said.

"Most are things you know already. Norman had Marty killed. The friends of Archie say Norman smuggled drugs and guns into Priest River. That was why crime was so bad."

Hank and I looked at each other. "How did Norman manage this?" I said.

Bongo shrugged. "They didn't know. They only knew who and what. They don't know why or how. Smuggling ganja is one thing. Government look the other way. Take away the ganja trade, half the people in Jamaica lose money. But guns is another matter. Nobody tolerates guns. Not police, not government, nobody. Not even Chief Gordon. Jamaica has a thing called the Gun Court. If a person is found in the possession of a handgun, or even a bullet, it is mandatory life imprisonment with no chance of parole. Hard to make such a thing worth the risk."

"But Norman was doing it?"

"This is what people say."

"Never mind about all this," Hank said at last. "What about Stephanie? If she rented the car that means she's here. Or was here. Shouldn't we be looking for her?"

"She's not here," Bongo said. "I was checking the jungle when you came. I think she is on the boat with Norman."

"The boat?" Hank said. "Then what do we do? Is there a Coast Guard here?"

Bongo slowly shook his head. "Look on top that box there. The one by the sink."

I went to the box next to the sink. An American passport was sitting atop it. I flipped it open to see Norman's smiling face.

"Norman can't go anywhere without that," Bongo said.

"So we wait?" I said.

"It's a big ocean," Bongo said. "Norman has a big head start and in an hour it will be dark. It is better to wait."

So we waited. The twilight thickened, the humidity deepened. We kept the lights off, and for an hour we sat in the dark and talked. Hank told us Stephanie and Marty stories from the New York days. Bongo recounted happier times spent growing up with his lost friend, Archie. I sat and listened to their talk with total absorption. It was a way of keeping at bay the knowledge of the empty rented automobile out by the horseshoe pit. Of not thinking about what could be happening to Stephanie, or of what may have already happened.

Bongo heard the sound first. Hank was in the middle of a story and Bongo suddenly raised his hand for silence. We sat in utter stillness, and from beyond the walls of the dark beach house came the thick, spluttering sound of a boat motoring toward the dock at slow speed.

Bongo pointed at Hank, then at the kitchen. Hank went. Then he signaled me to go flush up against the wall behind a stack of boxes just to the right of the door. Bongo flattened himself against the wall to the left of the door. My eyes had grown accustomed to the dark, and I could see quite clearly the gun in Bongo's right hand.

The minutes dragged by. The boat noise drew very close, then the motor chugged one last time and came to a stop. We listened carefully to the sudden, overwhelming silence. Lapping water. A throat being cleared. Footsteps on the wooden boat ramp. But there was no conversation. No backing or forthing or a second pair of footsteps. A small sickness started in the pit of my stomach and then spread to the rest of my body like ink on wet paper. Norman Tollinger was alone. If he had left with a companion, he hadn't come back with one.

The footsteps were suddenly right next to us, up on the wooden front porch, and the doorknob began to move. Bongo braced himself, readied the gun, planted his feet.

The door jiggled, came open an inch, and

then stopped abruptly. Two seconds passed. Three. He knew we were inside. He knew something was wrong.

In the next moment Bongo reacted. He reached out with his free hand and yanked the doorknob in as hard as he could and Norman came in with it. He went down hard on his stomach and the gun that had been pulled from his shoulder holster was jarred loose at impact. Norman started to crawl for the fallen weapon, but Bongo was atop him in a flash, left hand pinning Norman's face to the floor, the other hand holding a gun at his head.

"No moves!" Bongo yelled.

"Okay!" Norman said, his voice muffled by the floor. "Jesus! I said okay!"

Bongo looked at me. "Turn on the lights."

I did as I was told. The brightness momentarily blinded me. Hank came out from behind the kitchen area, blinking and shielding his eyes. He was very pale and breathing hard.

"Get his gun," Bongo said.

I picked it up.

"Bring it over here," Bongo said. "Put it up to my nose."

I did as he said and Bongo sniffed at it.

"Okay," he said. "Take it out to the boat dock and throw it in the water. Be careful."

I went out into the night and walked unsteadily past the now-docked Chris-Craft and tossed the gun underhanded into the gently rolling sea. Then I stepped on board the boat and checked below. No Stephanie.

When I got back to the house Norman was sitting in a chair in the middle of the room, rubbing the back of his neck. Bongo sat ten feet away in another chair, straddling it backward, his arms outstretched and braced over the bamboo backing. The gun was steady and motionless and trained on Norman.

"Quinn," Norman said. He managed a smile while rubbing the pain from his neck. "Shit, this is getting to be like old home week around here."

"Where's Stephanie?" I said.

"Bongo here already asked that question while you were outside. I'm afraid that's gonna have to be my little secret for a while."

"You don't have the luxury for secrets," Bongo said.

Norman quit rubbing his neck. He was wearing new jeans and cowboy boots and a brown, Western-style shirt with designs stitched above the pockets. It almost looked like a costume.

"I have the luxury to do whatever I want," Norman said. "Because I know where Stephanie is and you don't. Fact is, I'm gonna have a steady diet of luxury from here on out."

"Only luxury you have," Bongo said, "is a fancy casket. Now where's Stephanie?"

Norman laughed and looked at the gun trained on him. "Casket? You're going to shoot me?"

Bongo didn't say anything. The weapon stayed on Norman.

"You're a lawyer, Bongo," Norman said. "You know all about the Gun Court." Then he turned from Bongo and looked at me. "What about you, Quinn? Ever heard of the Gun Court? Hank?"

"As a matter of fact," I said, "we were just talking about it."

"Were you?"

The room was silent. Norman's laughter was replaced by a hard, flat smile.

"Gun Court don't apply here," Bongo said.

"Bullshit, it doesn't!" Norman turned from Bongo and faced Hank. "Gordon or no Gordon, cops in this town still think fondly of old Norman. Spent a lot of time and money and effort over the years cultivating that friendship, if you know what I mean. Bongo here pulls the trigger and the three of you are locked up for life. Besides, you kill me and you'll never know where Stephanie is."

"Stephanie's already dead," Bongo said

suddenly. "Don't try to be bargaining with her corpse."

"She's alive," Norman said, still looking at Hank.

Silence filled the room. Norman went back to rubbing his head. "I think you fucked up my neck, Bongo."

"All right," Bongo said. "Let's pretend I believe you. Stephanie is alive. Where?"

"Okay," Norman said, "we'll do it like this." His tone was relaxed, confidential, like we were a group of businessmen who were closing in on an agreement after an especially fruitful three-martini lunch. "I don't want any more bloodshed. There's no need for it. I didn't kill Stephanie because I didn't need to. I *like* Stephanie!"

"Keep talking," Bongo said.

"The difference between the old Norman Tollinger and the new Norman Tollinger is that the new one thinks ahead. Plan A fails, you go to Plan B, and if that fails, you go to Plan C."

"What's your point?" Hank said.

Norman turned in his chair to face Hank. "My point is that Plan A failed. But I've had five years to put together Plan B and it's all ready to go. I've been tucking money away for a long time now. Mad money. Fuck-you money. Fold up the tent and start

413

all over again money. I get on an airplane tonight and I'm history. Vanished. Poof. I'm gonna disappear so bad nobody's gonna ever find me. It's all set up."

"All set up except for the airplane out," I said.

Norman looked at me. "Deal is this," he said. "You drive me to the airport in Kingston tonight, and when we get there I tell you where Stephanie is."

"Unh-unh," Bongo said. "You fly away and we come back and look and find nobody."

"One of you stays here," Norman said. "This phone works. Check it. Pick it up and check it."

Hank leaned over, picked it up, and listened for a dial tone. He nodded and put the receiver back on its cradle.

"There," Norman said. "We call from the airport and whoever stays behind checks it out. If I'm right, you let me leave. If I'm wrong you can toss me in the goddamn harbor."

Bongo took a deep breath and looked at me.

"Quit pretending you have a choice in the matter," Norman said, "because fact is, you don't. If I'm not on the nine forty-five flight out of Kingston tonight Stephanie *will* be dead."

"This place where Stephanie is," Bongo said. "Any of us here could find it?"

Norman gave his shoulders a little shrug. "Piece of cake."

"Then I'll stay," Hank said.

"You guys are doing the right thing," Norman said. "I mean that."

"Bring the BMW," Bongo told me, never taking his eyes off Norman. "Bring it right up around here to the front door."

I stood and Norman rubbed his hands together and blinked his nervous blink. "BMW?" he said. "All right! Leave this dump in a little bit of style!"

"If this is a trick," Bongo said. "You are going to die. If Stephanie is harmed, you are going to die."

"Everything's going to be fine," Norman said, standing and stretching. "I told you, this is the new Norman Tollinger. Plan B. Nobody has anything to worry about."

Bongo allowed him to stand, but the gun never wavered. I went outside and half-ran, half-walked down the dark road leading back to the BMW.

415

26

Bongo drove. Even in open country, on relatively quiet roads, I had found driving on the left-hand side of the road excruciatingly stressful. Shifting gears with my left hand was confusing. Oncoming traffic invariably made me flinch, and every intersection extracted of me a Rubik's Cube of intense and white-knuckled concentration. I was not prepared to negotiate the snarl and chaos of a strange city in the middle of the night.

So Bongo took the car keys and Norman and I climbed into the back seat, me turned sideways, facing him. Bongo gave me the gun and leaned close.

"You can do this, Quinn?"

"Do what?"

"Use a gun if you have to?"

I nodded, but it was not the kind of confident nod Bongo was looking for.

"Quinn," he said, putting his hand on my shoulder. "I need to know you can pull the trigger if you have to. It's important. If he makes a move while I'm driving . . ."

"Don't worry, Quinn," Norman said. "I'm

not going to give you any reason to blow me away. Plan B only works if I'm alive and healthy. Relax. Enjoy the ride."

I turned and kept my back up against the locked door and pointed the weapon in Norman's direction. Norman shrugged and looked out his window.

Hank came around to my side of the car and leaned in through the open back seat window.

"Go easy," he said.

"I will."

"Nothing stupid or brave."

I shook my head. "Not a chance."

"Stephanie and I will be waiting when you get back."

The hope didn't fly real well. It sounded hollow and unlikely. Then Hank straightened up and walked back toward the beach house and we pulled away.

"How far to Kingston?" I asked Bongo.

"Hour."

Norman leaned his head all the way back on the leather upholstery and sighed. "So this is how it ends," he mumbled. "Five years . . . good-bye house. Good-bye driveway. Been good to know you."

I didn't say anything. Norman closed his eyes and licked his lips, then turned his head sideways and gave me a weary smile.

Bongo got the car out onto the main road and headed left toward Priest River. We slowed briefly through town, then picked up the highway on the other side and accelerated toward Kingston.

"Been to Kingston yet?" Norman asked.

I shook my head. "No."

"It's an armpit. Big, ugly, dangerous . . . nowhere near as beautiful as Montego Bay."

I adjusted my back against the door. The gun was still resting in my lap, pointed at Norman. He looked at the weapon, smiled, and shook his head.

"Tell me about Plan A," I said.

"Ah, yes," Norman said with a sad shake of the head. "Plan A. How come I get the feeling you could tell me more about it than anybody else?"

"The Resort at Seven Altars," I said.

Norman nodded. "Yep. It was a great plan. Simple, clean, mostly legit. I guess I always sort of knew deep down that Russell'd fuck it up, otherwise I wouldn't've had Plan B."

"How did Russell fuck it up?"

"How do you think?" Norman said. "Building a model of the whole thing and showing it off to Meredith and God knows who else!"

"Who told you about that?"

"Russell himself. The putz. Stephanie figured it out somehow and got in his face. Demanded answers. Wanting to get to the bottom of things. Couldn't believe it," Norman muttered. "That's when I knew it was over. Really over."

"So you had Meredith killed?"

Norman gently shrugged his shoulders. "You saw Meredith. Is she the kind of woman you're going to let wander around, shooting off her mouth?"

The dark highway sped by. Bongo was utterly silent, now and then glancing up at us, his eyes flashing in the rear-view mirror.

"Too bad," Norman said after a while. "The resort would've been nice."

"Was the resort your idea?" I said.

Norman shook his head. "Incredibly enough, that was Russell's brainchild. Probably the only smart thing he ever thought up in his whole life. He came down shortly after I moved here. I was still fiddling with the ganja business and Russell and I went out on this sailboat he rented and smoked a little and he started in about how this was the perfect spot for a resort. He had a recreational brain. Could already see the golf course, where the sand traps would be."

"And you offered to help?"

"Eventually, sure. Russell went out and bought that bluff on the south end of the cove. Cost him a fortune. All I did was make a business proposition."

"You'd bring down the property values," I said.

"Exactly." Norman shrugged. "I told Russell I'd get the land around here affordable, and when the resort was built my payoff would be a job at a nice salary. A *real* nice salary. While away my golden years in style. Rum, girls, sunshine. Tighten the volleyball net every once in a while."

"So you brought guns into the Priest River area and scared off the landholders," I said.

Norman smiled. "Easiest thing in the world."

"How did you get the guns in?" I said.

Bongo's eyes flashed again in the rear-view mirror. He was watching Norman very closely.

Norman continued to smile and shook his head no. "Unh-unh. I'd love to tell you because it's really beautiful, but that part of it involved other people and they might not want me giving away all the secrets."

"So everything went as planned," I said, "except Marty wouldn't sell his land."

"You got it," Norman said. "Not for any price. Of course, I didn't tell Russell this. Far as Russell knew, the deal was close, but it had to be hush-hush. Russell'd believe anything you told him."

"Like Marty dying tragically in a drug deal?"

"Right. I mean, you saw what happened when he finally started to add two and two. He freaked. Called me up and said he was going to blow the whistle on the whole deal. He didn't care if his ass got cooked, as long as mine did, too."

"Which is why he went over the balcony of his terrace?"

Norman shrugged. "I like my ass uncooked, thanks."

"Who did it for you? Gary?"

Norman looked surprised. "You knew Gary?"

"We met once or twice. I thought he worked for Russell."

"He did. But, hey . . . Gary's just like you or me. Keep the career options open. When this resort business started getting serious I knew I'd need somebody on Russell's end to, you know, keep an eye on things. First time I visited and saw Gary. Shit . . . central casting. I made it worth his while to shift loyalties."

"There was no need for Meredith to die," I said quietly. "No need."

"That so?"

"You know it as well as I do."

Norman sighed. "I guess you would've probably wandered up to Russell's office on your own. Accidentally bumped into the mock-up."

"She was just a messed-up girl. Harmless."

"Right," Norman said. "A harmless girl who every time she has a fight with her boyfriend goes out and blabs more secrets."

I looked at him without saying a word. Norman sighed again and shifted in his seat. "Look, Quinn. For Plan B to work there can't be people hanging around who can scream too much. Like Russell. Like Meredith."

"Like Stephanie . . ."

Norman leveled a hard and cold stare about halfway down my throat. "Stephanie came looking for me, don't forget. It wasn't the other way around. If Stephanie needed to be dead, she would've been dead a long time ago."

We fell silent, and nobody spoke again until a half-hour later when we saw the first twinkling lights of Kingston on the horizon.

"Here we are," Norman said quietly, almost to himself. "Practically home."

We descended into the city. Tall buildings, lots of people, a park. Nothing especially distinctive. Bongo drove through some spacious and manicured residential areas, then past the University of the West Indies, and on into town. Though night had fallen, the traffic was heavy and the urban heat oppressive. We went past a sign that indicated the airport and continued west.

"Missed the exit," Norman said, sitting up on the edge of his seat.

Silence.

Norman leaned toward Bongo. "I said, you missed the fucking exit."

Bongo's eyes found mine in the rear-view mirror. "Keep the gun on him, Quinn," Bongo said. "Concentrate."

Norman looked from Bongo to me and then back to Bongo again. "All right," he said. "What's the game?"

"No game," Bongo said. "Many ways to get to the airport. I used to live here, remember?"

We continued west and with each block the neighborhood deteriorated significantly. I felt the dangerous whiteness of my skin. The conspicuousness of the sleek and streamlined BMW. Bongo drove as one who has a specific destination in mind.

"Don't be stupid," Norman said to Bongo. "Take me to the airport and I fly out of here and everybody goes home safe. Don't blow it."

"Bongo," I said. "What's happening?

Where are we going?"

"Trench Town," Bongo said. "This is the place where Archie and I grew up."

We pushed deeper and deeper into West Kingston. It was like entering a war zone. The streets were filled with flattened tins, smashed cartons, vegetable husks, vacant television shells spilling the last of their electrical guts into desolate gutters. Jukeboxes blared. Abandoned cars, stripped of everything that had even remote value, sat rusting next to the garbage in the gutters. The streets and alleys were mobbed with ramshackle buses, honking automobiles, pedestrians, rattle-trap bicycles, broken-down handcarts, rib-cage dogs, and an occasional goat or donkey. The air smelled like pale, day-old urine, and piles of excrement lay in the streets and on the sidewalks.

We drove through a shantytown of haphazard dwellings that formed two long rows on either side of the street and then climbed up into the hills beyond. Some were made of concrete or cinderblock, others of plywood or corrugated tin, still others of automobile tires strapped together. They all had low roofs, no windows, no visible light from within, and I was reminded of crudely built fallout shelters — dank, concrete pits where the few forlorn survivors of nuclear madness might huddle together, fearing what they would find when they eventually had to surface. Dead eyes looked out of the doorless darkness as we inched through the chaos. The eyes showed no life at all. They were eyes that were capable of doing anything. Anything.

Norman was right at the edge of his seat, both hands gripping his knees. His eyes flashed from one thing to the next. His nervous blink was going double time.

Bongo took the BMW over a series of railroad tracks, past an abandoned warehouse, and pulled to a stop.

"Where the fuck are we?" Norman demanded.

"This is Plan C," Bongo said, and he gestured to the right. "The Dungle."

I looked out the window. Fifty yards away a swell of dark rose up out of the earth, a massive semicircle against the softer darkness of the night. For a moment it had no relation to anything I'd ever seen before, then I recognized it for what it was. The Dungle was a garbage dump. It sprawled for acres and acres, bulging from the earth in a festering heap like an inflamed chancre sore. The smell was suddenly overpowering. People were atop the pile, rummaging through the garbage. Men, women, children. They nosed through the trash, picking up this, discarding that. Their ghastly silhouettes moved over the skin of the garbage heap.

"What's your point?" Norman said. "Educate the white boy about how bad the ghetto is?"

Bongo got out of the car and came over to my side and took the gun from my hand. Then he went over to Norman's side and opened the door and motioned for him to get out.

"You're out of your fucking mind," Norman said. "They'll kill us all. You think just the white boy is going to get it? You don't think they're going to have fun with the Rasta in the BMW?"

Bongo waved the gun again. "Out!"

Norman sat for a moment, thinking it over, then slid heavily across the leather seat and stepped outside. "Congratulations," he said coldly. "You just killed Stephanie."

Bongo shook his head.

"He's right, Bongo," I said. "Stephanie's the only important thing now. Let's do it the way we planned it."

"Whatever happened to Stephanie already happened," Bongo said. "A phone call from the airport is going to make no difference."

"Then I'll tell you now!" Norman said, the panic building. "Why don't I do that?

Tell you now and then we get back in the car and get the fuck out of here!"

Bongo shook his head.

"She's in jail!" Norman shouted. "Okay? She came to my house waving a fucking gun and I had her tossed in jail. Call Trevor right now if you don't believe me! That's the goddamn truth!"

"Trevor?" Bongo said.

"Yes! He was out at my place getting his last fucking payoff when she showed. On a gun charge she'll rot in there forever, but one phone call from me and she's sprung! You know that's true, Bongo! You goddamn know it!"

Bongo shrugged like it didn't matter much one way or the other.

"All right," Norman said, changing tactics. "You want to make a deal? We can deal."

"What deal?" Bongo said.

The glimmer of hope animated Norman. He pulled his shirttails out and removed a money pouch that fit around his waist like a second, inner belt. "Money," he said. "Lots of it. That's where I was in the boat when you came to the house. Picking up my stash."

Bongo didn't say a word. Norman held up the pouch and waved it at him. "Three hundred thousand bucks!" he said. "You can have a hundred of it. I got more tucked

427

away so it don't matter. You can have half! Half of it! But let's get the fuck out of here before we get killed."

A bottle flew from the darkness and shattered on the ground a few yards away. Norman skipped out of the way of the flying shards and stared wildly in the direction the bottle came from. "Shit!"

"This is the money you make from selling guns?" Bongo said.

"The what?" Norman said, half-listening, still gazing back in the direction of the thrown bottle.

"I said is this the money you got for bringing more weapons into Jamaica? Making Trench Town such a happy place?"

Norman's face grew dark. The excited tone left his voice. "I get it," he said. Bored forthrightness. Eyes that had grown weary of a game played too long. "Poetic justice, right? Bring the bad guy to the belly of the beast."

Bongo didn't answer right away. He concentrated on the people crawling like maggots across the infected skin of the Dungle. Some of them had noticed the BMW, and they were moving closer, in small groups of three and four. At last he licked his lips and nodded a small nod. "Yes, mon," he said softly. "Poetic justice."

"You're out of your mind . . ." Norman said.

"You know," Bongo said. "Me and Archie, when we were boys, we used to look up and watch the planes fly away, and we had a game to guess where they went. No winners in the game because there was no way to know the final destination, but that didn't matter. Every plane was going to a better place than Trench Town."

"I'm all choked up," Norman said.

Bongo ignored him. "Archie'd close one eye and hold his finger up and pretend to touch the airplane. I remember the way his arm moved slowly across the sky."

"So that's what this is all about?" Norman spat out the words. "Homage to Archie Barrett? Hate to clue you, Bongo, but your old buddy was a killer. Enough money and he'd kill anybody, including you and your friend here."

"Airport's only two miles that way," Bongo said, waving the gun toward the south. "Two miles. Not far." Then he focused suddenly and ruthlessly on Norman. "You have an advantage. You've got money and a passport. All you got to do is walk."

Norman looked at me. "You going to let him do this, Quinn?"

Bongo shook his head. "This business

doesn't concern Quinn. This is our business. Yours and mine."

Bongo circled around the front of the car, keeping the weapon trained on Norman, and slid in the front seat. Another bottle hurtled out of the darkness and exploded against the side of the car. This time Norman didn't even flinch.

Bongo started up the engine, and the car began to inch away. Under the washed-out yellow of the faded streetlamp Norman stood and watched us. He was suddenly old beyond his years. Old, and haggard. He was in the process of dying already. Bongo pulled fifteen feet away and then leaned out of his open window.

"I'm going to give you the same chance you gave these people," Bongo said. With the car idling he held the gun out the open window and dropped it onto the pavement below. Then he put the car into gear and accelerated away.

I turned and watched Norman. I thought he'd bolt for the weapon, but for a long, long time he didn't move. It was as though he knew the end was near, and a small hand-gun wasn't going to make much difference.

"We can't do this, Bongo," I said.

"It's done," Bongo said.

People were closing in on him slowly from

both sides, but still Norman just stood and watched us drive away. Sanity dictated that I drain him of every residual drop of humanity he might have possessed. There would be no grieving loved ones. He had never been a laughing child. He'd never felt the first flush of love, and he'd never stumbled awkwardly over the lips of the first girl he'd kissed. Norman Tollinger had to be abstracted into a sinister vehicle of black, opportunistic evil, but the longer he stood and watched us go the harder it was.

Then he suddenly bolted. Raced for the dropped gun. He picked it up, and, looking this way and that, rushed off into the night. Several of the figures that had been closing in on him gave chase. There was a determination in Norman's action that scared me. A desperate, nothing-to-lose abandon that might make him the worst of the worse, even at this level. It suddenly occurred to me that he might survive.

"You shouldn't have given him the gun, Bongo," I said. "He'll get out of this and come back for us."

Bongo shook his head. "If he gets out of this he will go ahead with Plan B. But he won't get out of it."

"How can you be so sure? Did you see the way he — "

Bongo turned and smiled at me. A weary smile. An unhappy smile. He reached into his pocket and removed a half-dozen bullets.

"The gun's empty?" I said.

"I told Norman the truth," Bongo said. "Now he has the same chance as any man in Trench Town, no?"

He put the bullets in his pocket and went back across the railroad tracks and headed east toward Kingston proper, toward Priest River.

I sat next to the window and pinched my upper lip. My gaze wouldn't penetrate the night. Instead it was reflected in the vibrating window; gaunt, pale, with eyes anxious and tired. The reflected face bothered me. It was too shadowy and hollowed out . . . not like I remembered my face at all. It reminded me of a painting, one of those ravaged self-portraits where the artist turns Lizzie Borden on himself and hacks away at his own features to create an effect. I turned uneasily from the black mirror and closed my eyes, and we drove east in utter silence.

27

We got back into Priest River late, and a single light was burning in the police station off the main square. It was hot, and the double door of the police station was open to the street in an attempt to get some air. Moths threw themselves furiously at the bare light bulb, and the crickets were going like they were on amphetamines. I could feel droplets of sweat in my eyelashes, and I tried to blink them away.

"Wait here," Bongo said.

I stayed put while he went in through the open door. My heart was in my throat. If Stephanie wasn't here . . . if Norman had strung us along . . . I pushed the thought from my mind.

A cop moved out from behind a desk and met Bongo halfway. I watched. Bongo was talking and the cop kept nodding his head and looking nervously out the door, pointing. Then Bongo turned and came back out and climbed in behind the wheel.

"Blood-clot miracle," Bongo said. "Norman was telling the truth. Stephanie was here."

I shut my eyes and felt the tension release and drain from my body. "Thank God . . ."

"Now we must find her," Bongo said.

"Why did the police let her go?"

"Norman's instructions. They were to hold her for a few hours and then release her." Bongo started up the engine. "Norman's not stupid. Rich man's daughter from the United States locked away in a Jamaican jail could mean lots of publicity. Norman only wanted to buy a few more hours to get off the island. Once he was gone he knew Stephanie would never find him again. Easier to just let her go."

We drove back to Norman's house and Hank was out on the doorstep to meet us before we had a chance to come to a complete stop. The rented Nissan was missing.

"Stephanie was here!" Hank said breathlessly. "The goddamn police brought her back, dropped her off. I tried to stop her but she just got in the car and drove away."

"It's okay," Bongo said. "No more harm can be done."

"What happened to Norman?" Hank said. "Is he gone?"

"Yes," Bongo nodded. "Norman is gone."

"Then why the hell didn't you call me from the goddamn airport? Jesus Christ! I've been sitting here all by myself going nuts!"

"We didn't go to the airport," I said.

Hank looked from Bongo to me and back to Bongo. "What's that supposed to mean?"

"Why don't you tell him?" I said. "I've got an idea where Stephanie went."

Bongo nodded, put his arm around Hank, and the two of them began walking back to Norman's house. I slid over on the seat to the driver's side and put the BMW in reverse.

The Nissan was parked there, on the crushed seashell driveway. I eased up next to it and cut the engine. There were no lights on at Seven Altars, and for reasons still unclear to me I refrained from turning any on. I felt my way around the living room, softly calling Stephanie's name. Nothing.

I rolled the sliding-glass door back and wandered out on the terrace and that's when I saw her. She was at the end of the empty boat dock, legs tucked up under her chin, replicating the pose I'd seen that first evening in Jamaica after we'd all come back down from the waterfalls.

I stepped down from the terrace and walked out to the edge of the dock and stood next to her. She didn't react. There was a soft, warm breeze coming off the water. Moonlight shimmered on the calm and soundless sea.

I got down into a crouch and positioned my face so she would have to look at me. "Are you okay, Stephanie?" I said.

"Where's Norman?" she said.

"He's gone."

"Does that mean dead?"

"That means he's gone."

Stephanie nodded at the information. "What a fool I was. Going off in the middle of the night. Superwoman. Corrector of wrongs. It's a miracle I didn't get somebody killed."

"Come on home with us," I said. "It's over now."

Stephanie shook her head. "No. I'm going to stay here a little while. A week or two, maybe. Figure out what to do next. Do you think Hank would mind if I stayed in the house?"

"Of course not."

Stephanie nodded. "Would you ask him for me?"

"Sure." I stayed in my crouch and ran my finger along the smooth, worn wood of the dock. "Would you like me to stay with you?"

"No," Stephanie said. "I have a lot of thinking to do. Decisions to make."

"Leaning in any particular direction?"

Stephanie exhaled and shook her head and

looked up at the starry sky. "You know what they tell skiers to do if they get buried in an avalanche?"

"No."

"You're supposed to scoop out a little pocket of air and take a piece of snow and hold it in the middle and then let it drop. See which direction it falls. Moral of the story is don't start digging until you've figured which way is up." Stephanie brushed away a strand of hair from her face and looked me in the eyes. "That's what I need to do now, Quinn. And to do it I need to be alone."

"Okay," I said. "Okay. But when you break the surface, you promise to call?"

"The minute I see daylight," she said.

I smiled, leaned down to kiss her, then walked back down the narrow wooden dock, shivering against the wind. I didn't know why I was suddenly cold. The breeze was warm, the air heavy and humid. It didn't make any sense, unless I was feeling a bit of the avalanche's snow myself.

28

"So the property's still mine?" Hank said.

"Still Matty's," I corrected. "Bongo put it all back together the way it was. You're twelve years away from joining the ranks of the millionaires."

"Like you."

"Like me."

Hank shook his head. "Mixed blessing."

We were nursing a couple bottles of cold Mexican beer in the Bus Stop on Union Street. The day was unusually warm. Bright, high sky. The whole city looked scrubbed clean and nobody was in a mood to work. For a Thursday afternoon the bars seemed especially full and the sidewalks especially crowded.

A month had passed since the night Norman was left to walk through two miles of the heavily armed hell he had been so instrumental in creating. Now and then I found myself wondering if he'd made it. If he'd taken his money pouch and bulletless gun and somehow clawed his way to the Kingston airport and lost himself in the world's five billion.

Shortly after Hank and I returned the San Francisco police decided Russell's death wasn't a suicide after all, and they nailed Gary at the Mexican border trying to slip across to Tijuana. As Russell had told me that afternoon on his boat, Gary had great instincts, but he just wasn't quick enough. When Norman's name came up the Jamaican officials cooperated as much as possible, but they had no record of such a person leaving the Kingston airport on the night in question. Or the next night. Or any night thereafter. Something told me Plan B had died on the drawing board. Like Bongo said, not too many people survive Trench Town.

"Oh, well," Hank said. "I should finish this beer and get back to work."

"What work?"

"Comedy. Tonight heralds my triumphant return to the Holy City Zoo. Howard's headlining me."

"Just do me a favor and stay out of the back alley."

"Very funny," Hank said. "By the way, Bongo called yesterday."

"What for?"

"A few legal loose ends that needed to be tied up."

"No gossip?"

"Stephanie left last week." Hank watched me and smiled. "Knew that'd get your attention."

"Where'd she go?"

"Bongo said here. San Francisco."

I nodded and sipped my beer. "No kidding?"

"She hasn't called you?"

"Nope."

Hank kept smiling, and he slowly shook his head. "I admire how you can pretend it doesn't matter. When I reach full maturity I hope to be able to do the same."

"When you reach full maturity, I hope you have the *opportunity* to do the same."

"Ouch!" Hank said. "Touché. I had that coming."

"Yes. You did."

Hank drained the last of his beer and set the empty bottle back on the bar. Then his eyebrows arched and he snapped his fingers. "Almost forgot!" he said.

"Forgot what?"

"Bongo said the mystery of the Priest River ghost got solved."

"How so?"

"Remember how you guys gave me such shit because I said it was somebody in a bedsheet. Turns out that was exactly what it was. Some retarded kid in town. Shoe-shine boy."

I put down my beer. "Winston?"

440

"Who's Winston?"

"Never mind." I sat up straighter. "What happened?"

"Some drunk with a machete apparently had enough and went out on the road to confront the ghost head-on. The drunk said if the ghost was really a ghost then it obviously had nothing to fear from a machete."

I felt my hands tightening on the beer bottle. "And?"

"And the drunk had his bluff called and the kid ended up dead. Bongo said he was standing on his shoeshine box. That's what made him so tall."

"Jesus . . ."

"Yeah . . . did you know him?"

"He shined my shoes a couple times. Always asked for five bucks."

Hank's eyes widened. "He did?"

I nodded. "It was a kind of game we played."

"That's strange."

"What was strange about it?"

"Bongo said when the kid went down the shoeshine box tipped over and it was stuffed with five-dollar bills. I mean, a couple hundred dollars' worth."

"U.S. money?" I said.

Hank shoved himself off the barstool and tucked in his shirt. "I don't know. Bongo mentioned it in passing and I didn't pump him for information. Anyway . . . hell of a town, hunh? But Bongo did say that was the last of it. With Norman out of the picture things are already getting back to normal. Who knows? Maybe I can get some short-term rental out of this thing yet."

"Maybe," I said, still thinking about Winston. A white man sits in the plaza and you ask for five dollars. Why? Because maybe when another white man sits there that's what he gives you. The exaggerated winking. Almost like a nervous blink. Rent-a-Ghost.

Hank walked away, out onto the street, then stuck his head back in. "You're coming to the Zoo tonight, right?"

I nodded. Hank gave me the A-OK sign and continued on down Union Street.

Roger the bartender tried to force another beer on me, compliments of the house, but I begged off. Had to get home and feed a hungry parrot and ravenous cat.

I strolled the five blocks back up Union Street, taking it slow. I crossed the busy four lanes of Van Ness and the sidewalk went into its up-the-hill tilt. I had the apartment key partially in the lock when I heard a woman calling my name. I looked around and saw Stephanie on the other side of Union Street. She was wearing faded jeans tucked into knee-high boots and a plaid L.L. Bean-ish shirt. She smiled and waved and waited for a car to pass, then half-walked, half-ran to where I stood.

We hugged each other and then I held her at arm's length. "You look good," I said.

"Thanks. You too." She pointed up at my door. "I just tried ringing your bell . . ."

"When did you get back?"

Stephanie put a finger to her head and looked at the ground. "When did I get back . . . day before yesterday. No. The day *before* that. Three days ago." She laughed sheepishly. "Brain's scattered."

"Setting up house in the cottage?"

She shook her head. The smile faded. "I'm going away, Quinn. This trip is just to wrap things up."

"Going away?"

She nodded.

"Come on upstairs and tell me about it," I said.

"No . . ." She put her hand on my hand. "I'm real lousy at this, so I'd rather make it quick."

We fell silent for a moment or two. Finally she exhaled loudly and looked up at me with a forced smile. "The woman you thought about marrying . . . Mady?"

"Yes?"

"She didn't prejudice you against women who are looking for themselves, did she?"

I smiled. "No."

"Good," Stephanie said. "Because that's exactly what I'm about to go do. Look for myself."

"How do you mean?"

"I mean that somewhere along the way I've lost whatever it was that used to comprise Stephanie Axton back in the days when I thought highly of Stephanie Axton. I don't even know where to start . . ."

"Where did you see it last?" I said.

Stephanie shook her head and swept back a lock of hair. "God, Quinn. I have no idea. Not in Jamaica, and certainly not in Idaho." She looked off to the right and thought for a second. "I think I may have laid it across the back of a chair in a restaurant in New York about a dozen years ago."

"Then maybe you should start looking there," I said.

Stephanie focused on me, silent and serious. "Maybe I should," she said. "What about you?"

"Me?" I took a deep breath and let it out. "I feel like my heart and soul just got tossed in the Gone-Till-June Box."

"The what?"

I smiled and shook my head. "A long story."

We were silent for a while, then Stephanie cleared her throat. "Well . . . I'd better go," she said.

"Okay. Keep in touch."

We kissed, then she turned and did her half-run across Union Street again, looking left and right, soft brown hair sweeping the tops of her shoulders. I was prepared to wave when she turned around that one final time, but she never looked back.

I opened the front door and took one look at the stairs in front of me, and suddenly home was the last place I wanted to be. Oscar was squawking and Lola came running down to the first landing. They didn't appreciate me. They didn't have any true love in their souls. All they wanted was food.

Animal maintenance ranks right up there with plant maintenance as one of my all-time favorite things, so I went back out the door, relocked it, and walked instead the dozen blocks down Polk Street to Ghirardelli Square. The pets could wait another hour. A little hunger builds character.

I found an empty bench out by the fishing boats and I sat and spent an hour watching the seagulls circle the blue, blue water. I resisted the urge to contemplate events, to track down clues, to mull over love and romance and sand through the hourglass. All

I wanted to do was lean back. Smell the breeze. Look through my eyes.

When the hour was up I stood and noticed that a boy had set up a shoeshine stall at the other end of the square, so I went over there. The kid was maybe seventeen, with a baseball cap turned on backward, dark haired and pimply faced. His friend sat on the bench next to him. Plump. Blond. They talked the whole time he did my shoes.

When it was over I stood and said, "How much?"

The kid kept talking to his friend. We hadn't made eye contact yet. He held up three fingers.

"Don't you want five?" I said.

The kid stopped talking and looked at me suspiciously. The four-second, up-and-down, what-the-hell's-your-problem assessment. "Don't I want *what?*"

"Five dollars?"

"Shoeshine's three bucks."

"You don't want five, then?"

The two friends looked at each other and smiled. "Look, mister," the pimply-faced kid said. "You wanna give me five, I'll take five."

I handed over the five-dollar bill and he shoved it in his pocket. I lingered, expecting something else. I don't know what I was